MW01194575

POISON IN PICCADILLY

A FIONA FIGG & KITTY LANE MYSTERY

KELLY OLIVER

Boldwood

First published in Great Britain in 2024 by Boldwood Books Ltd.

Copyright © Kelly Oliver, 2024

Cover Design by Alexandra Allden

Cover Images: Shutterstock and iStock

The moral right of Kelly Oliver to be identified as the author of this work has been asserted in accordance with the Copyright, Designs and Patents Act 1988.

Every effort has been made to obtain the necessary permissions with reference to copyright material, both illustrative and quoted. We apologise for any omissions in this respect and will be pleased to make the appropriate acknowledgements in any future edition.

A CIP catalogue record for this book is available from the British Library.

Paperback ISBN 978-1-80483-206-6

Large Print ISBN 978-1-80483-207-3

Hardback ISBN 978-1-80483-208-0

Ebook ISBN 978-1-80483-205-9

Kindle ISBN 978-1-80483-204-2

Audio CD ISBN 978-1-80483-213-4

MP3 CD ISBN 978-1-80483-212-7

Digital audio download ISBN 978-1-80483-211-0

Boldwood Books Ltd
23 Bowerdean Street
London SW6 3TN
www.boldwoodbooks.com

1

TROUSSEAU SHOPPING

The first item on my trousseau list was a sleeping suit for these new air-raid nights. I wanted something attractive but also practical. After all, vanity wouldn't keep me warm hunkered down in a London Underground station. Then again, that job should be reserved for my intended, Lieutenant Archie Somersby. Otherwise, what was the point of marriage? Companionship? You could get that from a dog. Fellowship? You could get that at church. Love? You could get that from friends and family. What unique pleasures did marriage add to life? Mark Twain claimed it made two fractional lives a whole and added new mystery to life. Mystery was right!

My last nuptials added a mystery that ended in divorce before it could end in widowhood. The affair, the divorce, my husband —ex-husband—dying in my arms from mustard gas, rather put me off matrimony. Yet here I was, in June 1918, in the middle of the Great War, shopping for my trousseau. Miss Fiona Figg, soon to be Mrs. Archie Somersby. Now there was a mystery! Archie. His entire life was classified.

"How about this one?" Clifford held up a sheer pink envelope chemise. Captain Clifford Douglas. My friend and sometimes chaperone assigned against my wishes by the War Office. He'd offered to come shopping with me on the pretense of needing a new cravat. Why I'd accepted his offer was another question. He was a nuisance under the best of circumstances.

"I say." Clifford looked at me through the fabric. "There's not much to it." His cheeks turned the color of the combination.

I fingered the fine silk. "Except the price tag." On my paltry wages from the War Office, I should be ordering my trousseau from Freeman's instead of shopping at Harrods. But shopping always lifted my spirits. The deeper the melancholy, the higher the prices. And ever since I'd accepted Archie's proposal, I'd been haunted by the strangest feelings of remorse. My espionage partner, Kitty Lane, claimed I just had a case of "cold feet." She also said I'd better marry Archie to "cool my hot blood" before I got myself in trouble. By trouble, she meant Fredrick Fredricks, the prime target of British counterintelligence who gave England's *Most Wanted* list a whole new meaning. The rogue.

"I suppose you'll have to quit your job," Clifford said, fiddling with a silk petticoat.

"Why?" I looked up from a lovely lacey lilac combination I'd picked out.

"You'll be married." He clamped his pipe between his teeth. "No self-respecting Englishman would allow his wife to have a job." He chuckled. "Especially not dressing up in disguises and trotting across the globe to catch spies and murderers."

A lump formed in my throat. I hadn't thought of that. What if Archie expected me to quit my job? He wouldn't. Would he? Of course not. Archie respected me as a colleague and as a woman. I could be both... and a wife, to boot.

"I don't see why marriage should stop me from catching spies and murderers." I adjusted my wig. "I'm perfectly capable of both homemaking and espionage." And if not, there was no question which one would get the axe. My espionage skills were far superior to my homemaking skills.

"What's this doohickie?" Clifford pointed to the dagger-shaped petticoat hook dangling from the front of a pretty cream corset.

"Don't tell me." I rolled my eyes. "Forty years a bachelor and you've never seen a woman's corset?" Although Clifford was perpetually enthralled by some young woman or other—the more distressed and pathetic the better—he'd never been married. Pity. He was a decent chap and not bad looking... for a man with a receding hairline and a face like a horse.

"Good Lord," he sputtered and blushed. "You say the darndest things, old girl."

A society woman dressed to the nines carrying a Japanese parasol stopped to stare. It was obvious from the purse of her lips she did not approve of a man shopping in the women's lingerie department. The society lady tutted and gave us the evil eye. Did she think Clifford was my fiancé? Bad enough he was stuck to me like a sheep tick.

"Let's go look for a honeymoon hat." I took Clifford by the arm.

The hat section was my favorite department. And the most important. A good hat was my only hope to soften my features and achieve a halfway feminine look. Without an elaborate hat and a few frills, whenever I glanced in the mirror, I saw my Uncle Frank looking back at me. Even with a fancy hat, you'd be hard pressed to call me pretty. At best, if I kept myself neat and clean, I might be considered handsome.

I made a beeline for a smart tailored azure turban with a pretty brooch gathered around a stalk of scarlet silk. I tried it on. "What do you think?" I turned to Clifford.

"Reminds me of a time I was hunting mandrills in Africa." His eyes lit up. "Did you know, they have blue faces with red snouts, and beautiful feathery fur sticking up from their foreheads. Anyway, I'd just come out of a stand of fever trees and—"

I patted his sleeve to stop him before he could launch into a boring hunting story. "Thank you, dear." Colorful African ape was *not* the look I was going for on my honeymoon. I replaced the hat on its stand.

A lavender cartwheel caught my eye. I placed it atop my wig. More subdued than the mandrill turban, and yet quite appealing with its flowers and feathers. I wasn't about to ask Clifford his opinion and risk being compared to an Indian rhinoceros or an American grizzly bear or some other poor creature he'd killed. I admired my reflection in the mirror. Yes, it would do.

"Ouch!" Clifford yelped.

"What in the world?" I glanced over to see what he was doing.

Playing with the hatpins, Clifford had managed to stab himself. I plucked the offending hatpin from his hand, pulled a handkerchief from my bag, and wiped blood from its tip. With its eight-inch steel shaft and gorgeous emerald pinhead, it was perfect for my new hat.

"Bloody nuisance." Clifford sucked at his finger. "No wonder uncapped hatpins are illegal."

"You choose your weapons, and I'll choose mine," I said, plunging it to its hilt into the crown of my new hat.

After I'd racked up quite an astounding bill at Harrods, Clifford drove me to Fortnum and Mason's tearoom where we were to meet Kitty. I hadn't seen her since she returned from Ireland where she was visiting an old school friend. No doubt someone from that spy school in France where she'd learned foot fighting —along with several languages and other less savory skills.

This morning, Kitty was practicing her foot fighting for an

upcoming competition nearby at the Piccadilly Dojo, London's premier jujitsu club, or so she said. I knew nothing of foot fighting. In my opinion, it wasn't very ladylike, but it had come in handy on several occasions. Still, almost out of her teen years, the girl should consider more appropriate pastimes for an active young lady. Riding or tennis, instead of fencing and fighting. For my part, I preferred curling up with a good detective story and a nice cup of tea. Speaking of tea.

Fortnum's tearoom was my favorite café in London. On this fine April afternoon, no less than three dozen people—mostly women showing off their finery—were seated for tea. Sun streaming in from the enormous windows shimmered green and blue off the backs of stuffed peacocks standing atop pedestals. Tall palms gave diners the illusion of privacy as they gossiped and traded secrets. On one side, our table had a lovely view of the orchestra, which was encircled by bouquets of pink and white flowers. On the other, we could look out the window onto busy Piccadilly, where the pavements were full of people coming and going.

"I say." Clifford looked up from his newspaper. "Have you read the new column in the *Daily Chronicle*?" He chuckled. "Apparently, Randolph Kipper's wife was seen practicing self-defense with a group of those women's suffrage people."

"Society pages?" I sighed. "Really, Clifford, don't you have something better to read than gossip?"

"Mr. Kipper, you see, is staunchly anti." He raised his eyebrows. "Doesn't approve of votes for women, says they're too emotional for politics—"

"Rubbish." I scowled at him. "Women are just as rational and capable as men."

His blue eyes sparkled. "I don't know of any man who spends thirty minutes deciding between two shades of purple," he said into his napkin, no doubt referring to my recent harrowing deliberation over two equally lovely shades of sleep suits.

"Violet and lavender are distinctly different colors," I huffed.

"If you say so," Clifford's smug smile told me otherwise, "it must be true."

Luckily, the waitress arrived to take our order before I threw a teaspoon at him.

Clifford went back to his newspaper while I tallied my receipts. After the honeymoon, I was going to have to work overtime at the War Office to keep up with expenses. Who knew an emerald hatpin could be so expensive? And a quid for silk drawers. Talk about rising prices. I still needed to get my wedding dress fitted. I'd ordered a lovely ivory silk gown from Ellis Bridal Boutique. I was hoping to enlist Kitty to help with that errand. She was my maid of honor, after all. I glanced at my watch. Where was she? Late as usual.

The waitress returned wheeling a cart laden with tea paraphernalia and a gorgeous plate of scones. The tea service was a darling royal blue and gilt porcelain complete with teapot, cups, saucers, milk jug, and sugar bowl—I knew what I wanted as a wedding present from Archie. Forget about diamonds or pearls. I'd take a fancy teapot any day. I admired the rose-petal ring on my finger. My engagement ring from Archie. It had been his grandmother's. So romantic.

As the waitress laid out the tea and scones, Clifford folded his newspaper. "New columnist, Ed Aria, is dishing the dirt on those horrible Pankhurst suffragette ladies." Admiring the scones, he giggled and rubbed his hands together—whether his delight was at the scones or the society dirt, I couldn't say.

"The Pankhursts have done more for this country than most of our prime ministers." I plucked a scone from the plate and broke it in two.

"I hate to think of the next election with all those women carting their screaming brats on their hips to the polls." He munched on a scone.

The mention of children cut deep. Unfortunately, my first marriage did not yield such fruits. Even worse, it was entirely my fault—as I later discovered when my ex-husband remarried and had a son. My body was defective in that department. I had yet to tell Archie. I winced. Would he still want to marry me when he learned I was barren? I couldn't even stand to think the word, let alone say it out loud. What kind of woman was I?

"Are you listening, old thing?" Clifford was still nattering on about women clogging up the polling places.

"Only propertied women over thirty will be able to vote." I poured a bit of milk into my teacup and swirled it. "Not all women." I didn't need to read the society pages to know there was a split between the Pankhurst sisters. Christabel and her famous mother Emmeline were content to have won the vote for certain women. Sylvia wanted votes for all women, especially working women. As a working woman under thirty myself, I didn't see why I couldn't vote. After all, I was serving my country at the War Office, even risking my life from time to time. Surely, I could handle the responsibility of political enfranchisement.

When my cup was sufficiently warm, I added the strong tea. After Clifford's talk of other women's rights and other women's babies, I needed fortification. Maybe something stronger than tea. "Where is that girl?" I changed the subject. "Kitty is twenty minutes late."

"She probably had to stop for Poppy to do her business." Clifford drained his teacup. "Poppy is very particular about where she—"

I held up my hand. "Not while I'm eating."

For a grown man, he was inordinately fond of Kitty's

Pekingese dog. He was always fawning over the furry little carpet. For my part, I tolerated the creature, and then only when absolutely necessary. The beast was nicknamed "Poppy-poo" for a reason.

As I sipped my tea, I gazed out onto Piccadilly, watching army lorries, motorcars, and a few stray horse-drawn carriages pass by. On the pavement, a large woman stopped and bent down right in front of the window. If it weren't for the glass, I could have reached out and touched her. When she stood up again, she was holding a furry little dog wearing a pink bow in its topknot. Speak of the devil and she shall appear. If I didn't know better, I could have sworn it was Poppy.

"Doesn't that dog look exactly like Poppy?" I discreetly pointed toward the window. "Down to the pink bow in its topknot."

"Good Lord." Clifford jumped up. "That *is* Poppy!" His napkin fell to the floor, and he dashed toward the exit.

Oh dear. Where was Kitty? Why in the world would Poppy be wandering the streets alone? Had something happened to the dog's mistress?

2

LOST DOG

It was Poppy, alright. As we stood outside on Piccadilly, Clifford held the little monster, but that didn't stop her from reaching out with her long, warm tongue and licking my face. "Yes, yes," I said through clenched teeth, not daring to open my mouth while patting the beast on the head. "Where is your mistress? Where's Kitty?"

"It's not like her to let our sweet Poppy-poo run wild." Clifford nuzzled the dog. "You could have been killed, poor dear," he said into the dog's topknot.

"Kitty was practicing foot fighting just up the street." I pointed in the direction of the Dojo, which was just two streets away. "Perhaps Poppy escaped when she was changing for tea. Maybe the girl got so involved in her practice she lost track of time and her dog."

"We'd best go find out." Clifford hugged the Pekingese to his chest. "Sorry I can't help carry your packages, old girl." He shrugged. "I have my hands full."

With heavy shopping bags bouncing off both of my legs, I waddled behind man and dog until we reached Piccadilly Dojo.

Outside, the building was unassuming brick like its neighbors. Its most remarkable features were the two uniformed coppers flanking the entrance. You'd think we were entering the Houses of Parliament or Fort Knox.

Inside, the Dojo was pleasant. The walls of the reception area were adorned with Japanese hangings featuring pink blossoms and calligraphy. A string of paper lanterns hung across the entrance. The lobby was empty except for a pretty little cat lounging on a chair near a wooden table. As we passed, the cat looked up with wide eyes, no doubt wary of Poppy. "Don't worry, little pussy cat," I said. "Uncle Clifford won't let the beast loose."

Voices emanated from the next room. Following the sound, we found ourselves in a large gymnasium with thick mats on the floor and an impressive rack of swords and wooden pole weapons along one wall.

A petite woman was leading a class of about a dozen women dressed in white smocks over black stockings. In pairs, they practiced throwing each other to the ground. Quickly, I scanned the faces. None of them were Kitty.

"Ladies." Clifford tipped his hat.

They stopped their fighting and stared at him.

"Can I help you?" the petite woman asked. "I'm Mrs. Edith Garrud, the instructor." Mrs. Garrud was a striking woman with arched brows, thin lips, a mop of curly hair, and a confident stride that made her seem bigger than she was. She put me in mind of a red fox. Small, sleek, and deadly.

"You're teaching ladies to fight?" Good old Clifford, always pointing out the obvious.

"These are not just *any* ladies." Mrs. Garrud adjusted the black belt at the waist of her smock. "These are Sylvia's bodyguards."

"Bodyguards?" Clifford chuckled. "Why does she need body-guards? Is her husband such a bounder?"

"We're looking for Miss Kitty Lane," I interjected before Clifford could embarrass me any further. "My niece." Kitty wasn't really my niece. But that was the cover story we'd used since we started working together six months ago—although, at twenty-five, I was only seven years her senior.

"Has anyone seen Miss Lane?" the instructor asked.

"I saw her in the locker room just before class," a pale woman said, smiling as she came over to pet Poppy. "Poppy-poo, darling, why aren't you with Kitty?" Obviously, Poppy-poo was well known at the Dojo.

"Which way is the locker room?" I asked. "Clifford, why don't you and Poppy wait here while I go find Kitty." I assumed the Ladies' locker room was no place for a man, even one as harmless and silly as Clifford.

"Members only," Mrs. Garrud said. "I'm afraid you can't go back there."

"I'll go." The pale woman gave Poppy one last pat. The woman looked soft and doughy with thick brows and heavy eyelids, an older, heavier version of Kitty. Her hair was perfectly coiffed into neat blonde finger waves, a style I associated with younger women. Swinging her ample hips, she strolled across the gym, presumably in the direction of the Ladies' locker room.

"Who was that woman?" I asked, since obviously she was on familiar terms with Poppy and a first-name basis with Kitty.

"Ellen Davis," the instructor said. "She has just started learning jujitsu with us."

"I say," Clifford interrupted. "Aren't you one of that famous suffragette's daughters?" He approached one of the women.

"Shhhh." Mrs. Garrud put her finger to her lips. "We must keep Sylvia's identity a secret. The police follow her everywhere, playing their horrible game of cat and mouse, always ready to lock her up."

"All women should learn to defend themselves." Sylvia Pankhurst gave an embarrassed smile. "I'm no different from anyone else." She was an attractive woman in her late thirties with sad eyes and lovely fine hair. "The police love playing cat and mouse with all of us."

"Pash." Mrs. Garrud waved as if shooing flies. "Now that women over thirty have the vote, you're the leading spokes-woman for *universal* suffrage." She turned to me. "The police would love to get their hands on Sylvia, which is why she needs bodyguards." She gestured toward the other women, who joined in the pledge to protect Sylvia Pankhurst. "We have vowed to protect her."

A loud shriek made all heads turn in the direction of the locker rooms. *What in heaven's name?* Frozen like statues, we all stood for a few seconds staring across the gym. I was the first to bolt. At full tilt, I headed to the back of the gym. Beyond a door was a hallway and down it were two more doors: one marked *Gentlemen* and the other marked *Ladies*. No doubt the locker rooms. My heels clicking along the parquet floor, I dashed into the Ladies. Inside, bamboo mats padded the floor, various-sized wicker baskets sat along one wall, with clothes lockers along another. The smell of lye soap and something darker and more sinister assaulted my nostrils.

"Kitty?" I stepped around the lockers and found an alcove with stalls. "Mrs., er, Miss Davis? Are you in here?" Gingerly, I pushed at the door to one of the stalls. It was an empty toilet stall. I looked in the other stalls. "Kitty?"

Around another corner were a series of dressing areas hidden behind curtains. "Anyone here?" Nothing. Where in blazes was Ellen Davis? Had the scream come from the Gentlemen's dressing room? Or elsewhere? I glanced around, then moved a curtain aside and peeked behind it. Empty. I moved to the next one. Empty.

I heard whimpering coming from further down. As I advanced, I noticed a glimmer on the floor. My breath caught. I rushed to pick it up. Kitty's favorite silver hair comb. As I reached for it, I gasped. There, under the curtain, was a black and white tangle of fabric and limbs.

Heart racing, I pulled back the curtain. "Kitty!"

Kitty lay in a heap, apparently unconscious on the floor. In the corner, her hand over her mouth, Ellen Davis stood pressed against the wall.

"What happened?" I asked.

"I found her like this." Ellen's voice trembled. "Is she... dead?"

I knelt beside Kitty and gently shook her shoulder. "Kitty, dear, wake up." She was warm but unresponsive. I felt her neck for a pulse. *Thank God.* She was still alive. I looked up at Ellen. "Stop whining and help me." I was beginning to wonder if she'd done this to Kitty.

Her lip trembled but she stopped whimpering. Together, we straightened Kitty's limbs. I sat on the floor and placed Kitty's head in my lap. "Go call for an ambulance."

Still simpering, Ellen nodded and left the locker room.

By this time, all the Suffrajitsu ladies plus Clifford were gathered around. Yelping, Poppy squirmed out of Clifford's arms and ran to her mistress. The loyal little creature stopped licking Kitty's face only long enough to bark in her ear. If that didn't wake up the girl, nothing would. What had happened here? Had she simply fainted? Or had someone attacked her?

"When was the last time you all saw Kitty?" I asked. Best to start an investigation while the memory—and evidence—was fresh. "Ellen saw her in the locker room just before class started. How long ago was that?"

"Not long." Mrs. Garrud looked at her watch. "Maybe twenty minutes ago now. Right after William's class ended."

"William?" I asked.

"My husband, William, teaches the men's classes." She peered over my shoulder as I examined Kitty for signs of a struggle. "Advanced jujitsu."

Apart from Kitty's kimono being askew, there was nothing obvious. I ran my fingers through her golden locks. Aha! There was a large lump on the back of her head. She'd hit her head—or been hit—very hard. It was doubtful that a bare fist could have struck such a blow. Unless it was a very large fist. The skin wasn't broken, which suggested whatever hit her was blunt and not sharp. One of those wooden poles along the wall of the gym, perhaps?

"Who else has access to the dressing rooms?" I shifted Kitty's head in my lap. "Did you see anyone here who didn't belong?"

The women mumbled and shook their heads. "No one."

"What about the students in the men's class?" I asked.

"William usually has four or five students in that class," Mrs. Garrud said. "But they use the Gentlemen's locker room." She gestured toward the door.

One of them could have entered the Ladies' locker room, accosted Kitty, and disappeared. "Could I get a list of all the students in that class? And in the suffragettes' class, too?"

Mrs. Garrud stood blinking at me. "I'll have to ask William."

I looked around the small dressing area. There was no furniture or bench or other corner where the girl could have hit her head. If she fainted and fell directly to the floor, she shouldn't have such a well-defined lump on the back of her head, especially since I found her face-down. The lump or bump would have been on her face. And if she fainted and hit the wall and then fell to the floor, she should have bruises. It was possible she could have fallen backwards and hit her head against the wall. Still, it seemed unlikely. I lifted the sleeve of her smock and checked for bruises. No, I didn't think she'd fainted.

Perhaps a well-trained fist could have struck such a blow. "Could a judo chop render someone unconscious?" I asked.

"We don't call it a chop," Mrs. Garrud said. "And yes, a well-placed hit could knock out its recipient... or worse."

I was certain someone had come into the locker room and attacked Kitty. And most likely, it was one of these ladies. Possibly even Ellen Davis. Perhaps she found Kitty, attacked her, and then pretended to be shocked at finding the poor girl unconscious. I'd read enough detective fiction to know about such tricks.

But why? Why would any of Sylvia Pankhurst's bodyguards attack Kitty? Kitty was no threat to Sylvia. If anything, she was in league with the radical socialist and her ilk.

Who would want to attack Kitty? I knew so little about my erstwhile espionage partner. Her past was a mystery to me. For all I knew, she could have dozens of enemies just waiting to pounce.

Right now, it was Poppy who was ready to pounce. "Clifford, be a dear and take Poppy away before the creature has a conniption." I nodded toward the little dog, who was pawing at Kitty's smock as if digging a hole to escape an approaching predator. Poor little thing. Where was the blasted ambulance? "And send in those police officers from outside."

"Come on, sweetheart." Clifford lifted the beast into his arms and cradled her. "Aunt Fiona will see to your mama." No doubt for the pup's sake, his voice was chipper and reassuring, but his face was long with worry. "We'll go fetch the police."

"Tell them I suspect foul play," I whispered.

His eyes went wide and he hurried his pace.

* * *

Kitty was still unconscious when the ambulance arrived. The medics loaded her onto a stretcher. Only when I told them I was her aunt would they allow me to ride with her to hospital. Sitting next to her in the back of the vehicle, I gazed at her sweet face. Just eighteen she looked the perfect angel. I knew otherwise. Within two weeks of our meeting, she'd tied me to a toilet. I'd seen her foot fight her way out of nests of enemies, and she'd gunned down several Bolshevik operatives. Hard to believe the vulnerable injured girl laid out in this ambulance was a highly trained British agent.

I reached out and took her hand. Poor girl. Truth be told, I'd grown quite attached to her. I don't know what I would do without her. "Hold on, sweet Kitty." I squeezed her hand. "We're almost there." At least I hoped we were. Riding in the back of the van was deuced uncomfortable. And the sooner we reached the hospital the better. I only hoped it wasn't too late. I knew from volunteering at Charing Cross Hospital that the longer the patient remained unconscious, the worse the prognosis.

Again, I felt for a pulse at her wrist. It was weak but there. Must have been quite a blow on the head to render her unconscious for this long. "Please, Kitty, wake up." I brushed a blonde curl from her face. Such a pretty face. With her rosebud lips, long lashes, and sweet ringlets, she could pass for a Hollywood starlet, which was probably why she made such a good spy. No one ever suspected her of anything except maybe stealing an extra biscuit at teatime. She did have a terrible sweet tooth. "Oh, Kitty, please wake up."

The girl's eyelashes fluttered. She groaned.

"Aunt Fiona is here." I leaned closer. "Dear Kitty, can you hear me?"

More groans. She put both hands on her head. "It hurts."

"Can you hear me, dear?" I asked, hoping she hadn't been permanently damaged by the blow.

She opened her eyes. When she turned to look at me, her eyes filled with terror. "*Cá bhfuil mé.*"

What in the world? Why was she speaking Irish "Kitty, it's me." I stroked her hair.

"Where am I?" she asked, thankfully this time in English. "You must tell Kell about Fianna Éireann and Cumann na mBan."

The poor girl. She was obviously delirious.

"I'm afraid there's been... an accident." I patted her shoulder. "You're in an ambulance on the way to hospital."

"An accident," she repeated as if in a dream. She squinted at me for a second. "Are you a nurse?"

Didn't she recognize me? *Oh, dear.* "I'm your Aunt Fiona."

"My aunt?" She blinked at me.

Not wanting to confuse the girl, I reconsidered. "We're work colleagues, remember?"

"Work," she repeated. "MI5?"

"No, the War Office." *What in blazes?* Didn't she remember anything?

Her gaze turned hard and her eyes glinted like sharp-cut emeralds. "I've never seen you before in my life."

Her words sank in my stomach like a rock.

She got a puzzled look on her face. "Who am I?"

"You don't remember?"

"No."

Good grief. The girl had amnesia.

3

HOSPITAL VISIT

The next morning, I visited Kitty in hospital. The girl looked well enough. But speaking with her was disconcerting. She remembered nothing. Not even her own name. And what she claimed to remember was preposterous. She was no more a secret operative for MI5 than I was.

The staff had just delivered Kitty's breakfast when Clifford arrived with Poppy. The pup wagged its tail so fast it looked like a child's top. Kitty claimed she'd never owned a dog. Her joyous reaction to the pup betrayed her. Obviously enamored, she caressed and cuddled the furry beast.

"And if I did," she said, "I'd never name it something as silly as Poppy."

"Poppy is a jolly fine name," Clifford said, tapping tobacco into his pipe.

Kitty tickled the dog under its chin. "Right, Poppy-poo."

"Aha!" I took heart. "That's what you always call her, Poppy-poo."

Kitty scowled. "Don't be ridiculous." She picked at her

porridge and added an obscene amount of sugar to her tea. That much hadn't changed.

Clifford took out his lighter, and I glared at him. Surely, he wouldn't light that foul pipe in the girl's hospital room. He took the hint and clamped the unlit pipe between his teeth.

"Do you remember anything of yesterday?" I asked, straightening Kitty's bed covers. "Anything at all from the Piccadilly Dojo."

"Sadly, nothing." She shook her bandaged head. "My mind's a complete and utter blank. How is that possible?" Deep in contemplation, she sipped her tea and stared out the window.

"Was anything missing from your person?" I asked. "Your bag or wallet or jewelry?"

"You tell me." She pointed to a cupboard. "My personal effects are in there."

I went to the cupboard and, with her encouragement, rifled through her belongings. As far as I could tell, nothing was missing. Her adorable beaded bag with a kitten on the outside was intact and filled with a modest amount of money. A jade brooch was still attached to the lapel of her pink and white sailor dress. Whoever had hit her wasn't after her money or her jewelry.

In silence, Kitty continued her vacant stare. She was so altered from the Kitty I knew, it was uncanny. No longer the silly, chatty schoolgirl, she'd become brooding and pensive. Not one single giggle had escaped her lips. The seriousness of her expression was unsettling and gave her the air of someone much older than her eighteen years. I was beginning to wonder if I knew her at all.

"Wait." Her face lit up. "I remember something." Poppy sat at attention next to the girl's pillow. Given the little dog's concern for her mistress and the calming effect the pup was having, I refrained from commenting on the offense to hygiene of having an animal so near one's pillow.

"What, dear?" I removed my notebook from my bag and readied myself to take notes. "What do you remember? Anything, no matter how insignificant, could be important." I sat on the edge of my chair.

"Does the name Jane mean anything?" She troubled the edge of the blanket.

"Jane." I wrote the name at the top of a page in my notebook. "Possibly the name of one of the suffragettes at the Dojo. One of Sylvia Pankhurst's bodyguards."

"Or someone from MI5?" She looked at me expectantly, as if I knew what she was talking about.

MI5 again. *Oh, dear.* "Do you remember your uncle, Captain 'Blinker' Hall?" I patted her hand. "We work for him at the War Office in the Old Admiralty Building."

"Fine chap, Blinker," Clifford said. "His eyelashes flash like a darned Navy signal lamp." He chuckled. "Did I tell you about the time Blinker and I went bird hunting at Lord Curzon's estate in Derbyshire? Rum do, that. We'd already bagged a dozen pheasants when the beater—"

"Clifford, dear," I interrupted. "I don't think your hunting stories are going to help poor Kitty regain her memory. Can we focus on who might have attacked her and why?"

"Righto." He cleared his throat. "Sorry, old thing," he said, tucking his pipe into his breast pocket. "So, you think this Jane person tried to brain you?" he asked and then snapped open his newspaper and disappeared behind it.

"I don't know." Kitty retied the bow in Poppy's topknot. "What do you think, Poppy-poo?" She smiled down at the dog —shades of the old Kitty shining through the mask of this nervous young woman who was nearly unrecognizable with the bandage swathing her curls and the worry shrouding her face.

"We'll find out." I closed my notebook. "Never fear." I resolved that my next stop would be the Dojo to investigate and find this Jane woman, even if I had to join as a member to gain access. Anyway, it wouldn't hurt to learn a little self-defense, especially in my line of work. I smiled to myself. It would be worth it to see the look on Fredrick Fredricks's face when I deployed my first jujitsu move on him.

South African huntsman Fredrick Fredricks was a known German spy and my arch-nemesis. I'd been following him across Europe and beyond for almost a year now. With his broad shoulders, muscular physique, devious head of thick black hair, and wicked smile, he was the most vexing person of my acquaintance. Since my engagement to Archie, Fredricks had disappeared from the scene. He was probably off in some far-flung land fomenting unrest against the British or poisoning a duplicitous countess at her afternoon tea.

Archie! I looked at my watch. Not yet eleven. I'd almost forgotten I was to meet Archie for luncheon to discuss our wedding plans. My return visit to the Dojo would have to wait until after.

"I say." Clifford let out a guffaw. "Listen to this." Eyes dancing, he peeked over the top of his newspaper and then disappeared again. "This new society columnist claims Lords Battersea and Balfour are covering up a secret ring for untoward liaisons with boys," he sputtered. "Preposterous." When he emerged from the paper, his cheeks were bright red. "Arthur Balfour is an admirable fellow. Just because he's a confirmed bachelor—"

"Like you," I interjected.

"Steady on. I'm not confirmed," he stammered. "I just haven't found the right woman yet, that's all."

"Yes, dear." I bit my tongue rather than speculate on what type of woman would put up with Clifford and his incessant hunting stories.

"Lord Balfour is horrible," Kitty said. "He is staunchly anti-suffragette, anti-home-rule for Ireland, and a terrible bigot." She kicked off the blankets and swung her legs over the side of the bed. "He believes in a hierarchy of men, with white Englishmen at the top."

"How do you know this?" My eyes went wide. I'd never seen Kitty interested in politics before. Her idea of scintillating reading material was the latest fashion magazine, and even then she only looked at the pictures.

"I have no idea." She shrugged.

"Good Lord," Clifford sputtered. "This damn journalist claims Balfour is a hermaphrodite." He blushed all the way to the tips of his ears.

"Hello." A bright voice came from the doorway. "Kitty, darling, how do you feel?" It was Ellen Davis. She breezed in with a bouquet of flowers. "I hope they're taking good care of you." She handed the flowers to me. "Be a dear and find a vase."

With a sigh, I took the flowers and surveyed the room for something to put them in. I settled on a small steel water jug on Kitty's side table.

"Thank you." Kitty stood up. "I'm afraid I don't remember you." The hospital nightgown looked two sizes too big for her.

"Dear me." The doughy woman clutched her breast. "She has brain damage?" She looked from Clifford to me.

"No." At least I hoped it wasn't brain damage. "Amnesia," I said, rearranging the flowers.

"I've never met anyone with amnesia." Ellen clapped her hands together. "How exciting."

"Exciting is not the word I'd use." Kitty crossed the room and opened a small cupboard. "I've got to get out of here and find out who I am."

"You mustn't. It could be dangerous." Clifford plucked Poppy off the bed. "The person who brained you may try it again... and next time it could be worse."

"Worse than not knowing my own name?" Kitty removed a stack of neatly folded clothes. "I don't think so."

"We have to find this Jane person." I turned to Ellen. "Do you know of a suffragette or one of the bodyguards named Jane?"

"Jane," she repeated. "There's Lady Mary Jane Russell." Her face lit up. "She'll be at Lady Battersea's Suffrajitsu tea party tomorrow afternoon." She looked around the room, and, not finding an empty chair, sat on the edge of the bed. "Are you going, darling?" she asked Kitty.

"Am I invited?" Kitty pulled a yellow frock over her nightgown.

"Of course you are, darling." Ellen waved her hands. "And so are your friends."

"Lady Mary Jane Russell, you say." Clifford looked up from his newspaper. "I should be glad to meet her." He folded the paper and tucked it into his jacket pocket. "I say, Mrs. Davis, what do you make of Ed Aria's new gossip column in the *Daily Chronicle*?"

"I rather like it." Ellen tugged off her gloves. "Why do you ask?"

"It's ridiculous at best," Clifford said, clamping his pipe between his teeth. "And libelous at worst."

"Ha!" Ellen scoffed. "Why don't you tell us what you really think?"

"Why would anyone write such stuff?" he asked.

"Because people like you eat it up," I said.

"To support themselves," Ellen huffed. "Even journalists need money to live on."

"What do the society ladies make of it, I wonder." Clifford tilted his head thoughtfully. "I think I'll ask them tomorrow at tea."

"Apologies. My mistake." Ellen tightened her lips. "It's a *ladies only* tea party. All the bodyguards will be there. And Mrs. Garrud is giving a demonstration on how to use a hatpin as a weapon. It's going to be so much fun."

"We'll be there," I said. "Right, Kitty?"

Slipping her feet into her boots, Kitty didn't reply.

"Darling, I hear you're recently engaged." Ellen smiled at me. "To the handsome Lieutenant Somersby."

"How did you know? Are you acquainted with Lieutenant Somersby?" Had there been a piece in the society pages about me and Archie? I sincerely doubted it. Neither Archie nor I warranted the society pages. I was a mere file clerk who'd become an intelligence agent for the War Office. And he was a Flying Corps pilot who flew secret missions for the admiralty. Perhaps she was a friend of Archie's.

"I have my ways." She sniffed. "A woman never betrays her sources."

"Excuse me." A redhead poked her head into the room. "Is this the room of Mrs. Smith?" She spoke with a thick Irish brogue.

"No, darling," Ellen said. "Miss Kitty Lane."

"Oh, apologies, Miss Lane." The woman bowed a quick curtsey.

"I'm not Miss Lane," Ellen said, but the woman had already vanished.

No sooner had the Irish woman left than the doctor arrived

carrying a clipboard. With people coming and going, Kitty's room was beginning to resemble a railway station.

The doctor scowled when he saw Kitty out of bed and Ellen taking her place. He bade his patient sit and then listened to her heart with his stethoscope. "Other than your memory, you're as healthy as a horse," he said, shining a light into her eyes. "Best resume your normal daily activities."

"You mean she's free to go?" I asked in alarm. How could she resume her normal daily activities when she didn't know who she was?

The doctor turned to Ellen. "Are you her mother?"

"Oh, no, darling." Ellen guffawed.

"Her sister, then?" the doctor asked.

Ellen shook her head.

"Apologies." The doctor looked chagrined. "The resemblance..." He turned back to me.

I hope he doesn't think I'm her mother.

"One more night here for observation," the doctor said, "and then first thing tomorrow, you can go." He scribbled on his clipboard. "The best chance for regaining your memory, young lady, is to get back to familiar places and people." He nodded. "Unless you need me, I'll check on you in the morning before you're discharged." He handed her his card. "After that, Miss Lane, call me if you have any new symptoms or if your memory doesn't return within a month."

"A month!" Kitty gasped. "You mean I may not remember anything for a month?"

"Usually, patients recover from amnesia within a month." He shrugged. "In rare cases, they never do."

Kitty's mouth fell open. She sat blinking, the color draining from her cheeks.

My heart sank. What if Kitty never recovered her memory? To

distract myself from the awful thought and my general feelings of helplessness, I concentrated on a plan to find out who attacked Kitty, starting with Sylvia Pankhurst's bodyguards and this mysterious Jane.

"What time is Lady Battersea's tea party?" I asked, gathering up my bag.

Ellen pulled a card from her purse and read aloud, "Constance Flower requests the honor of your presence at her home at 148 Piccadilly at three o'clock." She looked up. "Three o'clock, tomorrow. Bring your best hatpin!"

"One of those bodyguards must know something," I said under my breath and quickly jotted down the time and address. I went to Kitty. "I intend to find out who attacked you and why." I put my arm around her narrow shoulders. "I'll be back first thing in the morning, my dear."

"What if I never get my memory back?" Kitty's lip trembled.

"Let's cross that bridge when we come to it." I kissed her on the cheek. "Are you coming, Clifford?"

"Can the dog stay?" Kitty asked, swinging her legs up onto the bed. As if she understood, Poppy hopped onto the girl's lap and licked her chin.

"Of course," Clifford said. "Poppy will help you regain your memory." He stood up and crossed over to the bedside. "She's your very best pal." Patting the pup's head, he cooed at the creature. "Right, Poppy-poo?" Silly man.

"If the nurses allow it." I shook my head. As a volunteer nurse at Charing Cross Hospital, I'd never have allowed it. Hopefully, Kitty's nurses were more tolerant of muddy paws and dog slobber.

4

LUNCHEON INTERLOPER

Archie had insisted on champagne and oysters at Wiltons to celebrate our engagement. Dark and heavy with cigar smoke, Wiltons was not my cup of tea. Given the war and so many going without, it seemed a great extravagance. Plus, I was not partial to oysters or drinking in the middle of the day. I only agreed to the plan to make him happy... and because Wiltons was around the corner from the Piccadilly Dojo. So, I could pop over after lunch and investigate.

Radiant in his dress uniform, Archie more than made up for the stuffy restaurant. He waved at me from a corner table. Smiling back at him, I weaved my way through the diners. Archie greeted me with a kiss on the cheek and a lovely bouquet of pale pink camellias accented with sprigs of lily-of-the-valley. Archie was as handsome as ever—that lock of chestnut hair cascading onto his forehead, those sea-green eyes framed by long dark lashes, and his lovely smile punctuated on either side by adorable dimples. I got butterflies in my stomach just being near him.

"Where did you get these beautiful flowers?" When I lifted

the bouquet to my nose, I was rewarded by their sweet fresh scent resembling jasmine and rose petals.

"I picked them for you this morning, first thing." Cap in hand, he was beaming as he pulled out a chair for me.

"Where do they have such magnificent camellias?" I hadn't seen luscious flowers like these except in royal gardens.

"That's classified." He tightened his lips, but his eyes did a mischievous dance.

"Now that we're engaged..." I sat down and pulled off my gloves. "You shouldn't keep secrets from me."

"I promise, in matters of the heart, I have no secrets." He put his hand over his heart. "You're my best girl."

"Best?" I raised an eyebrow. "There are others?"

"You're the bee's knees." He grinned. "A real brick."

I ignored the fact that he hadn't answered my question.

"I wish we could get married right now." He reached across the table and took my hand. "I can't wait to hold you in my arms all night—"

"Shhh." I leaned closer and whispered. "What will people think?"

"Hang them." He squeezed my hands. "I adore you, Fiona." His eyes shone. "Why do we have to wait to get married? Why not do it now?" He was always so impatient. Insisting we get married right away. Maybe because he was a soldier and so many soldiers left and never came back. The war tended to put life in perspective. Grab your happiness where you could. Every moment. Of every day.

"The wedding is less than a week away." I freed one of my hands from his. "And I still have the last gown fitting... and to finalize the flowers... and confirm the cake order..."

"I don't need flowers, or cakes, or gowns." He lifted my hand to his lips. "All I need is you."

"And the guests and the music for the reception in King's Square. There's just so much to do in just over a week." I was practically hyperventilating. Listing everything I needed to do made me dizzy.

"It's just you and me, Fiona." When he smiled, dimples formed on either side of his lovely mouth. "Just us. That's what matters."

The waiter delivered the oysters and champagne in the nick of time. A few more minutes and Archie would have convinced me to elope. The waiter poured out two flutes and laid out two plates.

"To my beautiful bride." Archie raised his glass. His gaze was so intense and sincere that I had to look away. He clinked my glass. "To you, Fiona."

"To us." I took a sip. The bubbles tickled my nose and made me let out a little giggle. "Can I ask you something?" I said when the bubbly sensation subsided.

"Anything." He smiled.

"When we get married, you won't expect me to stop working, or anything?" I used a tiny fork to slip an oyster from its shell.

"Why would you want to work?" He had a puzzled look on his face. "Don't you think I can provide for you... and our family?"

The word family stabbed me like a dagger through the heart. I still hadn't mentioned my faulty reproductive system. How did one bring up such an indelicate topic? "That's not it." My cheeks warmed. "I'd prefer to keep working is all."

"But why, when you don't need to?" He narrowed his brows.

"I enjoy it." *Enjoy* wasn't quite the right word. Working and travelling took me out of myself and my failures. My failed marriage. My failed attempts at a family. More than that, I craved the adventure the way a drug addict craved morphine. I didn't just enjoy working. I needed it to survive. The money was not the point. I couldn't imagine sitting home all day sewing or painting or baking—especially since I had no talent for any of those pastimes. No, I wanted the excitement of my life as a spy.

There was nothing as thrilling as chasing Fredrick Fredricks across the continent. And if there was something untoward about a married lady following such a cad across the globe, I could follow other spies and traitors. Or, at the very least, I could work with the men in Room 40 to intercept and decode secret messages. On that score, I did have a talent for breaking codes. My photographic memory came in handy, too. I didn't need to carry a spy camera. I could simply take a mental picture and recall it to my mind's eye later.

"I prefer that my new wife not work." Archie's voice brought me out of my reveries. "Eventually, there will be children and—"

"And what about what I prefer?" I dropped the little fork back onto the oyster plate. I didn't want to eat the nasty thing anyway.

"No need to raise your voice." Archie scowled.

"You don't seem to be hearing what I'm saying." I drained my champagne flute in self-defense.

"Let's not row." He reached across the table for my hand. "Everything will work out for the best."

I wanted to take his hand. I really did. To run away from the stupid war. From my solitary life. From trousseau shopping. Instead, I folded my hands in my lap.

"Fiona, please." His eyes implored with such genuine longing that I was about to relent when a youngster in a newsboy cap approached our table.

"Excuse me, sir, miss." He held out an envelope to Archie. "An urgent message from Countess Markievicz."

"Who is Countess Markievicz?" I stared across the table at Archie.

Archie's cheeks reddened. He ripped open the envelope and

quickly read the card. "So sorry." Standing, he reached into his trouser pocket, pulled out a few pennies, and dropped them into the boy's grubby hand. "So sorry," he repeated. "I've got to go." He ran a nervous hand through his hair and then clamped his cap atop his head. "Urgent business, I'm afraid." He picked up a black walking stick from the floor. I'd never seen him carry a stick before.

"Let me guess," I sighed. "Classified."

"I'm afraid so." He gave me a weak smile.

"Nice walking stick." I pointed to the stick. "A gift from Countess Markievicz?"

He shrugged and took off after the boy, leaving me with an open bottle of champagne, a plate of oysters, and the unpaid bill.

I poured another glass of champagne. Did he really expect me to leave my job? And who was this countess? I knew he was working for the War Office on top-secret projects, but how would I cope with being married to all those secrets? His entire life was classified. Surely, when we were married, he'd tell me everything. And I'd do the same.

"You know what they say about oysters?" A velvety baritone brought me out of my reveries.

I whirled around. "They're slimy and disgusting?"

"Fiona, *ma chérie*." With a broad smile, Fredrick Fredricks doffed his slouch hat and bowed. "The good lieutenant ran out on you, eh. Lovers' spat?" His dark eyes sparkled. As usual, he was enjoying my misfortune. And, as usual, he was wearing his ridiculous swashbuckler's outfit of tan jodhpurs, ruffled white shirt, tall black boots and carrying a swagger stick. The only thing missing was a bandoleer filled with bullets crisscrossing his chest. Instead, he carried a parcel.

"If you must know," I snapped my napkin open for effect, "he was called away on business."

"Yes, I know." He gestured at the empty chair. "May I?" He leaned his stick against the back of a spare chair and put the parcel down too.

I shrugged. I wouldn't have put it past him to have arranged for Archie's departure himself. "What are you doing here? And where have you been?"

His smile broadened. "Miss me?"

"Of course not." My cheeks warmed. "I'm engaged to Archie."

"Ah, yes. The good lieutenant." Rubbing his hands together, he surveyed the food and drink. "Called away on business."

"That's right."

"The business of Countess Markievicz and her younger sister, Lady Eva Gore-Booth." He helped himself to the oysters. "Lady Eva, whom the poet Yeats describes as having a gazelle-like beauty."

"A gazelle." I chuckled. "We should introduce her to Clifford." At the mention of a large beast, he'd probably ready his hunting rifle. And if Archie had actually left me stranded here to meet another lady, then I might provide the ammunition.

"Dare I say, she's already caught the eye of your beau, the good Lieutenant Somersby." He filled Archie's champagne flute and took a sip. "Umm. Your betrothed has good taste... in wine. I couldn't have done better myself." He drained the glass. "Now, how about we get down to our own business, *ma chérie*?" He leaned closer.

"What are you doing here?" I demanded. "Are you following me?" Fredricks had a habit of showing up in my environs. And, as to our business, we had none, despite his claims to the contrary.

"First, I have a gift for you." He smiled. "A very practical gift for a very practical woman." He lifted the parcel off the chair and held it out to me.

He must want something. Why else would he give me a present? With some trepidation, I took the parcel.

"Go on, it won't bite," he said encouragingly.

Reluctantly, I opened the box. Inside was a leather bag attached to a belt, like a holster in those films about the American West. "What is it?"

"A combination chatelaine bag and belt to hold all your necessaries..." He leaned closer and whispered. "And spy gear."

I held it out. I had to admit, it was jolly handsome. "Thank you." I gave him a genuine smile. "It will come in handy." In fact, it was perfect. Now I could dispense with my silly handbag. And, as an added benefit, I would have my hands free for other purposes. "Very kind of you." I meant it. I reached out and patted his hand. Immediately, I regretted it. A spark of electricity travelled up my arm and made my cheeks warm.

"Second..." His tone turned serious. "I came to warn you. Your beloved is playing a dangerous game."

"Archie?" I fiddled with the corner of my napkin. "Whatever do you mean?"

"You won't believe me, *ma chérie*." He sighed. "You never do."

"Tell me." I levelled my gaze. "If Archie is in danger, I want to know." Was Fredricks threatening to harm Archie?

"*You* are in danger, *ma chérie*." With desperation in his eyes, he reached for my hand, triggering my heart to beat faster. To think, a few minutes ago, it was Archie doing the same but with much less effect. Now this bounder had taken his place.

"Me?" Staring down at the panther insignia on his pinky ring, I tried to ignore the unwelcome heat travelling up my arm and into my chest... and beyond.

"For months, I've been telling you the good lieutenant is not what he seems." He sucked in breath. "He's toying with you."

"Oh, please." I rolled my eyes. "We're engaged." Would

Fredricks stop at nothing to ruin my nuptials? I withdrew my hand and cradled it in my other hand as if it were a wounded bird.

"Why has he been so desperate to marry you?" Fredricks asked. "Insisting he can't wait?"

"Because he loves me?" I closed my eyes and shook my head, wishing I could shake away the doubts Fredricks was trying to plant in my mind. With any luck, when I opened my eyes, he would be gone.

"There's no easy way to say this…"

No such luck. He was still there, his countenance full of tenderness and concern. The scoundrel.

"*You* are your fiancé's assignment." Fredricks twirled his hat in his hands. "I'm sorry, dearest Fiona, but the good lieutenant's intentions are far from honorable."

"I don't believe you." My eyes burned.

"Ask yourself…" He put his hand on my sleeve. "Why is he always in such a hurry to get you married off and out of his way?"

"You're a liar and a cad." I jerked my arm away. "You've gone too far this time." I grabbed my handbag and gloves. "Are you trying to ruin my last hope for happiness?"

"I'm trying to protect you from heartbreak." He closed his eyes. "Fiona, *ma chérie*, please listen—"

"No." I stood up. "I've had enough of your malicious slander."

"Don't forget your present." He held out the belt and bag.

I huffed. It was nice. I snatched it out of his hands, turned on my heel, and darted out of the restaurant. Wiping my eyes, I hurried around the corner toward the Dojo. I wished the War Office would just haul him in once and for all. But Captain Hall insisted he was of more use to us free than in captivity. Too bad.

What did the bounder mean, *I* was Archie's *assignment*? That Archie wanted to marry me to get me out of the way? Ridiculous.

It made no sense. And who would assign Archie to me? Unless... unless Captain Hall had assigned him to keep an eye on me. But to get me out of the way? No. The captain's faith in me had been hard won. But won it, I had. In fact, I'd even won an award for my service. Perhaps, in the beginning, months ago, Archie had been assigned to trail me while I trailed Fredricks. But now there was no need. Was there? And Archie and I had fallen in love somewhere along the way.

By the time I reached Piccadilly Dojo, my head was spinning. I fastened my new belt around my waist. To distract myself from Fredricks's cruel words, I threw myself into my investigation. Kitty had been attacked. *She* could be in danger. *She* was the one who needed protection. *She* was all that mattered now.

Midday and between classes, the Dojo was quiet. I found Mrs. Garrud putting away bamboo sticks. Again, she reminded me that I needed to be a member to get access to the gym and the locker rooms. This time, she questioned my authority, suggesting the attack was a matter for the police and not a mere acquaintance of the victim.

"I'm Miss Lane's partner," I pointed out. "We are both employed at the War Office and the attack could be related to our work there." I didn't mention that we were espionage agents. Although it was unlikely that my work as a file clerk would precipitate an attack. But, given the sensitive nature of the files in Room 40, it was possible. I opened my purse and withdrew my wallet. "How much to join?"

The door swung open. Cape flapping, Fredricks entered with his usual flourish.

How dare he follow me?

"Captain Soughton," Mrs. Garrud greeted him with a big smile.

Captain Soughton, my emerald hatpin. What was the scoundrel up to now?

"I'm here on behalf of Miss Lane," he said, winking at me. "Miss Figg and I have been entrusted with investigating yesterday's mishap."

Mishap? The girl had been brained to the point of amnesia.

"Of course, Captain." Mrs. Garrud gave me a sideways glance. "Anything to help." The way the jujitsu instructor fawned over Fredricks turned my stomach. "Right this way." She led us back through the gym to the locker room.

Under Mrs. Garrud's watchful eyes, Fredricks and I searched the Ladies' locker room. When it came to crawling around on the floor, he had the advantage of trousers.

Examining the stall where I found Kitty, I noticed a fresh dent in the back wall. Upon closer inspection, I saw scratches inside the dent. My hypothesis was the object used to strike Kitty had also hit this wall, perhaps as it ricocheted off her head.

Running my hand along the wall, I followed it down to the floor. *What have we here?* Embedded between the wall and the floorboard was a tiny bronze leaf with an even smaller green stone in its center. Removing my lockpicking set from my bag, I crouched down and then used my hook rake to maneuver the ornament loose. Carefully, I flipped the decorative leaf into the palm of my hand. About the size of a penny, it had three leaves, which were scratched and worn.

"I found something." I stood up and held out the ornament for inspection. "Do you recognize this bejeweled clover?" I asked Mrs. Garrud.

She plucked it from my palm, examined it, and pursed her lips. "It does look familiar. But I can't place it." She returned it to me. "Do you think it's related to the attack on Miss Lane?"

"Could be." I wrapped the ornament in a handkerchief and tucked it into the bag on my belt.

"If you remember where you've seen it before..." Fredricks removed a small card from the pocket of his vest. "Please let us know."

"Of course." Mrs. Garrud took his card. "Happy to help, Captain Soughton."

Happy to help, Captain Soughton. Annoying man. What did he think he was playing at? Once I got him out of the Dojo, I planned to find out. In the meantime, I might as well make use of him. "And those lists of students in the advanced class and in the suffragettes' class?" I turned to Fredricks. "We need those, too, don't we, *Captain*?"

"Indeed." He smiled. "But I can tell you who was in the advanced class." He twisted the end of his moustache. "I was there."

My mind raced through the reasons Fredricks might have for attacking Kitty. She always did warn me against him. And there was no love lost between them. Could *he* be the culprit?

I made a mental note to put him at the top of my list of suspects. I planned to give him a thorough interrogation whenever I got him alone. What fun. I couldn't wait.

5

KITTY'S INTERLUDE

Outside her window, it was pitch black. She didn't know what time it was—sometime in the middle of the night. The hospital was quiet except for an occasional groan or moan from the girl in the next bed.

The prissy woman and fussy man who had visited her earlier insisted that she worked for the War Office and Captain Hall. And yet, when Captain Hall had visited her earlier, all he could tell her was he'd plucked her off the streets as a girl and sent her to boarding school. He didn't even know where she lived. And he pretended to be her uncle! Both Fiona Figg and Clifford Douglas had told her that her name was Kitty Lane, but it didn't feel right. She rubbed her hurting head. Her mind was a blank. Well, not quite a blank, exactly. More like a redacted document with half her memories blacked out. Pacing back and forth in her hospital room, she felt like a caged animal. She had to get out of there and discover the truth.

With every step she took, the dog, Poppy, was practically glued to her leg. With its squished face and black mask, it was an adorable little thing. She bent down and scooped it up. "Hello, you." The effort made her head spin and she had to sit on the edge of the bed to avoid falling over. "Do you know who I am?" she asked the dog. "Poppy. What kind of silly name is that?" The dog licked her face, and it made her laugh. It felt good to laugh. She had the sense that she didn't do it often. At least not for real.

Who are we but our memories? What if hers never returned? She would be nobody. Did she have friends? Family? A sweetheart? Aside from Miss Figg and Captain Douglas and that Davis woman, she hadn't had any other visitors. No one else had come to claim her. She'd been told the "accident" happened at a jujitsu Dojo in Piccadilly. Did she practice jujitsu? She extended her right leg and stared down at it. She tried her left. Carefully, she removed Poppy from her lap and sat her on the bed. "Let's see what they can do." She jumped off the bed and kicked the air. It felt good. She did a butterfly kick, and it was like her legs had a mind of their own. Her body remembered. If only her mind would cooperate.

She dropped back onto the bed. "I'm pretty good." She sighed. "But who am I?" And why did she know more about Lord Balfour than she knew about herself?

A squeak from the other side of the curtain made her prick up her ears. She listened. Was someone else in the room? Someone besides the girl in the next bed? Surely, the girl couldn't have a visitor at this time of night.

Suddenly, she was afraid. Why? An instinct kicked in. She grabbed the dog and dove under the bed. "Shhh," she said to Poppy, hugging the dog to her chest. She held her breath and waited.

A pair of black boots appeared at the foot of her bed. Men's boots. They moved around to the side, and then back again. The scent of cedar and citrus attacked her nostrils. Her heart was racing. Poppy squirmed in her arms. Tears welled in her eyes.

She fought the urge to burst out from under the bed and attack. She didn't remember being this terrified in her life. Then again, she didn't remember much. She watched the boots moving. She listened. Who was he? What did he want?

The girl in the next bed groaned. The boots stopped in their tracks. The girl yelled out. The boots zipped past and disappeared from sight.

She listened and waited. A nurse came to check on her roommate. "There, there," the nurse said. "It was only a nightmare. You're alright."

She wished someone would wake her up and tell her this was only a nightmare. Still crouched under the bed, she held the little dog tight to her chest. It let out a whimper. She made a hand signal and the dog quit squirming and was as quiet as a mouse. How did she know that signal? How did the dog know it?

Her foot was cramping, and her head still hurt. But she didn't move a muscle. She continued to wait. Finally, stealthy footfalls receded from the room. Was he gone? Slowly, she scooted out from under the bed. Who was he?

She didn't need to ask. She knew. He was an MI5 assassin. She didn't know how she knew. But she knew. MI5 wanted her dead. Her life was in danger. She had to get out of this hospital and go into hiding. At least until her memory returned. The sooner the better.

He was gone now. But she was sure he'd be back for her.

6

POSH TEA PARTY

Early the next morning, Clifford picked me up outside my flat and we went together to collect Kitty from hospital. As we roared through North London, the fumes from his motorcar were making me nauseous. Probably because Fredricks had kept me out late drinking something called "Midnight Stingers." Unfortunately—thanks to the Stingers—Fredricks had got more out of me than I had out of him. When I asked him what he meant, telling me I was Archie's *assignment*, he replied, "What better way to get you out of the field than marrying you and starting a family?" I'd cringed when he mentioned family, and promptly changed the subject to Countess Markievicz.

I'd learned Countess Markievicz and her "fetching" gazelle-like sister Eva were not only suffragettes but also Irish activists who engaged in protests, both against conscription and for Irish home rule.

Of course, I'd read in the newspapers about the conscription protests. The Irish weren't the only people tired of the war. We all were. So many boys were dead or wounded. At Charing Cross Hospital, I'd seen my share of shattered lives. Those poor broken boys missing limbs and disfigured for life—and those were the ones who made it home alive.

According to Fredricks, like Sylvia Pankhurst, the countess and her sister were pacifists working to end the war, and as such they were old friends of his. He always was espousing the virtues of pacificism, especially if it meant defeat for the British. Over Stingers, he told me he'd helped the sisters write an open letter to the women of Germany urging them to unite in the cause of peace. I was all for peace, but not if it meant conspiring with the enemy. Except, of course, taking a few Midnight Stingers for Old Blighty when my intelligence work required it.

When we arrived at her hospital room, Kitty was pacing around like a caged tiger waiting for her discharge papers. By the time an orderly finally arrived with the papers, it was well past lunchtime, and we were all on tenterhooks. We still had to go home and change for Lady Battersea's tea party. I wasn't about to miss my chance to question the jujitsu suffragettes and their ringleader, Sylvia Pankhurst.

Clifford thought reacquainting Kitty with Captain "Blinker" Hall and the staff at the War Office might jog her memory. So, once she was discharged, we all loaded into his motorcar and headed to the Old Admiralty. Using his pipe to point to this or that, Clifford explained the workings of the War Office. Starting at the entrance to the building, he told stories about every room and every employee as we went. Of course, he knew everybody who worked there.

To my mind, he was taking a bit too much pleasure in giving Kitty a grand tour of her own life. Anything for a captive audience. He reintroduced her to the men in Room 40. The code breakers were only too happy to chat with the pretty girl and to pet Poppy. None of them knew Kitty well—certainly not well enough to know anything useful, like where she lived. Odd that none of us knew that essential titbit.

Clifford walked us up the stairs and pointed out the various departments and explained their charters: the Royal Navy, the Air Ministry, Medical Army Board, Censors Bureau, and Paymaster General. Captain Hall should consider Clifford for a tour guide position if the Old Admiralty ever became a museum.

Even when he didn't know their names, Clifford was only too happy to chat them up. We poked our heads into every door in the building. Peeking into the censor's office, Kitty pointed to a fellow sitting at a desk in the far corner. "Who is that?" She squinted. "He looks familiar. Do I know him?"

"Let's find out, shall we?" Cradling Poppy, Clifford led the way.

The gentleman's name was Jules Silver. He was one of the censors who read all the mail that went to and from any branch of the military, along with other mail the British postal service deemed suspicious. Without giving us a second look, he proclaimed he'd never seen Kitty before in his life. "And I never forget a pretty face," he added. "So, I'd definitely remember the dog." He smirked.

Poppy growled in disapproval.

"Apologies," Kitty said, shaking her head. "I could have sworn..."

Declaring her head hurt, Kitty begged off going to the tea party. I hated to leave her, but I had to interrogate those suffragettes, especially Lady Mary Jane Russell. I made Clifford promise he and Poppy would look after the girl.

After an exhausting grand tour of the entire building, I left Clifford, Kitty, and Poppy munching on stale biscuits over tepid tea in the tiny kitchenette in Room 40, and then I took a taxi to

Lady Battersea's tea party. I hadn't had time to change, of course. My plain wool skirt and blouse would have to do.

Lady Constance Battersea's posh townhouse at 148 Piccadilly was near the entrance to Hyde Park, where a battalion of soldiers was doing exercises. An ambulance stood at the ready. I wondered what kind of exercises they were doing if they were expecting accidents.

On the outside, the Battersea townhouse with its brick façade and plate-glass windows was commonplace. Inside, the house had been transformed into an Italianate mansion complete with a front portico sporting double Doric columns that opened onto a grand marble staircase and spacious reception rooms. A butler named Toogood led guests into the drawing room, where a long table was set for tea. Given the afternoon's entertainment was jujitsu fighting, I expected something less formal. In my grey wool skirt and white blouse, I felt excruciatingly underdressed. At least I'd worn my new hat with the emerald hatpin. I stood in the entrance, considering returning home to change.

I'd turned to go when Ellen Davis caught my elbow. "Miss Figg, how wonderful to see you again, darling. I'm sure Toogood will take your coat and hat... and hatpin." She was a walking Victoria sponge in yellow satin and raspberry lace with matching shoes. Although the shoes looked a bit worn. Come to think of it, the dress did too.

On cue, Toogood the butler appeared out of a hidden alcove and held out his gloved hands.

"Where is Miss Lane?" Ellen asked. "Is the darling girl quite recovered?"

"She's on the mend, but poor girl still can't remember anything." I gave the butler my coat and reluctantly removed my hat. In the process, I managed to prick myself with the new hatpin. A tiny red spot blossomed on my white gloves. "And her head hurts."

"Oh, my," Ellen said, looking over my shoulder. "It's the darling countess and her sister from Dublin."

I glanced at the Irish sisters. They made a striking pair. One dressed like a man and the other an angel holding a large bunch of flowers. The angel tilted her head and stared at me. Did I know her?

Ellen took my elbow again. "We'll get to them later. Now, let me introduce you to our hostess, Lady Battersea." She pulled me back into the drawing room.

The large drawing room had rust-colored wallpaper and a beautifully ornate cornice ceiling decorated with gold and turquoise shapes and figures. From every wall, almost life-sized portraits of the family and their ancestors looked down at the guests with scorn or delight. A fire blazed in the marble hearth and gave the room a cozy glow.

Lady Battersea wore a double string of pearls so tight around her neck it looked like they were strangling her. Her gown was darker and heavier than a typical tea dress. And her hair was a remarkable shade of yellow. She had a round face, kindly eyes, and a wonderfully soft and raspy voice. Her manner of running her household and the party put me in mind of a puppeteer quietly pulling the strings from behind a screen.

Lady Battersea announced tea was ready and asked us to take our places. I found my place card and Kitty's too, which was next to mine. When Ellen sat in Kitty's place, I pointed out the card to her. She waved me away, saying, "Everyone who's anyone knows who *I* am."

Funny. I didn't know who she was until I met her two days ago at the Dojo. I assessed the other guests to formulate a plan for interrogation. Around the long table sat a dozen women. There was the doughy Victoria sponge Ellen Davis to my immediate right, followed by the foxish jujitsu instructor Mrs. Edith Garrud, and then ringleader Sylvia Pankhurst flanked by four body-guards, two on either side. At the head of the table sat our hostess Lady Battersea with her tight pearls and to her right Lady Mary Jane Russell. And then the two sisters—the ones Ellen noticed just before she whisked me away. The taller of the two was wearing a black tunic with an insignia on the collars and black trousers with braces. Had she mistaken the tea party for a fancy dress party? The shorter wore an ivory chiffon gown that gave her the look of an impish angel.

Given Kitty's fixation with the name Jane, I trained my sights on Lady Mary Jane Russell. She was an elegant woman with small features, a bonnet of curly brown hair, and soft eyes. From conversation, I gathered she was the Duchess of Bedford and had founded several army hospitals. An avid suffragette and practi-tioner of jujitsu, she had been featured in a series of instructional photographs in a guidebook. Like Mrs. Garrud, she was slender but obviously tough. Was she capable of delivering a damaging blow to the head? To Kitty's head in particular? Was that why Kitty was fixated on the name Jane?

A freckle-faced maid with her hair neatly tucked up into a tall cap poured tea. Over strong tea and buttery cucumber sand-wiches, the conversation turned to that horrible column in the newspaper. Was I the only person in England not interested in such gossip?

In hushed voices, the women expressed outrage over this mysterious new columnist and the dirt dished in the *Daily Chron-icle*. None of them knew the journalist's identity, although they were quick to speculate. Apparently, Lord Battersea wasn't the only person maligned by the journalist. Sylvia Pankhurst had been accused of encouraging cowardice and draft-dodging in the face of conscription, along with being an anarchist, going so far as rejecting the institution of marriage and refusing to take her husband's name. Her bodyguards were called "harpies" and blamed for luring unsuspecting police into boobytraps. Reportedly, Lady Mary Jane Russell was going deaf and enjoyed the company of wild birds more than her own family. And the two mystery women were Irish suffragettes and militants, none other than Countess Markievicz and her gazelle-like sister Eva Gore-Booth, who was indeed lovely except for her nose, which was a bit *too* gazelle-like for her otherwise angelic face.

After an hour of listening to the high society women complain about being the targets of Mr. Ed Aria's new gossip column, I was glad to be a lowly, and very middle-class, file clerk whose life was of interest to absolutely nobody.

As we nibbled on watercress sandwiches and small salads adorned with wild berries, our hostess, Lady Battersea, lambasted the "vile" column for spreading rumors about her husband.

I turned to Ellen. "It seems you and I are the only persons not mentioned in this horrid column." I took a tiny bite of sandwich. Scrummy.

"So it seems." Ellen's cheeks turned the color of the berries skewered on her fork, which, I had to admit, looked more appetizing than the anemic pale berries on my salad. She washed them down with a quick sip of tea.

Lady Battersea tapped a crystal water glass with her fork. "Ladies, can I have your attention? After we finish our tea, we will transition to the ballroom upstairs for a demonstration on self-defense techniques using hatpins as weapons."

How exciting. There were murmurs from the guests.

"Then, we will come back to the drawing room for sponge cake, biscuits, and another round of tea before the last demonstration of the afternoon." She stood up. "How to use parasols as swords." With a broad smile, she laid her napkin on the table. "For now, Toogood will deliver your hatpins."

Toogood appeared in the doorway with a tray. On it, neatly laid out, were our hatpins. As we passed by, we each selected our own hatpin from the display and proceeded upstairs to the ballroom where Mrs. Garrud was waiting with two of the bodyguards.

The hatpin demonstration was thrilling. Mrs. Garrud showed us how to use an attacker's own strength and momentum against him. She brandished a parasol like a sword and used a hatpin as a dagger. My new hatpin was a smashing success and the envy of all. By far the longest at the party, Mrs. Garrud called it the perfect "saber."

It was an educational afternoon. I couldn't wait to try out what I'd learned on some adversary or other. If Archie got out of line on our honeymoon, I knew exactly what to do. And Fredricks. What fun it would be to try it on him.

As we went back down to the drawing room to finish our tea party, Toogood collected the hatpins. With pride, I laid mine in the center of his silver tray. Lady Battersea assured us that Toogood would return them to our hats, claiming he had a masterful memory for details. A man after my own heart.

Once we were back in our assigned seats, the maid served a lovely sponge topped with more berries. We were enjoying our pudding course when a commotion in the entryway turned all heads. Four jovial men wearing top hats and evening capes stood gaping at us.

"What's all this?" The speaker was a rather pretty man with a mane of silky hair and matching beard that made him look like an attractive lion.

Lady Battersea rushed to greet them. "Dearest," she blushed.

"I told you about the Suffrajitsu party." She laid her hand on the sleeve of the lion, whom I assumed must be Lord Battersea.

"Suffrajitsu, you say?" He surveyed the room.

"A new breed of suffragette?" one of his companions tutted. "That's the last thing we need." With his greying hair parted down the middle, large handlebar moustache, and the eyes of a sad hound, I recognized him as former prime minister Arthur Balfour. The very man the gossip columnist accused of covering up Lord Battersea's "boyish indiscretions." The man Kitty described as a terrible bigot. Even I remembered he was forced to resign after only three years because of his unpopular policies in Ireland, the barbarism of the Boer Wars, and the importation of Chinese labor, which the newspapers compared to slavery. If memory served—and it always did—he claimed that women didn't really want the vote.

The bodyguards sat up at attention. All but one. She shrank into her chair and stared down into her lap. Did she know these men? Or was she merely containing her rage?

"Worse, yet, Arthur, old boy," Lord Battersea said with a laugh, "these are suffragettes learning Japanese martial arts." He slapped his companion on the back. "Any one of these ladies could kick your behind. And you'd deserve it, too. Why shouldn't women have the vote?"

Lord Balfour knew better than to list his reasons against suffrage in front of a dozen foot-fighting suffragettes ready to pounce.

"Why don't you take your friends into the library?" Lady Battersea suggested. "I'll ring for Toogood and he'll see you're taken care of." She patted her husband's arm.

"May I say hello to some friends?" One of the men entered the drawing room and made a beeline for Countess Markievicz and her sister Eva. I recognized him as Jules Silver from the censor's office. With thick dark hair, a goatee beard, and an intense gaze, he was an attractive fellow, despite his big ears. Under his cape, he wore a high-collared starched shirt and silk cravat. He was carrying a heavy black walking stick, which he swung as he crossed the room. He took the countess's hand and kissed it. "Good day, ladies. I see you brought a bouquet from your homeland." He pointed to the centerpiece. "I always did admire your gardens."

"Good day, Jules," the countess replied, in a cut-glass English accent.

"Carrie, is that you?" Mr. Silver made his way around the table to where the demure bodyguard was still staring down into her lap. He waved over to the other men. "Kipper, look who's here." He bowed to Carrie. "Why, it's your wife."

"My wife wouldn't be caught dead at a meeting of bitter old maids." Kipper stepped out from behind Lord Balfour. He wore tiny round wire-rimmed spectacles and a bushy moustache.

Murmurs from the women suggested they knew him. Ellen turned to me and whispered, "That's Randolph Kipper, the poet."

Of course, Randy Kipper. A target of the nasty new gossip column, the one Clifford loved so much. Supposedly, he was a staunch anti-suffragette whose wife was secretly attending meetings for women's rights. Not so secretly, now.

"Come on, Carrie," Mr. Kipper said, crossing over to his wife. "Let's get you home."

"Will you watch my bag?" Ellen asked, laying her reticule handbag on the chair. She looked flushed and wobbled a bit as she stood. I noticed she hadn't touched her cake. She excused herself to go to the powder room. Perhaps the palpable tension in the air was too much for her. Or maybe she just wanted a better view of Mr. Kipper dragging his wife from the house.

Without a word, Carrie Kipper folded her napkin, stood up,

and followed her husband out. Once they were out of sight, their raised voices could be heard echoing through the foyer. And quite a row it was. Mr. Kipper threatened her, and she gave as good as she got. The Kippers were not a model of marital bliss. I made a mental note to ask Archie how he felt about votes for women. If he didn't want his wife to work, did he think she should vote? What other restrictions did he have in mind for marital life? I hoped Kitty was right and my fears were merely "cold feet."

After the noise from the Kippers subsided, Lady Battersea apologized for the intrusion and suggested we head upstairs for the parasol demonstration. I gathered up my large handbag. Since Ellen hadn't returned from the powder room, I took her small bag, too, and then followed our hostess out of the drawing room and through the foyer. As we passed the library, we met a great roar of men's laughter. The door was open, and I glanced over. *Oh, my word.* What was he doing here? Fredrick Fredricks again. Dressed up as Captain Soughton. He'd joined the other men for whisky and cigars. Of course, the bounder knew everyone. "Everyone who's anyone," as Ellen had said.

My cheeks warmed and I averted my gaze until we were out of sight of the library. I hoped the rogue hadn't seen me. Then again, he'd probably followed me here. The cad. Now that he was back in town, I couldn't seem to shake him.

The parasol demonstration was even more enlightening than the hatpin performance. Mrs. Garrud and the bodyguards looked like they were engaged in a graceful dance as they parried and lunged using their brollies as fencing foils. Mrs. Garrud promised that, at the next Suffrajitsu class at the Dojo, we'd all get a chance to try defending ourselves with both umbrellas and hatpins. One of the bodyguards flipped a hulking footman onto his back and then thrust her parasol toward his neck. The ladies clapped and cheered.

As the women filed out of the ballroom, I asked our hostess directions to the powder room. She directed me back downstairs. My heels clicking on the marble floor, I made my way to a door tucked away in an alcove under the stairs. The door was closed, so I knocked. No answer. I knocked again. Nothing. I turned the knob and made to open the door. It was unlocked, but the door wouldn't budge. Something was blocking it. A strange sensation crept up my spine. It was like a cold wind blowing across a grave. The hairs on my arms stood on end. Ellen Davis had gone to the powder room ages ago and never returned.

Two tiny white threads stuck out from under the door. I bent down, plucked them up, and tucked them into my sleeve. I tried the door again. It budged but wouldn't open.

"Ellen?" No answer.

With all my effort, I pushed the door. It moved an inch. I took a deep breath and gave it my all. Another inch. After much exertion, I managed to push the door open just a crack. Breathless, I peeked inside. *Good heavens.* My hand flew to my mouth. Splashed across the bathroom floor was a streak of yellow satin with raspberry lace.

7

PRIME SUSPECT

When the police arrived at 148 Piccadilly, they corralled the tea party into the drawing room, along with the servants and Lord Battersea and his gentlemen friends, including Fredrick Fredricks. It wasn't lost on me that the bounder had conveniently been present at both attacks, this afternoon's fatal attack on Ellen Davis and the thankfully not-so-fatal attack on Kitty at the Dojo. The ladies milled around and snacked on leftover biscuits while the gentlemen smoked. If the dead body didn't kill my appetite, the men's foul smoke filling the drawing room certainly would.

Given that Ellen Davis had collapsed against the door of the lavatory, and given that the door opened inwards, it would have been impossible for someone to have killed her and left the room. So, unless the police found the culprit tucked in a corner of the powder room, out of view of the door, Ellen Davis must have died of natural causes. Still, as I'd learned from experience, one could never be too cautious when it came to guests dying at posh house parties.

My notebook in hand, I took the opportunity to observe the guests and formulate a list of possible suspects just in case it was murder. Had I known Ellen Davis was going to die, I would have paid more attention to the comings and goings of the ladies during tea. Who, besides Ellen, had left the room? Of course, we had all traipsed through the house and up the stairs to the ballroom. During that time, anyone could have peeled off and made a detour to dispose of Ellen.

But why? Why would anyone want Ellen Davis dead? To determine a motive, I needed to learn more about Ellen and her relation to the suffragettes. Luckily, I still had her bag. I'd tucked it into my own handbag, along with the threads from the bottom of the lavatory door, which I'd wrapped in a handkerchief. I just needed a quiet spot where I could examine the contents of her bag—in private. With everyone crammed into the drawing room, privacy was sorely lacking.

Biding my time, I circled the room, writing down the names and descriptions of persons and their postmortem demeanor, keen to discover an especially nervous lady or loquacious gentleman. Our hostess, Lady Battersea, was beside herself as she leaned on her husband's arm. Was she distraught because Ellen Davis was a good friend? Or because a murder in the ground-floor powder room had ruined her tea party? Given her prominence at the head of the table, I think I would have noticed if she had left the room after Ellen did. Then again, she could have invited Ellen to the party with the express intention of killing her. If only I could have got the door open and done a proper investigation before notifying the police.

But with Ellen's body sprawled in front of the door, I never could get the darned thing open. My immediate assessment was made through a tiny crack in the door. And then all I could see was a shoe and the fabric of her dress. I did not see any blood, which was telling. Could the murderer have hit her on the head with a blunt object and then pushed her into the powder room and shut the door? No. That was not possible. The door opened into the powder room and not out of it, which is why I couldn't push the door open with the body in the way. So, if Ellen was murdered, how did the killer get out of the room and close the door? Again, the placement of the body suggested she'd died of natural causes. I wished the police would inform us of their findings.

Clifford would probably tell me my imagination was getting the best of me. Truth be told, there was no evidence it was murder. Perhaps, poor unfortunate Ellen had a heart attack or a stroke and simply dropped dead in Lord Battersea's posh townhouse powder room.

I paced the length of the room, taking in the guests as I went. Sylvia Pankhurst and her bodyguards, minus Carrie Kipper, had installed themselves in a corner where they had their heads together, whispering. Pretending to admire the wallpaper, I eavesdropped. To my surprise, they were speculating that the notorious anti-suffragette, Arthur Balfour, might have something to do with Ellen's death. Propertied women over thirty had just gotten the vote. So, why kill now? And why Ellen? If he'd wanted to make a dent in the movement for universal suffrage, he would have killed Sylvia Pankhurst. Perhaps Ellen was more important to the cause than I realized. I clutched my handbag to my torso and continued my rounds.

In the opposite corner, the men sat drinking whisky and smoking. Arthur Balfour looked tired. He had bags under his eyes, and elbows on his knees, he leaned his chin into his hands. Had murdering Ellen taken its toll? I imagined taking a life was exhausting. Chatting up Fredricks, Mr. Jules Silver—the censor employee who'd insisted on kissing the cheeks of the countess and her angelic sister—held a lit cigarette in one elegant hand but never actually smoked it. Every time I passed by, Fredricks gave me a wink. Did he know something? Of course he did. He always knew more than he let on.

The sisters, Countess Markievicz and Eva Gore-Booth, huddled near the fireplace. The countess seemed to be comforting her younger sister. The parlor maid had been allowed to fetch a glass of milk for the shaken young woman. The countess held her sister in her arms while the maid whispered reassurance to the poor girl. Was Eva Gore-Booth upset because she was close to Ellen Davis? Or perhaps she couldn't stomach death at a tea party? Or was she nearly hysterical because she'd just committed murder? Then again, in her all-black outfit, the countess looked every bit an assassin. As I watched the trio, I noticed the parlor maid's gaze drifting toward the men. One man returned her interest. Jules Silver. Unless my imagination was playing tricks, the two of them were exchanging meaningful glances. If only I knew what they meant.

After I made my list of suspects—Lord and Lady Battersea, Lord Arthur Balfour and Jules Silver, Countess Markievicz and her sister Eva, Sylvia Pankhurst and her bodyguards, Randy and Carrie Kipper (they still could have been in the house at the time of Ellen's demise), and, of course, Fredricks—I retired to the remotest corner of the drawing room in order to inspect the contents of Ellen's bag. I'd just opened it when Fredricks appeared in the shadows. I snapped it shut and buried it in my own handbag.

"Have you identified the culprit?" Fredricks asked, a twinkle in his eyes.

"For all I know, *you* are the culprit." I folded my hands over my bag in my lap. "If experience following you across the globe has taught me anything, it's that you are capable of cold-blooded murder."

"Moi?" He grinned. "I'm deeply hurt you think so poorly of me." He tilted his head. "And what of justice?"

"Is that a confession?"

"As you know, *ma chérie*, I'm a pacifist."

"For a pacifist, it's odd you're always surrounded by violence." To avoid staring into his belt buckle, which was at my eye level, I looked up and met his gaze. "How about you? Have you identified the culprit?"

"Not yet." He sat down next to me. "Why don't we work together?"

"Why don't you tell me everything you know." I fiddled with the handle of my bag.

"I know you're very clever and together we could end this bloody war." Fredricks was always going on about how together we could end the war. Who did he think I was, King George?

"I want the war to end as much as you do, but right now I have more immediate concerns." I scrutinized him. "Spill the beans. Starting with the attack on Kitty."

"Do you think the two are related?" Fredricks asked. "The attack on Miss Lane and the attack on Ellen Davis?"

"One thing they have in common is your presence." I levelled my gaze. "Did you attack Kitty and kill Ellen Davis?"

"Fiona, really." He waved me away. "Do you think I'd make such a mess of it?"

He had a point. Fredricks was nothing if not fastidious in every way.

"Assuming they were related, we should be able to narrow the suspect pool." All I had to do was determine which of the tea party guests were also at the Dojo when Kitty was attacked. "Are any of the men now present also in your advanced jujitsu class?"

"Actually..." He raised his eyebrows. "We all just came from the Dojo. Cyril invited us over for a pick-me-up after class."

"Cyril?"

"Lord Battersea."

"I see." So much for narrowing down the suspects. Any one of those men could have stayed around after class and hit Kitty. And they were all here when Ellen Davis died... or was killed. But why? What motive would any of them have for attacking both Kitty and Ellen? Was one of them so staunchly anti-suffrage that he'd kill? "Do you know why any of those gentlemen might want to dispose of Kitty or Ellen?"

"No." He pursed his lips. "I have no idea." His face lit up. "What about looking at it from another angle—what do Kitty and Ellen have in common?"

"Nothing that I know of." Then again, I didn't know all that much about either of them. "When I first met Kitty, she was going by the name Eliza, Eliza Baker. So, there's that. Both names start with E." Although I'd been working with Kitty for six months, I really didn't know much about her past. And I'd only just met Ellen Davis at the Dojo. "They're both blonde?" That was the best I could come up with. "And they both like, er, liked, bright, lacey frilly frocks." Kitty loved to dress up in frilly, lacey, hot pink or bright orange numbers whenever she got the chance.

"What about something more substantial than looks?" Fredricks asked. "For example, are they acquainted? Shared interests? Friends in common?"

"I don't know," I said with a sigh. "And with Kitty's amnesia, I'm not sure how to find out." Hopefully, Ellen's bag held a clue. If only I could get rid of Fredricks and search its contents. "Too bad the police won't let us near the crime scene."

"Indeed." He crossed his legs. "What do you think of the maid?"

That came out of the blue. I scanned the room. Surely, the maid hadn't been at the Dojo the day Kitty was attacked.

"Over there." Fredricks nodded in the direction of the maid, who was still attending to Eva Gore-Booth. "The three of them are thick as thieves."

"What of Toogood?" I glanced around to locate the butler. He was standing at attention near the entrance. I hadn't thought to add the staff to my list of suspects. Why would the maid or the butler want to kill Ellen Davis? Then again, why would anyone? As soon as Fredricks left me alone with my handbag, I would add them to my list. My list was quite long enough as it was. I needed to cut it down and not add to it. "Who do you reckon is our prime suspect?"

"Ellen Davis is new to London society." He sniffed. "No doubt, like every other society lady, she has her secrets."

I clutched my bag.

"If we learn her secrets, we'll be one step closer to identifying her killer." He stood up and held out his hand. "Would you care to take a turn around the room?"

"Why not?" Who knew how much longer the police would keep us here. I took his hand. It was warm and soft and electrifying. For some reason, after only one turn, I was quite out of breath. The scent of Fredricks's rosewood cologne made me lightheaded.

We'd made it halfway around the drawing room for a second time when a copper appeared in the doorway. Finally. Maybe now we would get some answers.

The officer cleared his throat. "Ladies and gentlemen." He held up his hand. "Can I have your attention, please?"

The guests quieted. The silence was filled with anticipation as the policeman made his way to the center of the room. "It looks like Miss Davis was the victim of foul play."

Murmurs ripped through the crowd and the copper put up his hand again. "We need to take down your names and addresses." He called back to an associate who appeared in the doorway. "And we'll need to take your statements."

Another policeman appeared. He was dressed in a suit and tie rather than a uniform. Presumably, he was the head detective. In one gloved hand, he held up a long emerald-tipped hatpin. "Whose hatpin is this?"

The guests looked at each other. My head was spinning in confusion. Where did he get my hatpin? And why was he brandishing it in the drawing room?

"Does this hatpin belong to one of you ladies?" Holding the hatpin out for identification, he circled the room.

Of course, I recognized it immediately as my new one. My heart leaped into my throat. "It's mine," I croaked. "Where is my hat?"

"And who are you?" he asked.

"Miss Fiona Figg." I felt the blood drain from my face.

"Miss Figg, I'll need you to come with me to the station." He made a beeline for me and took me by the elbow.

"Why?" I swallowed hard. "Was Ellen found wearing my hatpin?"

"In a manner of speaking." He tugged on my arm.

"Surely, I'm not a suspect." I pulled out of his grip.

"Not just any suspect." He clamped onto me again. "The prime suspect."

8

ELLEN'S DIARY

Although I couldn't persuade the coppers I was innocent, I did convince them to let me ring Captain Hall. Bile rose in my throat as I told him about my predicament. All he said was, "Why am I not surprised?" Then he asked to speak to the arresting officer. After moving up the ladder until he reached Basil Thomson, head of Scotland Yard, Captain Hall eventually secured my release, but only if I promised not to leave town until they concluded their investigation. Given I was busy preparing for my wedding and investigating Kitty's attack, not to mention my job at the War Office, I was deuced unlikely to fly the coop. I could *not*, however, convince them to let me take my new hatpin. My consolation was overhearing Basil Thomson repeating the captain's praise. "One of your best agents, you say. Absolutely necessary in the field. I see."

My stop at the police station hadn't been a total waste. While there, I'd learned that my hatpin had been found stabbed into Ellen's neck. Given her position against the lavatory door, the coppers suggested she might have used it to commit suicide. I shuddered to think. And yet, was a poke in the neck with a sharp pin usually fatal? Or had the shock of being stabbed with a hatpin given Ellen a heart attack? The police couldn't say for sure until they'd done an autopsy. In the meantime, I needed to come up with a way to get my hands on that autopsy report once it was ready.

One of the officers was good enough to drop me off at my flat. It was a relief to be home. I hung up my coat and pinless hat, which I'd had to carry since it wouldn't stay attached to my wig without the hatpin. Once inside, I went straight to the kitchen and put on the kettle. Waiting for the water to boil, I emptied the contents of Ellen's bag onto my table. Finally, I could inspect the contents. A nice cup of tea and a rifle through Ellen's bag would be just the ticket. I arranged the contents in a neat row: coin purse, lipstick, small mirror, tiny scent bottle, cards tucked into an interior pocket, an embroidered handkerchief, and a small blue diary. My kettle whistled and I made a strong cuppa with milk and returned to my treasures. Settling in at the table to relish whatever discoveries awaited, I sipped my tea and opened the diary.

To my surprise, it wasn't a date book or a diary at all. In tight, curly handwriting, Ellen had been making odd notes. The first was dated two weeks ago. It read, "Anti-RK's wife secret suffragette" and a page later, "CF caught with pants down. Lord AB covers for him" and then, "Lt. S cheating with E-G-B." Finally, "Maid's affair." I reread the pages. The names were in code. But the content was familiar from that horrible gossip column. RK could be Randy Kipper, whose wife Carrie was secretly attending suffragette meetings and learning jujitsu. CF could be Cyril Flower, known as Lord Battersea, caught in the boys scandal while Lord Arthur Balfour covered for him. LB could be Lady Battersea or Lord Battersea or Lord Balfour. I had no idea about a cheating Lt. S and E-G-B. Why was Ellen keeping track of this dirt? My eyes lingered on another notation: "Attacked KL."

KL. Kitty Lane? Attacked Kitty Lane. Did Ellen know who had attacked Kitty? If she'd seen the attacker, why didn't she tell the police? Did he threaten her, too? Was she too afraid to tell? That was certainly a motive for murder. If Ellen had seen Kitty's attacker fleeing the locker room, he could have murdered her to keep her quiet.

I had an idea. I went to the telephone and rang Clifford. "Do you keep old newspapers?"

"Fiona, old bean, what a pleasant surprise." He sounded chipper. "You'll never guess who came round my flat for a brandy."

He was supposed to be looking after Kitty and Poppy. "Kitty?"

"No." He chuckled. "Fredricks. We were just reminiscing about our last trip to Africa to hunt elephants." Why those men felt the need to kill beasts I'd never understand. It turned my stomach to think of them shooting such regal animals.

"Newspapers," I repeated. I loosened my collar. The mention of Fredricks had made me quite agitated for some reason. Probably because the blackguard was up to something. Clifford always underestimated Fredricks. He didn't believe him capable of being a German spy. I knew better. "Do you have the papers with Mr. Aria's columns? The ones you've been reading to me. About Kipper's wife and Lord Battersea's boys?"

"I can look."

I heard the receiver clunk. I stared at the scrap of paper tucked behind my telephone box. Archie's telephone number and address. He'd given it to me months ago. And although I had the number memorized, I kept the little piece of paper as a memento. I studied the way he wrote his name and number in stiff, bold letters. Was it odd that I'd never been to his flat? He'd never invited me. When we were married, would I move there, or would he move here? Perhaps we would get a new place alto-gether. The wedding was only days away and there was still so much we hadn't discussed. Where would we live? Could I keep working? Would he still love me if I couldn't have children?

"You still there?" Clifford asked, bringing me back from my worries.

"Did you find the newspapers?" I asked.

"Yes. Should I save them for you?"

"Good idea." I pulled my notebook from my bag, flipped to a blank page, and held my pencil at the ready. "For now, can you tell me the dates?"

"Dates?"

"The dates of those columns."

"Righto." The newspapers rustled. "Let's see. The Kipper story was last week, and the Battersea was this week. Column comes out every Thursday. Does that help?"

"Yes." So, Ellen made the notes *before* the columns appeared and not after. How did she know about the dirt beforehand? Perhaps she was friends with the gossip columnist. "What do you know about the journalist?" I asked. "This Mr. Ed Aria?"

"Nothing." He chuckled again. "Nobody does. That's part of his allure. His identity is a mystery."

"There must be some way to find out." I flipped through Ellen's notebook. Most of the pages were blank. Only the first few had notes. And, except for the ones about Lt. S, and "Attacked KL," all appeared to be related to the gossip column. My gut told me I was onto something. "Might you be good enough to drop by later and bring those newspapers? I'll break out the good whisky." I still had a bottle of Scotch my former husband had abandoned in the flat when he took off with his secretary. Some of his pals had given it to him as a wedding present when we got married—almost five years ago now, it seemed like an eternity.

Before the war. Before his infidelity. Before his gruesome death. Before I became a spy for British Intelligence. So much had changed since I was first a blushing bride. Hard to believe I was about to embark on my second marriage. Archie and I were meeting tomorrow to finalize the menu for the reception. I hoped he'd had time to reconsider my future working for the War Office. Thanks to espionage, in some ways, my life had just begun. I wasn't ready to end it, not yet.

"We'll come right over," Clifford said, never one to refuse a nice glass of Scotch.

"We?" I asked, but he'd already hung up.

Waiting for Clifford to arrive with the papers, I poured myself another cuppa and made a few notes of my own. At the tea party, a good number of the ladies were upset about Ed Aria's gossip column. Lady Battersea was especially angry over what had been printed about her husband. The suffragettes were not happy either. Sylvia Pankhurst had been called a coward and her body-guards, harpies. The countess and her sister had been attacked as militants. Nearly everyone there had a reason to despise this Ed Aria and his wicked gossip column.

What if Ellen Davis had supplied information to this Ed Aria? She could have been one of his sources, an informant. And what if one of the ladies had discovered she was betraying their confidence by feeding information to the journalist? That could be a motive for murder. If someone wanted to stop the gossip badly enough, they might have gone after the source... unfortunately, using my hatpin.

In that case, Kitty's attack was not related to Ellen's murder. Unless Kitty was somehow involved in, or implicated by, Ed Aria's gossip column. Like Clifford, Kitty loved to read the society pages. She cooed over the latest fashions and always knew who was doing what with whom. Of course, with Kitty, it could have been an act. She was a mysterious creature, especially now with her memory gone.

Stuck in the back of my notebook, I found the little clover charm from the Dojo. I unfolded my handkerchief and laid it out on the table. What was this jewel from? A charm bracelet? A cufflink? A tie pin? Something that had flown off Kitty's attacker's person during the attack in the locker room?

A knock on the door sent me scurrying to answer it. I hesitated a second. What if it was the police? I could swear they had a plain-clothed man following me. I took a deep breath and opened the door. Poppy trotted inside, her toenails tapping as she went. She was followed by Clifford, Kitty, and Fredricks. It was a regular party. I broke out the fancy whisky and poured us each a glass, mine smaller than the rest.

"Kitty, dear..." I handed her a glass. "How are you feeling? Any better?" What I really meant was *has your memory returned?*

"I feel fine." She plopped into a chair. "Now, if only I knew my name."

"Did you find a Jane at your tea party?" Clifford asked.

"Lady Mary Jane Russell, Duchess of Bedford, was the only Jane present, who, despite her staunch devotion to her causes, seemed a kind-hearted soul. Like the others, she was not a fan of Ed Aria's gossip column." I handed whiskys all around. "Did you bring the newspapers?" I wriggled my fingers.

Clifford produced a bundle of folded papers from under his arm. "Every Thursday's paper since Aria's column first appeared," he said proudly, handing them to me.

The sitting room was quite cozy filled with my colleagues... and Fredricks. With my travel schedule, it had been some time since I'd entertained. It was nice to have company. I dropped the newspapers on a side table and zipped back to the kitchen to search my cupboards for a tin of biscuits or some nibbles. My ice box was empty except for a bottle of milk. My cupboard wasn't much better. I found a half-empty tin of stale biscuits. I laid out the meagre offering on a plate. On my way out of the kitchen, I rewrapped the clover jewel in my hanky and tucked it into my pocket. After serving the stale biscuits, I produced the jewel. "Have any of you ever seen a jewel like this?" I held it in my palm and walked the small circle to show it around.

When I showed it to Fredricks, he got a funny look on his face. "Why do you ask?"

"Do you recognize it?" I brought it closer and turned it over.

"Where did you get it?" he asked.

"I found it in the stall where Kitty was attacked." I glared at him. "You know something. Spill it."

"In Irish mythology, the shamrock, with its three leaves, is a symbol for the goddess Brigid and her three functions, poetry, healing, and smithing." He tutted. "Saint Patrick used the shamrock to explain the Holy Trinity in his attempts to convert the pagans away from the goddess to his male tripartite god."

Shamrock. Was the clover ornament a proper shamrock? "Have you seen it before?" I asked, suspecting he knew more than he was letting on. "Forget about its meaning, do you know who it belongs to?"

"Do I get a prize if I do?" He winked at me.

"You'll get more than you bargained for if you don't tell me what you know." I put my hands on my hips. "Spill the beans."

"Maybe later." His eyes danced. "When we're alone."

I rolled my eyes at him and then went back to my seat. Between sips of whisky, I examined the newspapers. In the last month, there was dirt on almost every one of those ladies at the tea party. In fact, being the target of Mr. Aria's column united them as much as their commitment to women's rights.

"It's odd," Kitty said. "The way the name Jane Archer keeps

popping into my head." She shook her head, as if to empty it of the interloper. "And a school called *L'Espion*."

"*L'Espion*." I nearly spat out my whisky. "A French school called The Spy?"

Kitty had always maintained she'd gone to boarding school in France. But I'd always suspected her so-called boarding school was really something else.

"Who is this Jane Archer then?" I asked. "Does anyone know a Jane Archer?" I looked at Fredricks. He knew everyone. Everyone who was anyone.

"Archer the proper name or archer the bowman?" Fredricks grinned. "Or, in this case, bowwoman."

I hadn't thought of archery. Another of Kitty's hidden skills?

"I have memories of working with someone else, too." Kitty sipped her drink. "A Mr. Basil Thomson."

"I say," Clifford said, removing his pipe from his mouth. "Basil Thomson is the head of Scotland Yard."

"Is it possible I work for Scotland Yard?" Kitty asked, picking at the hem of her blouse. "I just remembered someone else." She let out a little gasp. "Vernon Kell... the man who attacked me." Her lip trembled. "He's coming after me. He wants me dead."

"If Vernon Kell wanted you dead, you wouldn't be here chatting," Fredricks said under his breath. "Vernon Kell is the head of MI5, the British secret intelligence service." He sat fixated on Kitty. "Kell doesn't have the power to arrest, so he enlists Thomson, who loves taking all the credit as a spy-catcher." He shook his head. "What is your relationship with Thomson and Kell?"

"I don't know." Kitty's cheeks turned pink. "I'm sorry."

"There, there, dear," I said encouragingly. "It's not your fault." I gave Fredricks the evil eye.

"Could MI5 want me dead?" Kitty asked. "I think they sent an assassin to my hospital room."

Not MI5 again. If I didn't know better, I'd think the girl had read too many spy stories. The Kitty I knew read only fashion magazines. "No one wants you dead." I let out a big sigh. "Your name is Kitty Lane, and you work with me at the War Office."

"And me," Clifford said.

"But I don't remember working with you." Kitty's voice was full of frustration. "Can't we find this Jane Archer and Basil Thomson or Vernon Kell and ask them who I am?"

"Of course we can, dear." I took the plate of biscuits over to offer her another one. "It will sort itself out." I held out the plate. "You'll see." I hoped I was right. "We just have to be patient." I patted her arm. "Your memory will return in time."

"In the meantime," Fredricks said, his voice stern, "perhaps you should keep your memories of Scotland Yard and MI5 to yourself."

"Don't be rude," I chastised him.

"I'm not being rude, *ma chérie*." He sipped his whisky. "I'm being prudent." He crossed his long legs. "If Miss Lane is indeed employed by MI5, her work is classified." He raised his eyebrows. "And there are many who would kill to keep it that way, including Vernon Kell."

A chill ran up my spine. Had Kitty been going around telling people she worked at MI5? Was she putting her own life in danger without realizing it? Then again, whoever attacked her did so before the amnesia and before her fantasies of working with MI5. "What else do you remember, dear?" I asked, trying to keep the sound of alarm out of my voice.

"A soldier named Somersby," Kitty said. "I think I work with him at MI5. Unless... he's the one who attacked me. Or the one who came to the hospital..."

"Archie!" This time I did choke on my whisky. "I'm certain Archie did not attack you." Talk about an overactive imagination.

"Archie is my fiancé." I dabbed my mouth with my napkin. "He works for your uncle, Captain Hall, at the War Office." I waved her away. "He does not work for MI5. Enough with all this nonsense about MI5."

"Don't be so quick to dismiss Miss Lane's latent memories," Fredricks said. "I know you don't believe me when I tell you that your fiancé is not what he seems." He stood up. "But Miss Lane is in imminent danger. I suggest we get her to a secure location immediately. Some place she will be safe while she recovers her memory."

"How about my old mum's place in Reading?" Clifford's face lit up. "Mum would love a visitor and that way I could visit Poppy... and Kitty, too, of course."

"Pash." I shook my head. "You're all talking nonsense. Kitty will stay here with me."

I dismissed the girl's delusions about Archie. Archie was exactly what he seemed. An earnest and kind man, and a loyal British soldier. And while he did engage in secret missions for the War Office—as did I—he was not an MI5 assassin. Then again, if Archie did work for MI5, that would explain a lot. Every time I asked him a question, his answer was "Classified." His entire life was classified. But if he did work for MI5, *surely* he would have told me, his fiancée. Within a week, we'd be married, for heaven's sake. The wedding. When was I going to get time to finalize arrangements for the wedding? I bit my lip. I really needed to talk to Archie. About the wedding. About Kitty. About our life together.

After Clifford and Fredricks left, I installed Kitty and Poppy on my living room sofa. Then, I went to the kitchen. I stared at the notecard with Archie's number. There was no way he attacked Kitty. He would never do that. But perhaps he knew something about the person who did. His clearance was higher than mine and he always seemed to have access to classified information. I lifted the receiver from its cradle.

The telephone rang and rang. No answer. I glanced at my watch. After eleven. Where could he be? The whole strange situation was making my head hurt. I took a packet of headache powders and went to bed. I would confront Archie in the morning.

For some reason, I couldn't get comfortable. The bed was too hot one minute and too cold the next. *What nonsense. MI5.* Tossing and turning, I thought of all the times Archie appeared out of nowhere and then disappeared again, all the times he told me his mission was classified, all his secrets. Truth be told, I was marrying a mystery.

9

KITTY'S INTERLUDE

Everyone kept insisting her name was Kitty Lane and she worked for the War Office. So, why didn't she believe it? Like a distant sound coming from a direction that she couldn't quite place, the name Jane Archer tugged at her consciousness. Why? Who was Jane Archer? Was it her name?

The only thing certain in her mind was MI5. And yet the more she said about the government's secret service, the more her "friends" balked. Trouble was, she didn't remember these so-called friends. Although "Aunt" Fiona's nagging was vaguely familiar.

She got up from the sofa and paced around Fiona's living room, careful not to run into anything in the dark. The dog followed on her heels. She stuffed her hands into the pockets of her kimono, the same one she'd been wearing when she was attacked at the Dojo, her jujitsu robe. Given she didn't know where she lived, she had exactly two outfits. The jujitsu kimono and a pink polka-dotted sailor's dress whose fabric matched the bow in Poppy's topknot. Hard to believe she was the sort of girl to wear such frothy clothes. She preferred an all-black riding kit. In her mind, she could almost see herself, hair flying in the wind, riding a chestnut stallion across the moors.

She stopped to gaze out the window onto the dark street. Poppy sat next to her and put a small paw atop her foot. She looked down at the dog. What a sweetie. She scooped her up. The dog's bow had come untied yet again. "Let me fix you up, Poppy-poo."

She leaned against the window frame and removed the pink ribbon. When she did, a tiny slip of paper drifted to the floor. "What's this?" She bent to pick it up. Interesting. An address in Finsbury. Was that where she lived? It would make sense it was tucked into the dog's bow in case the little darling got lost. Although putting it in her collar would make more sense. Then again, what made sense to her now might not be the same as what had made sense before her amnesia. There was only one way to find out.

Quietly, she changed into her dress and little brown boots. She went to the coat closet and slipped into one of Aunt Fiona's wool coats and grabbed one of her hats too. The coat was long on her. All the better to protect against the nippy night air. The hat was an ugly taupe cloche. But it would call less attention to her than a mop of blonde curls. She stuffed a couple of chair cushions under the blanket on the sofa, and then gave Poppy a command. The dog curled up near where her head would be if she were still lying there. "Stay." She patted the little dog's head. "Good girl."

She went to the side table near the closet and found Fiona's handbag. After a bit of searching, she found Fiona's keys in a small side pocket. She "borrowed" the keys and a few quid and then tiptoed to the door. Holding her breath, she turned the knob as slowly as possible. A squeaky hinge made her stop and listen.

Hopefully Fiona was sound asleep. She stepped out into the hallway and silently pulled the door shut behind her.

The brisk night air felt good against her cheeks as she hurried to the busiest corner. She didn't have to wait long for a taxi. Finsbury. For some reason, she remembered that part of London had suffered heavy bombing. Would she find her flat destroyed? As she rode through the dark streets of London suburbs, she took in everything, hoping something would jog her memory.

King's Road in Finsbury was lined with brick townhouses. They all looked alike. The driver asked her to point out which one, but she couldn't. He slowed to a crawl and they both studied the addresses, looking for number thirty-three.

"I'll pay you double fare if you'll wait here for me." She flashed what she hoped was a charming smile. She didn't know what she was walking into. And if he didn't wait, she'd be hard pressed to find another taxi out here at this time of night.

"What's that?" The driver cupped his ear.

She repeated her request, only louder this time.

The driver scowled. "How long?"

"Just a few minutes." She kept her tone light. "I want to pick up some clothes from my flat and then you can drive me back to my friend's place."

"What's that?" He cupped his ear again. Obviously, the fellow had hearing trouble.

She repeated what she'd said, only louder.

His eyes went wide. "I see."

Let him think whatever he would about her "friend," as long as he waited.

"Thank you." She hopped out and approached the front door.

Trouble was, she didn't have the key. If it was her flat, where was her key? Now what? She glanced back at the driver. He was smoking and staring straight ahead. She felt Fiona's hat for its hatpin and then pulled a pin from her own hair. Armed with hatpin and hairpin, she manipulated the door lock. Not stopping to consider how she came by these dubious skills, she maneuvered the two pins into the lock and popped it open. Quietly, she mounted the stairs and stopped in front of flat 2B, as indicated on the slip of paper she'd found attached to Poppy's ribbon.

The moment of truth. Was this her flat? Should she knock? For all she knew, she had a husband or little sister living with her. Then again, no one had come to claim her from hospital. Chances were she was alone in the world. She felt it in her gut. All alone... except for Poppy.

She stood in front of the door for a few more seconds. What if it wasn't her flat? What was on the other side of this door? Whatever—or whoever—was a clue to her identity. A clue she desperately needed. In the best case, it was her place, and she could gather some spare clothes and her toothbrush. In the worst case... well, she'd learn something about herself, but at what cost? She was about to find out.

She tried the doorknob. Locked. She inhaled deeply and inserted the pins into the lock. It was even easier to pick than the front door. She slowly pushed the door open. The room was pitch black. She waited a few seconds for her eyes to adjust to the darkness. The faint scents of citrus and cedar hung in the air like a memory. A memory that wasn't hers. The hairs on the back of her neck stood to attention. Muscles tight, on high alert, she entered the room. Nothing looked familiar. If this was her flat, she didn't recognize it. The sparse plain furniture. The heavy dark curtains. She crept through the living room and down a hallway toward an interior door. It was closed. She guessed it was the bedroom.

Just in case this wasn't her flat, she left the lights off. Despite the darkness, she had a cat-like sense of her surroundings. Ready to pounce at the slightest provocation, she continued toward the bedroom. When she reached the door, she stopped. Panting from anxiety, she took several deep breaths to calm herself. *Here goes.* She blew out a breath and then yanked the door open.

The barrel of a pistol was pointed right at her face. She winced. Not her flat, then. A man stepped out of the shadows.

"What are you doing here?" He lowered the gun. "How'd you get in?"

She squinted at him. He looked vaguely familiar. "Do I know you?"

"So, it's true, then." He sighed. "You don't remember?"

She shrugged. "Should I?"

"You can't be here." He ran a hand through his hair. "You're compromising our mission." He took her by the elbow. "Does Fiona know you're here?"

What did he have to do with Fiona? "So many questions." She jerked out of his grip. "How about you give me some answers." Looking into his eyes, she remembered something. She *had* seen him before. Yes. Her mind was clearing. He was her mark. The man she'd been assigned to follow. She'd been tracking his every move for the last six months. She tightened her fists. She couldn't remember his name. But she did remember he was the one they'd been looking for. The double agent. The mole in MI5.

The question was, did he know she knew? If he did, that would explain why someone was trying to kill her. She felt the blood drain from her cheeks. Hang it all. Why *he* was trying to kill her.

"Forget I came." She turned and sprinted toward the door.

Gun in hand, he charged after her. "He'll come after you."

She whirled around and kicked the gun out of his hand. It clattered to the floor. He lunged for it, but she was faster. She grabbed the gun, rolled out of his grasp, and pulled the trigger.

The crack of the shot was deafening. Her head spinning, still clutching the gun, she ran. As she took the stairs two at a time, she tucked the gun into her coat pocket.

Back outside, she dove into the back seat of the taxi. "Drive!"

"What's that?" He cupped his ear.

"Drive!" she shouted at the top of her lungs.

Her head in her hands, she squeezed her eyes shut and tried to catch her breath. She'd just shot a man. But who? She didn't even know his name.

10

THE GOSSIP COLUMN

After several hours of fitful sleep and terrible nightmares about Archie being shot and my spending the rest of my life in prison, I got up, tossed on my bathrobe, and padded out to the kitchen to make a cup of tea. On my way, I looked in on Kitty, who was sleeping as peacefully as an angel with Poppy curled around her neck. The dog lifted its head as I passed. I put my finger to my lips. Poppy put her head down and closed her eyes. Good doggie.

In the kitchen, I put on the kettle and then went back to the newspapers. Carefully, I cut the Aria columns out of every Thursday's paper and then laid them out side by side on the table. Head in hands, I studied the columns. There had to be some clue to Ellen's death. Something I was missing. If only I knew the identity of the mysterious Mr. Ed Aria and his relation to Ellen. Journalists—especially gossip columnists—often used bylines that were aliases or pseudonyms. Ed Aria might not be his real name. I stared down at the newspaper column to see if there was any indication of whether Ed Aria was his real name. *Wait a second*. The byline wasn't *Ed* Aria. But the initials E and D.

"E. D. Aria," I said into my teacup. *Good heavens*. E. D. Ellen

Davis. Of course, that would explain why Ellen's diary was filled with notes on the very same gossip that later appeared in the newspaper column. If Ellen Davis *was* E. D. Aria, that would also explain why any one of the ladies at the tea party might want to kill her. The killer must have learned her true identity and then disposed of her with my hatpin. With that column, she'd made a lot of enemies. The question was, who knew that E. D. Aria and Ellen Davis were one and the same?

E. D.'s devoted readers—if she had any besides Clifford— were going to be disappointed tomorrow (or should I say later today) when her column was missing from Thursday's *Daily Chronicle*. Unless, of course, she'd submitted the column before she died.

Sipping my tea, I reviewed my notes from the tea party. Considering my revelation about E. D. Aria, they appeared in a new light. Lord and Lady Battersea's world had been rocked by scandal since the gossip about his penchant for boys appeared in the newspaper. Lord Balfour's coverup hadn't gained him any favor, either. The suffragettes were very protective of their leader, who had been smeared in the column as an anarchist, and so had her bodyguards. Surely Lady Mary Jane Russell wouldn't have killed the columnist just because she'd claimed the lady was going deaf and preferred birds to people. And yet, any of the others could have conspired to kill Ellen Davis. Where my hatpin fit in was still a mystery. And then there was the matter of the lavatory door. How could anyone have killed Ellen and got out of that room? Either they would have had to move the body, in which case, it would not have been up against the door. Or... or, what?

And if the gossip column was the motive for Ellen's death, what was the motive for the attack on Kitty? There must be something to connect Kitty to the gossip columnist or the dirt in the newspaper. I unfolded my handkerchief and stared down at the shamrock. "Give up your clues, my little friend," I whispered.

"Aunt Fiona." Yawning, Kitty appeared in the doorway. "What are you doing up?" Poppy clicked along behind her.

"Couldn't sleep." I smiled at her. Poor girl. I took comfort in the fact that she'd called me *Aunt* Fiona. "Are you feeling better, my dear?" Hopefully, she was back to her old self. I missed that silly girl.

She looked down at my rows of newspaper clippings and the clover charm and her eyes lit up. "Do you have any face powder?"

What in the world did she want with face powder in the middle of the night? "Of course, but—"

"Go get it." She plunked down in the chair next to mine. "Hurry up."

She must be feeling better. She was back to bossing me around. I did as she asked and went to fetch my face powder. Poppy turned circles around my legs, making it more difficult to traverse my flat.

When I returned, Kitty had the shamrock charm laid out in front of her. I handed her the face powder, and she proceeded to dust the jewel with my powder brush.

"Look at this." She pointed to a fingerprint that appeared in the powder.

I bent down and examined it. "It's only a partial print."

"Part of a very large thumbprint, I'd say." She smiled up at me, obviously chuffed. Poppy sat at her feet and barked in agreement.

"But whose?" I sat down.

"It's too large for most women." She pushed the handkerchief toward me. "It belongs to a man." She tapped my notebook. "You can eliminate the suffragettes as suspects in my attack. If this charm came from my attacker, chances are he is a man. And a large one at that. Who are the men on your list?"

Was she back to her old self? She hadn't mentioned MI5 or strange men coming after her. No more talk of Basil Thomson or Vernon Kell. Neither of whom were on my list of suspects. I cracked open my notebook and read off the male suspects, which was comprised of the men from the advanced jujitsu class. "Fredrick Fredricks, of course, Randy Kipper, Jules Silver, Lord Battersea, Lord Balfour, and the jujitsu instructor, William Garrud."

"Do any of them have connections to Ireland?" she asked.

"I haven't the foggiest." But she had a good point. If the clover jewel was indeed a shamrock, then the assailant might have some association with Ireland. What about Ellen Davis? Did she have a connection to Ireland? The countess and her gazelle-like sister did. And what about Kitty? She woke up speaking Irish for heaven's sake. "What was your relationship with Ellen Davis?" I asked.

She gave me a puzzled look. "Relationship?"

Oh no. She didn't remember Ellen. Even though the woman had visited her at hospital. "I'm wondering if your attack and her murder are related."

"I think I only met Ellen last week when I started practicing at the Dojo." She shrugged.

What a relief. She hadn't forgotten Ellen. "Can you think of anything that links the two of you?" It *could* have been a coincidence that Kitty was attacked two days before Ellen was killed. Then again, probably not.

"Not really." She shook her head.

Whatever my instincts told me, prudence required I treat the two as separate. I didn't want to start with incorrect assumptions. "Have you remembered anything else?" I finished my tea. My stomach growled, and I went in search of any leftover biscuits.

"I work for MI5." Her voice was strong and confident... and deuced convincing. "Maybe my name is Jane Archer?"

Not that again. I sat blinking at her. Who was this girl? Eliza Baker, Kitty Lane, or Jane Archer. How many bloody names did she have? I thought of my own undercover aliases. It was possible she was telling the truth. Perhaps I didn't know her real name. Why should I? I shuddered. How could I have been working with her for the last six months, trusting my life to her, and still not have any idea of her true identity? "What are you saying? You're not really Kitty Lane?"

"I'm not sure." She let out a big breath. Poppy gave a reassuring little squeak. "What do you think, Poppy-poo?"

Aunt Fiona. Poppy-poo. We were making progress in getting our old Kitty back.

"What about the gossip columnist, E. D. Aria?" I stabbed at one of the newspaper clippings. "Do you have any connection to her?"

"Her?" She squinted at me. "I thought Uncle Clifford said the journalist was named Ed."

"He did." I passed one of the clippings to her. "But it's not Ed. It's the initials E. D." I pointed at the byline. "As in Ellen Davis."

Her mouth fell open. "Ellen Davis is... was the gossip columnist E. D. Aria?"

I nodded. "So it seems."

"Well, I'll be." Her eyes went wide. "Oh dear..."

"Oh dear, what?" Alarm bells went off in my head.

"That's why she was asking me all those questions after you and Uncle Clifford left the hospital the other day." She grimaced. "What if I divulged classified information? Or dangerous information? Information that got her killed?"

"What did you tell her?"

She blushed. "I told her about Jane Archer and MI5 and Lieutenant Somersby..." Her voice trailed off. "I just wanted someone to listen and believe me and not look at me like I'm mad."

"What did you tell her about Archie?" I dropped my teaspoon with a clank.

"Nothing much." She tightened her lips.

I levelled my gaze. "Tell me."

"Only that he and I worked together at MI5," she said quickly. "But now he was trying to kill me."

"Good heavens."

"I know." She sighed. "I just wanted someone to listen to me."

"I'm sorry if I haven't been listening." I'd been one of the people looking at her like she was mad. I should have taken her seriously and not doubted her—even when she said her name was Jane Archer and she worked for MI5. I really should have asked the doctor how to approach the situation. I'd never known an amnesiac before. Not even at Charing Cross Hospital. "I believe you." Saying it didn't make it so, but it was the best I could do. "I believe you, dear. I do. I really do." No, I didn't. But it wouldn't kill me to pretend, for her sake.

For the next hour, I told Kitty everything I knew about her and recounted our adventures together—Manhattan, Cairo, London, Italy, and Moscow. How could she forget narrowly escaping the Bolsheviks? Or our antics with Mussolini in the Dolomite mountains? Come to think of it, MI5 had a hand in our Italy mission. I just never quite understood what it was. But if Kitty and Archie were both working for MI5, then the whole queer situation suddenly made more sense. On that mission, I'd learned MI5 was paying Mr. Mussolini for information about German interests in Italy. And only then had Archie taken me to Mussolini's secret lair. As I recalled, Archie and Kitty were pretty tight-lipped about the whole operation.

"I'm sorry, dear." I dabbed my mouth with a napkin. "I have to get ready to go." I hated to leave Kitty on her own fretting about her lack of memory. But I had to meet Archie at Wilton's to finalize the menu for our wedding reception in King's Square Park across from the church. Needless to say, he'd chosen the restaurant. He'd better not dash off again and leave me holding the bag.

I went to the powder room to do what I could with my face. Although I was irritated by his behavior last time, and perturbed by the possibility he was really an MI5 agent, I still wanted to look my best. A woman should always look her very best, especially when preparing for a fight.

I picked out a lovely lavender wool frock, perfect for a brisk spring day. Instead of my practical Oxfords, I went with a pair of strappy Mary Janes. And for the hat... well, the hat was always the most difficult decision. I stood staring into my closet. The large purple bucket hat with white silk flowers? Or the close-fitting green cloche with black lace band? What the heck. I tugged the large bucket hat over the top of my blonde bob wig. I patted my new bag with my spy paraphernalia. Yes, we were meeting to discuss the menu. But one never knew when one might need a lock-pick set or a spy lipstick with its handy double mirror.

I arrived at Wilton's a few minutes early, despite taking a circuitous route in the hopes of losing the plain-clothed policeman who was following me. The hostess showed me to a table in the back where the owner was waiting with menus spread out on a table. He was a small balding man with a large belly, who, from the looks of him, sampled every dish they made. Leaning back in his chair, he sat reading the newspaper. I hated to disturb him. Especially since Archie hadn't arrived yet. I decided to wait up front instead. That way, I could mentally rehearse how I would confront Archie about MI5 and his secret life. How about, "Are you an MI5 assassin?"

I sat down on a chair at the front of the restaurant and

removed my gloves. I would give him an ultimatum. If we were to be married, he would have to tell me everything. *Everything.*

After ten minutes, I got up and went back outside. *No more secrets.* I strolled up and down the street, looking in the windows. *No more lies.* Another fifteen minutes of window-shopping and my legs got cold, so I went back inside. We would swear to always tell each other the truth. Where was he? He was now half an hour late. How much longer should I wait? *The truth and nothing but the truth.* I waited another fifteen minutes. *No matter what.*

Good grief. I tugged on my gloves and stomped to the back of the restaurant.

He wasn't coming. Archie had stood me up. I couldn't believe it. I was going to have to tell the owner that my fiancé didn't show. Anger didn't begin to describe my feelings. I was fuming. And after I'd so carefully planned how to present my ultimatum.

When I got to the back of the restaurant, the owner had vanished. The menus were there. His newspaper was there. But he was gone. A photograph in the newspaper caught my eye. I picked it up. I felt the blood drain from my cheeks. My breath shaking, I dropped into a chair. There in E. D. Aria's gossip column was a photograph of Archie and Eva Gore-Booth arm in arm, strolling down a garden path. I looked closer. I thought so. A garden path lined with camellia bushes and lily-of-the-valley. So that was where he'd picked those flowers. I was overcome with nausea as I focused on the caption:

The Markievicz estate in Dublin.

My heart raced as I read the article. It was entitled, "The Cheater." It went on to say:

Lieutenant Archibald Reginald Somersby...

Golly, I didn't know his middle name was Reginald.

...engaged to Miss Fiona Figg, has been seen two-timing her with Countess Markievicz's younger sister, Eva Gore-Booth, at the Markievicz estate.

My stomach sank. Lt. S from Ellen's notebook.

Oh, Archie, what have you done? Brushing away tears, I ran out of the restaurant.

11

ADVANCED JUJITSU

Running out of the restaurant, my eyes blurred with tears, I smacked into a man. He grabbed me by the shoulders. I struggled to get free. Had the coppers found more evidence against me? Was he apprehending me and taking me back to the station. A familiar scent of rosewood made me blink.

"*Ma chérie*, I was hoping to run into you." Fredrick Fredricks. Not the police. What a relief... of sorts. From the frying pan into the fire. "I just didn't know it would be so literal."

I sniffed.

His voice was full of concern as he pulled me into an embrace. "What's happened?" The bag he was carrying pressed against my back.

"Oh, Fredrick." I buried my face in his jacket. He smelled of rosewood, moustache wax, and something else... something stalwart and furtive. "You were right about Archie."

"This is one time I'm not pleased to be right." Fredricks stroked my wig. "If it would make you happy, I'll agree to be wrong from now on." He held me tight. "I'm so sorry, *ma chérie*." He kissed my cheek and then held me at arm's length. "I know what will cheer you up." Smiling, he took my hand. "Come on. I have a surprise for you." I let him lead me up the street and around the corner. He stopped in front of Piccadilly Dojo.

I looked up into his face. "Have you learned who attacked Kitty?"

"Let's find out together." He brushed a wig hair from my cheek. "Shall we?" He held the door open for me.

I didn't know his plan, but I sorely needed the distraction. The image of Archie with the beautiful gazelle-like Eva haunted me. Why did I ever think he would settle for me? Plain old Fiona Figg, file clerk from a family of farmers and greengrocers. Of course he would ditch me for the posh daughter of a baronet... and she was a poet, too.

Fredricks led through the foyer to the tearoom. With its bamboo screens and calligraphy wall-hangings, it was sparse but charming. He sat me down on a cushion on the floor at a low wooden table and ordered a pot of Japanese tea called Sencha.

A few minutes later, a waitress wearing a flowered pink kimono delivered a heavy black teapot and adorable little cups. Fredricks and I sipped the bright green tea from Japanese teacups and Fredricks told me his plan. To my surprise and delight, it involved false moustaches and a bushy beard.

"I know how keen you are to investigate the advanced jujitsu class," he said with a wink. "So, I've brought everything you need to pass as my cousin visiting from France." He placed the bag he'd been carrying on the table and slid it across to me. "In here, you'll find all the accoutrements to transform the beautiful Miss Fiona Figg into the fearsome Monsieur Marcel Désiré—excepting, of course, the accent and skill at martial arts." He smiled. "You, *ma chérie*, will have to provide those."

I was fluent in French, thanks to classes at North London Collegiate School for Girls. So, the accent should be no problem.

The foot fighting, on the other hand, would be a challenge. My mind may be agile, but my body was not. In fact, at school, I'd been known for my clumsiness.

"Don't worry." Fredricks must have sensed my unease. "Just follow my lead."

I nodded and picked up the parcel. "No shoes?"

"We practice bare footed." He got a mischievous twinkle in his eyes and looked me up and down. "Something to look forward to..." He twisted the end of his moustache. Cheeky devil.

* * *

My commitment to detection and the art of disguise did not extend to the men's locker room. Careful to make sure no one saw me, I carried the bag to the women's locker room, to the very stall where Kitty was attacked. I took the opportunity to conduct another quick search of the area. After several days, I didn't expect to find anything, especially since no doubt the cleaning staff had been in. But it didn't hurt to look. All I found were a couple of long hairs stuck on the corner of a bench. I wrapped them in my handkerchief for Kitty to analyze later. One appeared to be blonde and the other dark. The blonde one could be Kitty's. And the dark one?

Eager to make my transformation, I pulled the curtain and emptied the contents of the bag onto a bench. I couldn't wait to see what Fredricks had brought for me. The promise of facial hair made my pulse quicken. Ooooh. The bag contained: a tiny bottle of spirit gum. A lovely ginger handlebar moustache with matching bushy beard and neatly parted ginger wig. Oval wire-rimmed spectacles with rose-colored glass—Fredricks always was one for dramatics. And a belted jujitsu kimono. I stripped down to my smalls and slipped into the kimono. Wearing the heavy canvas robe and trousers, I felt stronger already.

Peeking out from the curtain, I glanced around the locker room, ears pricked. Once I was confident no one else was there, I took the spirit glue and facial hair to a mirror hanging over the sink. Unscrewing the top of the little bottle gave me a thrill. And when the pungent smell of the glue hit my nose, I smiled. Ahh. Nothing like a moustache to lift one's spirits. I painted my upper lip with glue and then carefully pressed on the moustache. As I did, Uncle Frank appeared in the mirror. I repeated the process with the beard and then stepped back to admire the transformation. I made a rather handsome gent. I straightened the short wig and wrapped the arms of the spectacles around my ears. I hardly recognized myself. Hopefully no one else would either.

How I loved being a man. The freedom of wearing trousers. I thought of my male disguises with the nostalgia of a long-lost friend: Dr Vogel, Rear Admiral Arbuthnot, Harold the helpful bellboy. A pang of regret stabbed at my heart. The first time Archie kissed me, in Paris, the city of love, I had been disguised as Harold the helpful bellboy. I had on a moustache then, too. Archie said it tickled. He still teased me about that moustache.

Oh, Archie. *Where are you? Why didn't you show up?* My breath caught in my chest. What if something had happened to him? Ours was a dangerous business. And he was still flying missions for the Flying Corps. So many fine men had been shot down, captured, or killed. I shuddered. Then again, if E. D. Aria was right and he was two-timing me with Eva Gore-Booth, I'd kill him myself.

Enough dillydallying. I had to get to the gym before class started. After one last glance in the mirror, off I went.

I was the first one in the gym, which was fine with me. The only way to the locker rooms was through the gym. I could observe the others enter before they went to change. I was here for my investigation, after all. And not just to enjoy spirit gum and facial hair.

The wood floor was cool against my feet. I leaned against the wall directly across the door to watch. Curling my toes against the chill, I levelled my gaze at Lord Battersea, the first to enter. He was as feminine as I was masculine. Was that the reason he wore such impressive facial hair? I was making good use of my androgynous appearance to pass as a man. If he shaved, he could make a very pretty woman. The next to enter was Lord Balfour. Slightly hunched over, he looked old and tired. Perhaps he took jujitsu for the exercise. I'd heard he was an avid tennis player and an amateur philosopher. Swinging a black walking stick, Jules Silver entered next. He was something of a dandy with the eyes and nose of a hawk. As he passed by, he doffed his hat.

I averted my eyes and hoped he didn't recognize me either from the tea party or the War Office. A glimmer drew my gaze to his walking stick.

"Admiring my Shillelagh, I see." He smiled. "She's a beauty."

Oh dear.

He approached me and held out the stick. "From County Wicklow, or so I've been told."

"Very fine." I nodded and took a closer look at his stick. *Crikey.* It was bejeweled with bronze shamrocks, each with a tiny green stone dotting its center—just like the one I'd found in the locker room. "May I?" I asked in my deepest tenor and held out my hand.

"Of course." He handed me the stick. "I'm Jules, by the way. Jules Silver."

"Fi, er, Finn. Fred, er, Captain Soughton's cousin." What name did Fredricks give me? I glanced around the room as if my imaginary surname could be lurking in some corner. Oh, right. "Monsieur Marcel Désiré, at your service." I turned the stick over in my hands. "She's a beaut, alright." I pretended to admire it as I looked for a missing shamrock. Was this the weapon used to brain poor Kitty? "Tell me more about it." I was stalling while I continued to examine it. "I've never seen a... what did you call it?"

"Shillelagh." Obviously very proud of his stick, he proceeded to tell me the history of such walking sticks. "Can also be used as a weapon," he said with a raise of the eyebrows. "They use magpie's blood and whale oil to give it the dark sheen."

Magpie's blood. Heavens. "I see." I did see. A spot on the bulbous head of the stick where it was missing a shamrock. "You've *been told* it's from County Wicklow. Does that mean it was given to you as a gift?"

"Why yes." He beamed. "How perceptive."

"How long has it been missing a jewel?" I pointed at the empty indentation.

"Damn." He took it out of my hands. "I hadn't noticed." He frowned. "That's unfortunate."

"Indeed." Dare I ask? "Where was your stick last Monday?"

His head jerked and he gave me a queer look. "I beg your pardon."

"Might you tell me where you got it?" I changed the subject. "I'd like to get one for myself."

"It was a gift from a lady." He smirked. "A very naughty lady." He smacked the stick against the palm of his hand. "Likes to play rough, if you know what I mean." He winked. "Don't know how I'd feel about sharing her, though, old boy."

"No. I wasn't..." I cleared my throat. "I didn't mean... I just wanted to know where..."

"You're too much of a gentleman for Molly." He laughed. "She likes a bit of a bad boy, if you know what I mean." He slapped his stick again. "One who needs a good spanking once and a while."

Good heavens. Did men always talk like this to each other? "Yes, quite." I forced a chuckle.

"Good chat, old boy." He cuffed me on the shoulder and nearly knocked me into the wall. "See you at practice."

I planned to keep a close eye on Mr. Jules Silver and his bejeweled stick. The way he talked, I wondered if his friend Molly was a prostitute. I hoped I wasn't going to have to dress up as a tart and infiltrate a house of ill repute. Then again, could a prostitute afford a stick like that?

The last man to arrive for class was Randy Kipper. A book tucked under his arm, he made a beeline for the locker room. There was something odd about his face. As he passed, I tried to get a better look. Behind his spectacles, one of his eyes was bruised and swollen. Had he been in a fight since I'd seen him last? Was his black eye a casualty of jujitsu or the result of an altercation? Perhaps a struggle with Ellen in Lady Battersea's downstairs powder room? Mr. Kipper was another one to watch. I made a mental note to make a physical note as soon as possible.

Fredricks finally appeared from the direction of the locker rooms. In his jujitsu costume—with his broad shoulders and flowing curls—he looked like a film star. Perhaps heartthrob Wallace Reid if he'd played Tarzan. Fredricks smiled as he came toward me, as if I were the only person in the world. He quite took my breath away.

When the other men arrived with Mr. Garrud, the instructor, Fredricks introduced me around as his cousin Marcel from France. I greeted everyone with a bow and my best accented English. Hopefully they would chalk up my eccentricities as a man to being French.

"To the mat." Mr. Garrud waved. "Today we're working on grappling positions." He demonstrated a move called Half Guard on Jules Silver, and then asked us to find a partner and practice.

Quickly, I snagged Fredricks by the kimono and asked him to be my partner. I didn't dare partner with any of the other men. Not only might they learn my true identity, but I might also get hurt. Hopefully, Fredricks knew better and would be careful with me.

As it turned out, the half guard position entailed one of us lying on the floor with the other on top, legs entangled. Fredricks gently pushed me to the bottom position and then slid one of his legs between mine. "Clamp on," he said, his voice hoarse.

I tightened my thighs around his leg. "Like this?" My breath caught. Golly. A jolt pulsed through me. Suddenly, I was hot. Very hot. Must be the moustache and full beard. My face felt flushed. I could feel Fredricks's breath on my neck.

"You smell like peaches," he whispered into my ear.

I pushed him off me.

"Good," Mr. Garrud said. "Now try the mount position."

Arms akimbo, I stood on my knees, glaring at my partner. "This time, I'm on top."

"I wouldn't have it any other way." Fredricks grinned.

When the instructor demonstrated the position, I realized why. *Good heavens.* "The mounted position is considered one of the most dominant positions," Mr. Garrud said, demonstrating on Jules.

"Marcel." Fredricks rolled onto his back and extended his arms to me. "Dominate me."

I crawled over to him and straddled his torso. He grabbed me by the waist. More than anything, I wanted to fall into him. To let him take me down. To lose myself in the reckless scent of rosewood.

"Move back a bit." Mr. Garrud pulled my shoulder. "Use your knees on either side of his pelvis to pin him down."

My heart racing, I inhaled a deep breath and slid back. When I did, what I encountered quite took my breath away. I gasped.

Mr. Garrud stood next to us, watching. "I think your cousin is getting the hang of it." He flashed a thumbs up. "You two should practice at home."

"Oh, we will," Fredricks said, his voice strained. "We will." He looked up at me with such longing in his eyes I was nearly overcome.

I tried to lift myself off him. He pulled me back down, and I fell forward, landing on top of him.

"*Je t'aime.*" His breath was warm against my face.

"*Je t'aime aussi.*" I don't know why I said it. The words just came out. As they did, my heart felt like it might explode and take the rest of my body along with it. I pushed myself up into the mount position again.

"*Ma chérie*, please don't marry him." Fredricks's eyes were pleading. He took my hand and pulled it to his lips. "Marry me."

For some inexplicable reason, tears welled in my eyes.

When I glanced around, everyone was staring.

12

THE LETTER

After my heated practice with Fredricks at the Dojo, I needed to be alone with my thoughts. What had I done? I'd just told the bounder I loved him. Was it true? Or was it just the effect of his knee between my thighs? Maybe Kitty had been right. I needed to marry Archie as soon as possible to cool my hot blood before I got myself into trouble. Then again, which was worse, Fredricks's uncanny effect on me, or Archie's philandering in Ireland, his missing our meetings, and his insistence that his wife wouldn't work? Was it possible my engagement to Archie was a defense against my attraction to Fredricks? I pushed the thought from my mind.

I changed into my own clothes and transformed back into plain old Fiona Figg. I returned the disguise to Fredricks, who was waiting outside the locker room door. Before I left the Dojo, Fredricks made me promise to dine with him tomorrow evening. I agreed, but only if he agreed to detain Mr. Jules Silver for the rest of the afternoon—and to leave off all talk of love or matrimony.

Speaking of matrimony, in just over an hour, Kitty and I were to meet at Ellis Bridal Boutique on Seville Lane for the final fitting of my bridal gown. To clear my head, I walked from the Dojo to the boutique, taking a detour through Green Park. With its canopy of flaming pink cherry blossoms overhead, the walking path was the perfect antidote to my swirling doubts. Until a placard reminded me the park's name was the result of King Charles II's wife ripping out all the flower beds after she caught him picking flowers for another woman. I thought of Archie and those pale pink camellias.

As I strolled through the park, I forced myself to leave off dwelling on Mr. Right or Mr. Wrong and concentrate on the case. For once, with no impending assignment from the War Office, I had the leisure to actually enjoy a murder investigation. Why squander it on worrying about my intended? Especially if my future husband planned to insist that I stay home with our imaginary children rather than don a moustache and investigate foul play.

I arrived at the boutique early, so I went to a café next door where I could sit outside and enjoy the warm spring afternoon and a cup of tea and biscuits. Fortification for the last stages of wedding preparations. I watched the man across the street who was watching me. When I waved at him, he ducked into a doorway. I smiled to myself.

Like the newly sprouted daffodils I passed on my stroll, I turned my face to the sun. I closed my eyes and soaked it in. It had been a long winter, what with the war and my missions behind enemy lines. Truly, I was lucky to be alive. And I wasn't about to let man-trouble—or that plain-clothed policeman—ruin a perfectly good afternoon tea.

Inhaling the scent of wisteria hanging from trellises overhead and sipping my tea, I watched the passersby. *Wait a blooming second.* Across the street, a woman who looked like Kitty was arguing with a man. I shielded my eyes with my hand and squinted into the sun. It *was* Kitty. And she was definitely arguing with a man. What in the world? The man grabbed her wrist and she jerked away. He leaned toward her and shouted in her face. He was wearing a uniform, but I couldn't get a look at his face. He lunged at her. She wheeled around and kicked him in the chin. What in heaven's name was going on? Obviously, the girl remembered her foot fighting.

I jumped up. A steady stream of traffic stopped me from getting across the street. By the time there was an opening to cross, the man was long gone, and Kitty was sprinting over to me. *Talk about gazelles.* That girl could run.

"What was that all about?" I asked when she reached me. "Who was that man?"

"He threatened me." She stomped off toward the café. "I need a drink."

Over brandies, Kitty told me how the man had threatened her life and then she'd kicked him. "I told you MI5 was trying to kill me," she whispered across the table. She sounded like a hissing cat.

Despite her insistence—and what I'd seen with my own eyes —I found it all hard to believe. There had to be some other explanation.

"What exactly did the man say?" I asked. "Tell me verbatim."

She rolled her eyes. "That my life was in danger and to shut up about MI5."

"Seems good advice, to me."

"I thought you believed me?" Her lip trembled.

"Of course, I do, dear." I patted her hand. "It's just that maybe he's right. If you work for MI5, perhaps you should *not* go around announcing it to the world."

She nodded.

"I shot him." Kitty stared down at her lap.

"Shot!" Good heavens. I'd seen her kick him. Did she shoot him, too? "When?"

"I went to his flat, took his gun from him, and fired." She bit her lip.

"When?" I asked again.

"Last night while you were sleeping." She gave me a sheepish look.

"Good heavens." I shook my head. The girl had snuck out in the middle of the night. With assassins chasing her. She was going to be the death of me.

"What about your fitting?" she asked, changing the subject.

After what I'd just witnessed, and this morning at the Dojo, and Kitty's story about shooting a man, I wasn't in the mood to be fitted for a bridal gown. In fact, my head was spinning. So, when Kitty suggested we order another brandy, I went along, hoping the strong drink would clear my head and calm her nerves, too.

"Where's Poppy?" I asked, changing to a more cheerful topic. Surely the girl didn't forget about the little creature. I took a sip of brandy. The alcohol burned all the way down.

"I left her at the War Office with Uncle Clifford." She drained her brandy and ordered another.

Goodness. I'd never seen the girl drink so much. And leaving Poppy behind. To say I was worried about the girl was an understatement.

"Speaking of the War Office." I leaned across the table. "We need to investigate Mr. Jules Silver in the censor's department." I proceeded to tell her about the shamrock missing from Mr. Silver's Shillelagh. The very shamrock I'd found wedged into the floorboard in the dressing stall where Kitty was attacked.

"So, you think this Mr. Silver was my attacker?" Kitty asked. "Could that be why I recognized him?"

"If not him, then someone wielding his stick." I sipped my brandy, wishing for a strong cuppa instead.

"Silver," she said. "That name rings a bell."

"A silver bell?" I couldn't resist.

"I think he's working for the Germans." Her face was animated. "He has been for months. I know it." She paused. A cloud passed over her face. "How and why, I don't know."

"All the more reason to search his office." I drained my cup. "I have a plan. Fredricks is detaining Mr. Silver, so we can search his office and then find out where he lives and search his flat."

"Fredrick Fredricks?" she asked. "You know that's an alias, right?"

I blinked at her. "Of course."

"One of many." She scoffed. "The man is very clever and extremely dangerous."

"And why do you say that?" I tightened my lips. Yes, Fredricks was a German spy. Yes, he had many aliases—I'd met two of them, Captain Claude Soughton and Duke Boris Zavrevsky. And, yes, he was definitely very clever. And dangerous, maybe. But, *extremely* dangerous? Perhaps to double agents... and the scores of women falling at his feet.

"I just do." She huffed. "How can I know things about other people but not about myself?" Her countenance softened. "And how can I be so certain of things you claim aren't true?" Her lip trembled. "You're probably right and I'm still delirious."

"Don't worry, dear Kitty." I reached across the table and patted her hand. "We'll get to the bottom of it, together."

"Thank you, Aunt Fiona." She gave me a weak smile.

"In the meantime, we need to settle the bill and get ourselves to the War Office." I placed a few coins on the table, along with my napkin. "Shall we?" Fredricks could only delay Mr. Silver for so long. "We have searches to carry out."

"You mean breaking and entering." She laughed. "Really, Aunt Fiona. You're going to get us arrested."

"Wouldn't be the first time." I waved for the waiter and paid the bill.

* * *

Long and narrow, Room 40 of the War Office felt like a bowling lane. Standing at one end, you could barely make out the other. Kitty and I had stopped there to see if any of the code breakers knew Mr. Jules Silver.

"I thought you'd quit us to get married," Mr. Dillwyn Knox said when he saw me. Dilly, as he was called, was a former classics scholar and papyrologist at King's College, Cambridge. A nosey rascal, he made it a point to know everyone's business.

"No." I glared at him. "I have a month off to get married. But I fully intend to return to work after the honeymoon." Despite Archie's objections to the contrary.

"I see." He grinned. "Your husband must be a forward-looking chap." He chuckled. "I supposed he's a suffragette, chaining himself to fences, and all that rot."

"Do you know a man called Jules Silver who works with the censors?" I asked, refusing to take the bait.

"Jules." His grin broadened. "Of course I've noticed him. Fine-looking man." Dilly was notorious for his flirtations with both men and women.

"What else do you know about him?" Kitty asked.

"Athletic fellow. Likes sports." He patted his ample belly. "My favorite sport is going to pubs." He chuckled again. "Why are you asking about Jules?"

"Top secret and confidential, I'm afraid." I took delight in knowing more than Dilly Knox for a change.

"We think he's a spy," Kitty said.

"She's joking." I gave her the evil eye. Her amnesia had made her even more rash and reckless than usual.

A high-pitched yip signaled the arrival of Poppy with Clifford in tow. The pup ran to her mistress and begged to be picked up. Kitty obliged, although not with her usual cooing and fussing over the poor little creature. Poppy must miss the old Kitty even more than I did.

"Good. You're here." I took Clifford's elbow. "Come along. I have a job for you."

"Righto." His face lit up. "Jolly good." He trotted behind me. "I hope it doesn't involve spirit glue. That wretched stuff gives me a headache."

"One man's poison..." I waved him away.

When we reached the censor's department, I asked Clifford (and Poppy) to stand guard outside the door. I instructed him to whistle if Jules—or someone matching his description—approached. Inside, the room was similar to Room 40, long and narrow with rows of desks. On the pretext of delivering a confidential letter, I went to Jules Silver's station. *Fiddlesticks.* Mr. Silver's desk was out in the open in a crowded room. It was going to be impossible to carry out a search without being noticed. At least it was at the back of the room.

I leaned over and whispered to Kitty, "You stay here and, when I get to Mr. Silver's desk, cause a distraction at the front of the room." Before she could object, I dashed down the center aisle. Even if the girl obliged, I wouldn't have much time to snoop. As I passed, I smiled at the upturned faces, hoping Kitty could get their attention away from me. When I arrived at Mr. Silver's desk, I nodded to Kitty.

"Uncle Clifford!" she yelled. "Bring Poppy!"

Clifford bolted through the door. He was holding Poppy, who

jumped out of his arms. Kitty was giving some kind of hand signals. Poppy started howling and limping. *Oh dear.* Had the little beastie hurt herself with that tremendous leap out of Clifford's arms? I hesitated for a second, wondering if I should go help. Then I noticed all eyes on the pathetic scene playing out in the front of the room. *Good girl.* Kitty was wailing almost as loud as Poppy. The two of them were putting on quite a show. Taking advantage of the distraction, I set to work inspecting the contents of Mr. Silver's desk.

The desktop was tidy. A man after my own heart. Quickly, I opened the desk drawers and inspected the contents. Nothing unusual in the top drawer. Extra pencils, eraser, stapler, rubber stamps and ink pad. The side drawers held files, which from a cursory glance seemed to be instructions and policies of the censorship department. I scanned the desktop. The inbox was full, and the outbox sported a neat stack of letters. The address on the top letter caught my eye. I picked it up. How odd. It was addressed to Captain Claude Soughton of the British Army. Captain Claude Soughton was one of Fredrick's aliases. The one he was using most recently to fool the posh men learning Japanese martial arts. Glancing around, I slipped the letter into my jacket pocket.

Kitty and Poppy were winding up their charade, so I had to cut my search short. Nonchalantly I strolled back up the aisle. When I reached the front of the room, Kitty gave another hand signal. In response, Poppy stood on her hindlegs and did a little dance. The crowd broke out into laughter and a round of applause. Kitty took a bow and so did Poppy, then we quickly exited the room.

"Well done." I congratulated Kitty and promised to give Poppy a biscuit when we returned to Room 40.

Back in Room 40, our little group convened in the kitchenette, which was barely big enough to hold the three of us, four if you counted Poppy.

"Well," Clifford said. "What was that all about?"

I opened the purloined envelope and scanned the letter. It was from Randolph Kipper. Hunting story, blah, blah. Anti-suffragette rubbish, blah, blah. Warnings of a German Plot in Ireland. I looked up at my colleagues. "Have either of you heard of a German Plot in Ireland?"

"Good Lord." Clifford's eyes went wide. "German Plot?"

"Let me see that letter." Kitty snatched it out of my hands. Concentrating as she read, her lips were tight. "Kipper is as bad as his pal Balfour." She thrust the letter at me. "I think I know why they're trying to kill me." She clenched her teeth. "Jules Silver was one of my targets. There are moles in British Intelligence. He's not the only one..."

"Targets? Moles?" I sighed. Not that MI5 business again. "Do you remember who attacked you at the Dojo?"

"No." She shook her head. "But I think I know why—"

"Why would anyone want to attack a delightful young woman like you?" Clifford interrupted. "It's absurd."

She turned to me. "Your sneaky friend Fredricks was right." She blew at her fringe. "I'd best not say anything to anyone." She lifted Poppy into her arms. "We need a safe place to think. Right, Poppy-poo?" She kissed the dog's wet little nose. *Disgusting.* "Some place they can't find me."

"Who is they?" I was growing impatient with her fantasies of assassins. Then again, her attacker was very real.

"My mum would love to have you at her place." Clifford scratched under Poppy's chin. "You'll be safe there. I can take you now if you like."

Kitty nodded.

"Thank you," I mouthed and patted his arm. Maybe some

time away from London would help Kitty regain her memories and shed her newfound paranoia about MI5 and assassins. "I'll report our findings to Captain Hall while you take Kitty to your mum's."

"Righto." Clifford scooped up Poppy and then took Kitty by the elbow. "My two favorite girls. Shall we?"

As soon as they'd gone, I marched up the stairs to Captain Hall's office. Of course, he wasn't expecting me. But I needed to report what I'd discovered. The letter from Mr. Kipper to Fredrick Fredricks addressed to his alias, Captain Claude Soughton. On the way up, I fabricated an explanation of how the letter came into my possession. I didn't dare tell him about our little charade in the censor's office.

I had a better idea. I'd tell him I'd stolen it from Fredricks. Surely, the captain would approve of my spying on the bounder. Hopefully, it wouldn't come to that. I'd hate to have to lie.

13

BATEMAN HOUSE

The next morning—with Kitty safely installed in Reading at Clifford's mother's house, and Captain Hall investigating Jules Silver and the suspect letter from Mr. Kipper he'd passed through the censors—I found myself on a train to East Sussex, which would be followed by a carriage ride to Bateman House, the home of Randolph and Carrie Kipper. Thankfully, the captain did not ask how I found the letter, so I didn't have to lie.

This time, I made sure to lose my tail before boarding the train. I tricked the plain-clothed copper by ducking in the lady's powder room at the station and exiting wearing a long black wig and sunglasses. He stood leaning against a pillar reading a newspaper and didn't even look up when I passed.

On the train, I reread the letter from Archie. It was waiting for me when I returned home last night.

Dearest Fiona,

My mother is ill, and I had to make an emergency trip home to Wales. I'm so sorry I missed our appointment. I promise it won't happen again. Depending on Mother's recovery, I may

be here for a few days. She is excited to meet you. Nothing
will keep me from marrying my best girl.
  All my love,
  Archie

I resisted the urge to crumple the letter and give it the defen-
estration it deserved. Instead, I folded it, replaced it in its envelope, and tucked it back into my new chatelaine bag. Evidence. I
might need it later when I confronted Archie about his secretive
life and presented him with my ultimatum. The truth or no
wedding. I shuddered. No wedding. I'd already made all the
arrangements. The guests, the flowers, the cake, the reception,
and church. It was too late to call it off now. Anyway, I didn't
really want to call it off. I just wanted to know what the heck
Archie was up to and why everything about his life was such a
big secret. "Classified." I was marrying Mr. Classified.

I reached into my bag and removed the *other* letter I'd
brought along. The one from the censor's office addressed to
Captain Claude Soughton, aka Fredrick Fredricks. Stamped
across the front of the envelope was the censor's seal of approval.
Why had this letter been approved by the censors? It was
addressed to a well-known alias of a suspected spy. Captain Hall
maintained Fredricks was more use to the War Office free than
imprisoned, which was why I'd been assigned to tail him on
many occasions. And that was why he was still on the loose. The
panther was more valuable in the wild than in captivity. I usually
didn't have to go far to find him, since he had an uncanny way of
showing up in my vicinity.

Jules Silver had approved the letter despite the fact Fredricks
and his alias were well known to the War Office. In the letter, Mr.
Kipper waxed poetic about the British Empire, blamed the defi-
ciencies of the British army for not winning the war already—

"have you lot learned nothing from the Boer War?"—and concluded, "Today, there are only two divisions in the world: human beings and the Germans." He reminded the captain that his son John had made the ultimate sacrifice. And encouraged the captain to stay the course against those "feeble minded" women and cowards "who in the name of pacifism would have us give in to the Huns." The letter ended with a caution to "watch out for the German Plot in Ireland."

Apart from the strange closing, I couldn't detect any sign of secret codes. Yet I intended to find out how Mr. Kipper knew "Captain Soughton" and why he was compelled to write to *him*. If Mr. Kipper wasn't also a suspect in the murder of Ellen Davis, I might have skipped the trip to East Sussex. But, when it comes to murder, Sherlock Holmes counsels there is no such thing as coincidence. Indeed, I couldn't rule out Carrie Kipper as a possible suspect either. In any case, it wouldn't hurt to interview them. Except for the killer, they were probably the last people to see Ellen Davis alive.

Bateman House was a lovely stone mansion with at least a dozen chimneys and several charming gables. It was surrounded by lush gardens in full spring bloom. The country breeze was fresh and brisk, with a scent of jasmine riding on its wings. The butler answered the door and led me into the morning room to await Mrs. Kipper—her husband, it turned out, was not at home.

The morning room was papered with delightful yellow flowered wallpaper and a vase of fresh daffodils sat on the center table. Large windows brought in the morning light and accentuated the bright cheerfulness of the room. The butler returned to tell me Mrs. Kipper would be down in a minute. I removed my gloves and waited. Fiddling with the handle of my bag, I wondered what could be keeping her. Had I caught her at a bad time? Perhaps she was busy. Perhaps I shouldn't have made the trip. Certainly, I should have telephoned first. And yet there was nothing like the element of surprise to catch a villain in his lair.

Carrie Kipper was indeed surprised to see me. Surprised to the point of alarm. Without the traditional greetings, she flew into the room and asked why I'd come. She was wearing a veil but underneath I could see she'd applied an extraordinary amount of face powder. She was an imposing woman who wore an impressive set of keys dangling from her waist like a prison guard. To top it off, she was an American. From New England, no less.

When I asked her about Captain Soughton, she said, "My husband is a writer, Miss Figg. He writes to a lot of people."

Judging by the purple blossoming along her cheek, her husband did more than write. When I'd seen him last at the Dojo, Mr. Kipper had a remarkable shiner of his own. Either the couple had an interesting love life, or they'd had a knock-down, drag-out fight.

"Do you know anything about a German Plot in Ireland?" I showed her the letter addressed to Captain Soughton (aka Fredrick Fredricks).

"I know little about Ireland." She shook her head. "And even less about Germany." She tightened her lips. "I'm really very busy, Miss Figg—"

"How did you get involved with the suffragettes?" I interrupted, changing course. Perhaps I'd come on a bit too strong. The woman had that effect. Her countenance was as steely as the side of a ship. Trying to gauge her mood was like trying to take the temperature of a brick wall.

"I've always believed women were as good as men." She lifted her chin.

"Quite so." I gave a quick nod of agreement. "But your husband—"

"Randy married me after my brother died." She gave a practiced smile. "They were best friends," she said with a sigh. "I think Randy felt he owed it to my brother." She closed her eyes for a long second, and, when she did, her bruises were more pronounced.

"If he mistreats you," I ventured, "you might be better off..." Easier said than done, I knew. Even after I discovered my ex-husband in the arms of his secretary, I still loved him and wanted him back. A month later, he died of mustard gas poisoning. And I mourned him just the same.

"I can't go back to Boston." She fiddled with her veil. "Randy has alienated me from my family, and I don't want to give my authoritarian father the satisfaction of an *I told you so*."

"I'm sorry." Caught between an authoritarian father and an abusive husband. Luckily, I wasn't in that position. My father was gone. And my betrothed might be an assassin, but I was confident that he would never harm me. "I don't want to take too much of your time, but might you tell me what you saw as you left Lady Battersea's tea party? Anything out of the ordinary?" I tilted my head. "Did you see Ellen Davis?"

She nodded. "Ellen took me aside and apologized."

"When was that?" I removed my notebook from my bag.

"Just before I got my coat and hat from the maid." She tightened her lips. "We were on our way out, and Ellen told me she hoped the column in the newspaper hadn't caused me any grief. I didn't know what she meant at first. Or why she would apologize on behalf of that horrible gossip person."

I knew why. Ellen Davis *was* that horrible gossip person. "Then what happened?"

"Ellen apologized and then continued down the hall, the maid fetched my coat, and we left." She opened her palms. "That's it."

"Was there anyone else around? The butler, maybe?"

"No one. Just the maid."

"And nothing out of the ordinary happened with Ellen?"

She shook her head. "Although... probably not important."

"Although what?" I gave her an encouraging smile.

"The maid tried to give me the wrong hat." She raised her eyebrows. "A hideous lavender cartwheel. I'd never wear something like that awful thing."

My cheeks warmed. The hideous, "awful thing" she described was no doubt my new hat. "Did you notice a hatpin stuck into the fabric of the hat?"

She narrowed her eyes. "I did not." She shrugged. "Then again, it wasn't my hat, so I gave it right back to her."

"Tell me more about this maid," I said, my pencil hovering over my notebook.

"Young, freckle-faced, red hair." She shrugged. "Nice enough looking girl."

"What was she doing when you left?" I made a note.

"I told you. She was coming up the hall. She was carrying a dirty towel. When she saw us, she popped into the coat closet and returned with the hat... the wrong hat."

Something was nagging at me. "Who took your hat when you arrived?"

"The butler." She sighed again. "Miss Figg, I don't know why you're asking me all these questions."

"My own freedom depends upon finding the killer." I tapped

my pencil on the notebook. "And you may have been the last person to see Ellen Davis alive."

"You don't think—" She huffed. "I didn't kill her, if that's what you think. Why would I?"

"Did you know that Ellen Davis was E. D. Aria, the gossip columnist who wrote about your suffragette activities?" I levelled my gaze. "And alerted your disapproving husband, not to mention the rest of the world, to your clandestine activities…"

"Ellen?" She sat blinking at me. "She did that to me?"

I nodded. "I'm guessing that's why you're wearing a veil in your own home."

She stared down at her lap. "He was angry." She looked up suddenly. "But I got the best of him." A sly smile played on her lips. "I gave as good as I got thanks to Mrs. Garrud's jujitsu training." She lifted her veil. "That man, or any other, dare not lift his hand to me again." A steely glint appeared in her eyes. "Or I'll kill him." At that moment, she seemed perfectly capable of murder. But her surprise at learning the identity of E. D. Aria was genuine and I doubted very much she'd killed Ellen Davis.

On the trip back to London, I reviewed my notes and pondered what Mrs. Kipper had told me. Something was off, but I didn't know what. If Carrie Kipper was telling the truth and she didn't know Ellen Davis was E. D. Aria, then she didn't have a motive for murder. But if she was lying, which I doubted, and she did know Ellen had betrayed her confidence—and in the newspaper, no less—then she had a motive. Because of the newspaper column, her husband had learned she secretly attended suffragette meetings. And, obviously, he wasn't going to stand for it, to the point of violence. *Then again*, if it was a matter of pride for Mr. Kipper, perhaps *he* wanted to dispose of the columnist who'd made his wife's "indiscretions" public.

I looked up from my notes in time to see him pass down the

aisle. The plain-clothed policeman. Drat. I thought I'd lost him. Had he followed me all the way to Bateman House? I buried my head in my notebook and pretended not to see him. Now, where was I? Right. Mrs. Kipper and my hat. The "hideous lavender cartwheel."

Why had the maid accidentally given it to Mrs. Kipper? Indeed, why was the maid giving out coats and hats at all? The butler, Toogood, should have been waiting with the coats and hats—not the parlor maid. Lady Battersea assured us that Toogood would see to our hats and make sure our hatpins were back in place. So why wasn't he handing out the hats? Why had the maid given my hat to Carrie Kipper? After all, the maid should have been busy serving luncheon and then picking up afterwards. I needed to question that maid. And the butler, too.

There was nothing to do but return to the scene of the crime and question the staff. Hopefully, Lady Battersea would receive me and indulge my investigation. If not, I'd have to find more covert means to get to the truth.

14

THE MAID

I arrived at Lady Battersea's by late afternoon. The policeman following me was getting brash. He stood nearby and watched as I presented the butler with my card. Lady Battersea received me in the morning room and offered me tea, which I gladly accepted. The dark circles under her eyes told me she hadn't been sleeping well since the murder. I wouldn't either if someone had died in my powder room.

There was no reason for Lady Battersea to confide in me or answer my questions, let alone give me access to her household. But I pleaded my case, nonetheless. I was still the prime suspect and unless I found the real killer *tout de suite*, I was destined for prison... or the gallows. Captain Hall couldn't keep them off me forever. The sooner I found the murderer, the sooner my name would be cleared, and perhaps then the police would finally return my emerald hatpin. Although, given where it had been, I wasn't sure I wanted it back.

Lady Battersea must have taken pity on me, for she gladly answered whatever questions she could. No, she'd never heard of the German Plot. No, she had no idea why anyone would want to kill Ellen Davis. Yes, the maid who served luncheon was on duty today. Yes, Toogood, the butler, was also on duty. *Maybe* she could allow me to speak to them after our tea... *if* I answered some of *her* questions. She quickly turned the tables on me and began her own inquisition. She insisted that I tell her everything I knew about both the attack on Kitty and the death of Ellen Davis.

What did I know? Not enough. The partial fingerprint on the clover jewel indicated the attacker was a man—or at least a man had touched the jewel. The clover appeared to be from Jules Silver's walking stick, which certainly looked like it could deliver an amnesia-producing blow. Mr. Silver had attended a jujitsu class at the Piccadilly Dojo and he was at the Batterseas' house when the murder occurred. He had the means and opportunity. But why would he attack Kitty? What was his motive? The girl seemed to know about Jules Silver's suspicious activities in the censorship office. Had she discovered he was a spy and he'd found out? That could be a darn good motive.

Then there was the matter of the suspicious letter addressed to one of Fredricks's aliases, a letter that somehow made it through Mr. Silver's censorship at the War Office. I needed to question Mr. Silver. The last time I'd tried, I'd been disguised as Fredricks's cousin Marcel from France. Perhaps I'd do better as Miss Fiona Figg. At least then he'd keep his florid comments about women to himself.

"Do you know why Jules Silver might have attacked Kitty?" I took a sip of tepid tea.

"You should ask my husband." She shook her head. "I hardly know the man. Do you think Mr. Silver attacked Ellen, too?"

"I don't know if he attacked anybody." I didn't want to start a vicious rumor about the man until I could be sure. "What I do know is Ellen was attacked with my hatpin, and your maid gave my hat to someone other than me."

"How ironic," she said in a whimsical tone.

"How so?" I narrowed my gaze. I failed to see the irony in a murdered woman, even if she was a gossip and killed with an extra-long hatpin, which happened to be mine.

"We'd just learned how to use hatpins as weapons." She shook her head. "Someone put the lesson into practice but, instead of using it against the police, they used it against one of our own." She sucked her teeth. "Such a shame."

"Indeed." It was true. We had just learned to use hatpins as weapons. Was the killer someone in attendance at the lesson? All the attendees were jujitsu-practicing suffragettes, except me.

I decided to spring the truth on her. "Did you know Ellen Davis was the gossip columnist E. D. Aria?" I tilted my head and watched her reaction.

"What!" she gasped. "Ellen wrote those dreadful things in the newspaper? I don't believe it. She was always so nice, so engaged, so easy to talk to... so..."

"Curious?" I thought of her sitting on Kitty's hospital bed, asking probing questions about Archie just two days before the story appeared in her column about Archie and Eva Gore-Booth. *Easy to talk to, my purloined hatpin!* Ellen Davis was adept at luring you in with her concern and interest, gaining your confidence, and then immediately betraying it. No one deserved to be murdered. But I could see why so many people might have wanted to silence E. D. Aria. That was the trouble. Too many suspects, all with the same motive. The question was who had the means and opportunity to kill poor Ellen? And how did they do it? The hatpin in her neck was a dead giveaway that someone else had been in the room. Surely, the woman hadn't used it to stab herself. Why would she commit suicide? Especially in someone else's powder room? If not for my hatpin stuck in her neck, the scene could have been simply one of a sick woman dying of a heart attack during afternoon tea.

A new idea sparked in my mind. What if Kitty's attacker had mistaken her for Ellen? They both had blonde hair, although overall Ellen was a bit wider than Kitty. Yet, from the back, in the locker room, the perpetrator could have thought they were attacking Ellen, trying to kill her. My head was spinning. They attacked Kitty thinking she was Ellen. But, when they realized their mistake, they'd tried again at Lady Battersea's tea party. Unfortunately, this time, they'd succeeded.

"Carrie Kipper told me that your parlor maid gave her the wrong hat when she was leaving the luncheon." I took a different tack with my investigation. "Unusual, yes?"

"No doubt upset by her husband dragging her out like that, Carrie was mistaken." Lady Battersea looked flustered. "Toogood was in charge of taking and returning coats and hats and hatpins, and he has a mind like a steel trap. He'd never give out the wrong hat."

"Carrie described the hat." I paused to take another sip of tea. "It was my hat."

"Your hat." Lady Battersea squirmed in her chair. "I don't see what any of this has to do with Ellen's death."

Incredulous, I raised my eyebrows. "My hatpin was involved."

"Oh, I see." She fanned herself with a napkin.

After another thirty minutes of speculation and chit-chat, Lady Battersea agreed to let me question the staff. It occurred to me that she had gotten more information out of me than I had out of her. Given her animosity towards E. D. Aria, if she had known Ellen's true identity, she could have disposed of the poor woman herself. Her alibi, however, was ironclad. She was at the luncheon the entire time and escorted us to the ballroom when it came time for the demonstration. The only way she could have been involved with Ellen's death was if she had an accomplice. One of the staff, perhaps? The hat-switching parlor maid?

Lady Battersea rang for Toogood, and a few seconds later he appeared at the threshold of the morning room. Standing erect and never making eye contact, he answered my questions without equivocation or hesitation. Yes, he oversaw the coats. No, he didn't leave his post, except to escort the gentlemen inside when they arrived and to take their outerwear. After which, he waited with coats and hats in anticipation of the guests' departures.

"So, except for when the gentlemen arrived, you were at your post the entire afternoon?" I asked.

He nodded. "Yes, ma'am."

Ellen Davis left to use the powder room after the gentlemen arrived. So, if Toogood was telling the truth, he would have been back at his post by the time of her death.

"Did you retrieve the Kippers' hats and coats?" I levelled my gaze at him.

"The Kippers, ma'am?" He glanced over at Lady Battersea. She gave him a subtle nod. "No, ma'am," he said, regaining his completely expressionless demeanor.

Now I was confused. "Why not?"

"I'd been called out to fetch one of the soldiers a glass of water." Red-faced, he cleared his throat. "It must have been at the same time as the Kippers' departure."

"What soldier?" An unhappy thought snuck in through the back door of my mind.

"Ma'am, it was one of the soldiers doing drill across the street in Hyde Park." He looked at Lady Battersea with concern. "He asked for water, so I gave it to him."

"You did the right thing," Lady Battersea said. "Of course you did."

"Can you describe this soldier?" I swallowed hard, dreading his answer.

"Tall, young, an officer." He shrugged. "Green eyes, maybe. Does that help?"

I exhaled. "Yes, thank you." No. It didn't help. It made everything much worse. A tall officer with green eyes. Means *and* opportunity. "Did you see Ellen Davis on her way to the powder room?"

"No, ma'am." He stared straight ahead. "As I said, I went to the kitchen to get water for the soldier." He waited a beat and then turned to Lady Battersea. "May I go now? The gentlemen may need me."

"Gentlemen?" I asked.

Finally, he looked at me. "His lordship has a guest in the library."

"Thank you, Toogood." Lady Battersea waved him away. "You may go to the men."

After the butler was out of sight, Lady Battersea turned to me. "Satisfied?" She smoothed her skirt. "Nothing nefarious, just Toogood offering a thirsty soldier a glass of water."

No. I wasn't satisfied. An unidentified officer had been thrown into my equation. One fitting the description of Lieutenant Archie Somersby. The parlor maid had given my new hat to Carrie Kipper. And unless Mrs. Kipper removed the emerald hatpin and followed Ellen to the powder room, the maid may have been involved in the killing. "Do you mind if I question the maid?"

Lady Battersea called for the parlor maid. A few seconds later, the girl appeared. She bowed a quick curtsey and stood blinking at me.

"Molly, dear," Lady Battersea said, "might you indulge Miss

Figg by answering a few questions?" She sighed. "We won't keep you long, right, Miss Figg?" She narrowed her eyes at me.

Molly. I'd recently heard that name. Of course, Jules Silver at the Dojo. He'd been bragging about his latest conquest, the one who liked bad boys and spankings. My cheeks warmed and I found that I couldn't look at the girl. Could this be the same Molly? Was Jules Silver having an illicit liaison with Lady Battersea's maid? *LB's maid's affair.* Ellen's notes.

"Did you give Carrie Kipper my hat after the luncheon?" I got right to the point.

"Apologies, ma'am." She blushed. To my surprise, Molly had a lovely Irish brogue. Perhaps that was why she was comforting her fellow countrywoman, Eva Gore-Booth, after the murder.

"Since I didn't take the hats when you ladies arrived," she continued, "I didn't know—"

"Of course," I interrupted. "Do you remember, was the emerald-studded hatpin still attached when you gave it to her?"

Her eyes moved back and forth from me to the door as if she were contemplating bolting. "I'm not sure, ma'am." She bit her lip. "You don't think I took your hatpin?" Her eyes flashed like a wild animal's. "I'm not a thief."

"No, dear," Lady Battersea said. "Of course not."

I had my doubts, but I kept them to myself. "How well do you know Mr. Jules Silver?"

Molly blanched. Her expression was all the answer I needed.

"Did you give Mr. Silver a walking stick as a gift?" I pushed images of spankings from my mind.

"Jules, er, Mr. Silver was kind to me... and I, um..." She sputtered. "It was one of my father's and Jules, er, Mr. Silver, admired it, so I gave it to him."

I wondered if she'd also "given it" to Kitty in the locker room. "How often do you see Mr. Silver?"

She tightened her lips but didn't answer.

"How often do you accompany her ladyship to the Dojo?" I changed the subject.

"Whenever she goes." Her tone brightened, obviously relieved at the change of subject.

"Is that where you rendezvous with Mr. Silver?"

More sputtering.

"Miss Figg, please," Lady Battersea said with a pleading tone. "Don't torture the poor girl." She gave the girl a stern look. "*I'll* deal with you later."

Did Lady Battersea know about her maid's affair with Mr. Silver? Was she covering for her? Taking her along to the Dojo to facilitate the liaison?

"No more questions." Lady Battersea pressed her palms together as if in prayer. "Apologies, dear Molly." Her tone was flustered. "Why don't you go ask cook for tea and biscuits to calm your nerves, dear girl." Her ladyship was obviously fond of the "dear girl." Her stern look earlier must have been for my benefit. And yet, given her agitation when I revealed Molly's affair with Jules, she seemed genuinely surprised.

"I'll thank you, Miss Figg, to stay out of my household affairs. Poor Molly has a romantic imagination is all, from reading the gossip columns. She's not a bad girl." Lady Battersea rang for the butler again and he appeared almost instantly. "Toogood, please show Miss Figg to the door."

On the way out, I heard male voices coming from the library. I stopped in my tracks. Not just any male voice. It was Fredrick Fredricks. "Excuse me," I said to Toogood as I pushed past him and peeked into the library.

Sure enough, there was Fredricks, smoking cigars with Lord Battersea. I waved my hand in front of my nose. Filthy pastime.

When I caught Fredricks's eye, he broke into a broad smile,

which exposed his shining canines—*or should I say felines*. He fancied himself stealthy like a big cat, ergo his self-given nickname "The Panther," echoed by the panther insignia on his pinky ring. He looked like the cat who ate the canary. I wondered if I was the canary.

"Fiona, *ma chérie*." He got up and came to the door. "What a pleasant surprise." He lifted my hand to his lips.

Heat from the kiss travelled up my arm and all the way to the tips of my ears. He moved closer and whispered into my ear. His breath sent a tingle up my spine as he said, "I've seen the preliminary autopsy report on Ellen Davis." He stepped back and winked. "Your hatpin is innocent."

"Really?" I smiled. "That is good news."

"The police concluded it only grazed her neck." He nodded. "It couldn't have killed her."

"Thank goodness." I clapped my hands together. "My name is cleared."

"Not quite, I'm afraid." He tilted his head. "The police still want to know why your hatpin was in her neck." He raised his eyebrows. "Perhaps the shock of being pricked with your elegant hatpin caused her heart attack." He tightened his lips to keep from laughing but I could see the mirth in his eyes.

"Heart attack?" Did that mean her death was from natural causes? It couldn't be. My hatpin was proof someone else had been in that room with her.

"The police are puzzled." He shrugged. "They have no idea how your hatpin is related to her heart attack. They may know more after they conduct more tests."

"It's odd." I squinted at him. "If she keeled over from a heart attack, then why would someone also stab her? And, more to the point, how did the killer exit the room with her body blocking the door?"

"All excellent questions, *ma chérie*." Fredricks sighed.

"And why *my* hatpin?" It was the longest at the party. Did someone want to frame me? Someone who wanted me out of the way. Could the whole horrible ordeal be the result of my espionage work? Perhaps the perpetrator wanted both me and Kitty out of the way and had devised this complex scheme to get rid of us. "Furthermore, will I ever see that hatpin again?"

"That reminds me." Fredricks pulled a narrow box from his interior pocket. "For you."

I took it and pulled off the lid. Inside was my emerald hatpin! "The police gave it to you?"

"No." He grinned. "But I couldn't let you go around defenseless. You never know when a beautiful woman might need to protect herself by pricking some masher." He laughed.

"Stop your laughing or I'll prick you." I stood arms akimbo, face to face with the bounder. Looking into his smiling eyes made it deuced difficult to concentrate on anything else.

He kissed my hand again and held my gaze in his. "You've already pricked my heart with the thorny rose of your loveliness." With all the drama of a theatre actor, he brought both hands to his heart. "My bounty is as boundless as the sea. My love as deep. The more I give to thee, the more I have. For both are infinite."

My knees went weak. Why did I feel so faint? It must have been from lack of food. "*Romeo and Juliet*." I steadied myself against the doorframe and averted my eyes. "And look how that ended!"

I prayed Archie's mother recovered soon.

15

THE ASSIGNMENT

Early the next morning, I got a call from Captain Hall ordering me to report to the War Office immediately. Even though I was on leave for the month, I didn't ask questions. Instead, I hurriedly slipped into the same clothes I wore yesterday and went to the railway station. What could be so important Captain Hall would call me away from my holiday? And my wedding preparations, no less. The rate I was going, I would have to get married in my silk air-raid pajamas. I'd missed the last fitting for my bridal gown, and my trousseau was almost nonexistent.

When I arrived at Captain Hall's suite, his secretary showed me through to his office. The small man seated behind a large desk looked like a boy playing at soldiers. His lashes beat like hummingbird wings as he stood up and bid me good morning and then asked me to take a seat. No wonder the men had given him the nickname "Blinker."

"Miss Figg," he said, tugging at the bottom of his military jacket. "We have a situation in Ireland." He dropped back into his chair. "Miss Lane was there investigating for us last month, but with her recent amnesia she's become a liability."

Liability. I didn't like the sound of that. Despite having once tied me to a toilet, Kitty was a good girl and an excellent spy.

"She was very close to getting a complete list of the members of the Irish Citizen Army." He shuffled some papers on his desk. "I'm sending you to Dublin to finish the job." He plucked a file folder off the top of a stack and held it out. "Since Miss Lane speaks Irish and I'm assuming you do not, we've arranged for you to take a position as British gardener at the estate of one of the ringleaders."

Gardener? Although I spent summers on my grandparents' farm, I was no gardener. As a child, I'd hidden in my room with the latest Sherlock Holmes story rather than go outside and play.

"I know how you love disguises." Captain Hall chuckled. "Unfortunately, you'll have to find a way to get from the garden inside the house and locate a list of members of the Irish Citizen Army. Fortunately, with your memory, if you do manage to find it, you can easily reproduce it for us upon your return."

"Yes, sir." To think he used to forbid me from wearing disguises and now he was arranging them for me. If only I didn't have a photographic memory, I might have got a spy camera. "How do you know there is a list? What does it look like?"

"We have it on good authority there is comprehensive list." He waved his pencil. "They have so many members, they keep a list. We're coordinating efforts with MI5 on this operation." He sighed. "Kell insisted—"

"Vernon Kell?" That was one of the names Kitty was bantering around in her delirium. That must be why Kitty was going on and on about MI5. She had been working with them in Ireland.

"Do you know him?" The captain tilted his head.

"No. Just that... never mind." I pretended to flip through the file folder.

"Anyway, you'll meet their operative in Dublin." He paused, lashes fluttering. "I told Kell I was sending our best undercover agent. Do not make me a liar, Miss Figg."

My heart skipped a beat. *Best undercover agent.* In a matter of months, I'd gone from mere file clerk to the best undercover agent. My chest expanded with pride, and I felt like the buttons might pop off my blouse I was so chuffed. I vowed not to let the captain down. "I'll do my best, sir."

"Good." He tapped his pencil, signaling the meeting was over. "Study that file. Let me know if you have questions." He stood up. "You leave this afternoon."

"This afternoon!" I hoped he meant late afternoon. I still had to study the file, go to Angel's Fancy Dress for a gardener's costume, pack, and get to the railway station. Unless the captain had arranged for Clifford to drive me. I should also ring and check on Kitty.

"Is there a problem, Miss Figg?" Captain Hall had already gone back to shuffling papers on his desk.

"No, sir."

"Then get going." He waved me away. "Captain Douglas will pick you up at fourteen hundred hours."

Two o'clock. That gave me five hours to get ready. "Yes, sir." I tucked the file under my arm and took my leave. So much for my wedding plans.

* * *

As I rode the bus to Angel's Fancy Dress Shop, I read the file. My assignment was to find a list of members of the Irish Citizen Army at the estate of Countess Markievicz outside Dublin. I did a double-take. There was a photograph of her and her sister Eva Gore-Booth in front of the hedgerow of camellias in full bloom. I recognized that place from Ellen's gossip column. I winced just thinking about it. I didn't believe for a minute Archie was having a liaison with Eva Gore-Booth. There must be some other explanation. Some completely innocent explanation. Like maybe they were distant cousins, or he was an adviser to the family, or he was there buying a bushel of Shillelaghs. Anything except what it looked like. Archie wouldn't do that to me, would he?

According to the file, Countess Markievicz and her sister were both involved in Irish revolutionary politics. And not just the Irish Citizen Army but other revolutionary groups called Fianna Éireann and Cumann na mBan. Those names were familiar. Apparently, the countess was a prominent figure in the Irish move for home rule. Her role in the Irish Citizen Army might explain her strange get-up at the tea party. She was dressed as a soldier. The War Office considered both the countess and her sister to be militant enemies of Britain.

Golly. They'd seemed like perfectly nice women when I met them. I never would have guessed. Although maybe I should have, given I met them at the Dojo where they were learning to throw down policemen.

When I flipped to the last page of the file, I was stunned by what I saw. "The German Plot." The exact words used in Kipper's letter addressed to Captain Claude Soughton aka Fredrick Fredricks. According to the file, the Irish Citizen Army was collaborating with the Germans against England. I couldn't believe it. They truly were conspiring with our enemy. It was up to me to get a list of these traitors so the War Office could stop them.

I had to find out from Kitty what had happened in Ireland. Had she been working with MI5 before she returned to London? And why did Captain Hall say she'd become a liability? Surely he didn't mean it. She was his niece, after all. Well, not exactly his niece. But he'd saved her from the streets by sending her to spy school, for heaven's sake. And she called him "uncle." And he treated her as family.

By the time I reached the stop for Angel's, I'd worked myself into a tizzy. I would get my disguise in order and ring Kitty at Clifford's mother's house. He'd said his mother would be delighted to have the girl and pup stay with them as she often complained about rattling around in the empty old house and wished Clifford would get married and give her some grandchildren. It wasn't for lack of trying that Clifford hadn't managed to grant her wish. Since I'd known him, he proposed to nearly every single woman of his acquaintance, particularly if said woman had befallen some crisis or calamity. Clifford was a good sort of chap. I was half surprised no one had accepted him yet. In the first months of our acquaintance, he'd proposed to me at least once a month. Now, he knew better. He'd learned I could take care of myself—at least most of the time and certainly better than he could. Especially when I had a good disguise. Eager to find a new one, I hurried off the bus and into the fancy dress shop.

Angel's brightly colored costumes and countertops lined with beards and moustaches made me forget all about fussing over the liabilities of the War Office. The only War Office liability I was worried about now was the invoice I planned to present to Captain Hall. I passed my hand over a rack of trousers. What would a gardener wear? I'd need trousers, of course. And braces. A white shirt and collar. A tweed jacket. And a tie, tie clip, collar pin, and armbands. And moustaches. Lovely huge moustaches. Given the countess and her sister had met me already, I decided a full beard was in order. I didn't want to risk being recognized. Colored spectacles would help, too.

My pulse quickened as I dashed around the shop gathering the raw materials to create Mr. Horace Peabody, groundskeeper extraordinaire. Brown moustache and matching beard. Short brown wig. Denim overalls. Newsboy hat. My only regret was putting aside my investigation into the attack on Kitty and Ellen Davis's murder. I was making real progress. But duty called.

As I rounded the corner to the moustache counter, who did I see but Fredrick Fredricks? *What's he doing here? Is he following me? Stalking me like a predator does his prey?*

"Ahem." I cleared my throat.

Holding an impressive black beard to his chin, he spun around. "Fiona." He placed the beard back in its display case. "Or should I say Dr Vogel, or Harold the bellboy, or Rear Admiral Arbuthnot." He grinned. "Who are we today, *ma chérie*?"

"I could ask you the same thing." I hugged the makings of Horace Peabody to my chest. "Captain Claude Soughton? Duke Boris Zavrevsky?"

"A rose by any other name, and all that." He brandished a moustache and waved it in my direction.

"Not *Romeo and Juliet* again." I joined him at the facial hair counter. "Fake beard, fake identity." I held up the beard he'd been trying on.

"All identity is fake." He paused. "As Heraclitus says, you can't step in the same river twice. Everything changes. Nothing stays the same." He put both hands on his chest. "Except my love for you. Only the stirrings of the heart are real."

I ignored his overly dramatic proclamation of love. "Whether I'm wearing trousers and a moustache or a ballgown, deep down I'm still plain old Fiona Figg."

"There's nothing plain about you, *ma chérie*." His dark eyes danced. "Deep down, you are extraordinary."

Why did I feel more comfortable wearing trousers and a moustache? Hiding behind a disguise. Even dressing in a ballgown and evening slippers felt like a costume. Who was I really?

How could Fredricks be so sure when I wasn't sure myself? "I'm quite ordinary. Whatever else you think I am is counterfeit, made up, make believe."

"And better for it! How meagre life would be without imagination." He sighed. "You are no more than the sum of what you can imagine." He reached out and touched my cheek. "And you, *ma chérie*, dream of a world more perfect and just than the one we inhabit. How can we make the world a better place without first imagining it so?" His full lips turned up into a smile. "I can't begin to tell you about the worlds you conjure in me..."

"And what if I change?" After all, I'd gone from a girl to a woman to a wife to a file clerk to a spy to the best spy. "Feelings change, too." The image of my husband in the arms of his secretary flashed through my mind. "You say you love me, but—"

"Love is not love—which alters when it alteration finds—" He reached out and caressed my hand.

"Love doesn't alter." I took a step backwards. What was I thinking? Talking about love with Fredricks when I was engaged to Archie. Had I lost my mind? My wedding was in less than a week. Come on, Fiona, pull yourself together. "Which is why I'm marrying Archie." I swallowed hard.

"You know how I feel about that." He raised his eyebrows. "But if it will make you happy—"

"It will." My arms were tired from holding every bit of Horace Peabody so tightly I didn't drop anything. "I have to go now." It was true. And even if it weren't true, I had to get away from Fredricks before I lost my resolve. There was something about the bounder that was almost irresistible.

Almost.

16

THE JOURNEY

By the time I got back to my flat, Clifford was waiting for me in front of the building. I recognized his burgundy car, which he kept polished to a sheen. I waved. He sat in the driver's seat, his pipe clamped between his teeth. When he saw me, he rolled down his window.

"Where have you been?" he asked impatiently. "I've been driving around the block for the last half hour."

"Sorry. I'll just grab my things." I reached in and laid my hand on his shoulder and then handed him the package containing Horace Peabody. "Only take a minute." It was unlike him to be early. Something must be wrong. I left him puffing and dashed upstairs, threw things into a suitcase, then hurried back out to the curb. When Clifford pulled up again, I tossed my case into the back and climbed into the passenger's seat.

"Captain Hall said two o'clock." I smoothed my skirt. "Why are you here already?"

"You're always complaining that I'm late and now... now when I'm early..." He threw up his hands.

"How is Kitty?" I regretted I hadn't had time to check on her. "Is her memory getting any better?"

"Good Lord, no." Clifford removed his pipe. "She won't stop talking about assassins." He shook his head. "Poor girl is delirious. I couldn't take another minute of her ranting about the shortcomings of Arthur Balfour, Basil Thomson, and other pals of mine." He replaced his pipe and puffed. "They're not bad chaps. Just because they're patriots and don't believe women should run the country."

Did he say "run" or "ruin"? I glared over at him. "We'd be a lot better off if women did run the country," I huffed. "All men do is make war and enslave other men."

"And you think women could do better?" He glanced over at me. "I mean, all women aren't like you... They're not as clever and level-headed." He chuckled. "You're practically a man."

Some compliment. Although I did enjoy the comfort of trousers, especially on a cold day. But clothes don't make a man. Women didn't need to be like men to run the country. Women were perfectly capable of being feminine *and* clever *and* leaders. If only men thought so too. Thankfully, some men did—or at least they'd voted for suffrage. I was looking forward to the day that I could vote. Another five years and I'd turn thirty. Then I could finally go to the ballot box.

"Except for your aversion to hunting." He puffed his pipe. "Foxes are one thing. You should try lions in the Serengeti." He laughed again. "I remember this one time..."

Here we go. I closed my eyes and leaned my head against the window.

I must have slept through the Serengeti. When I awoke, Clifford was recounting hunting tigers in India. "Ghastly sport. Taking another life just to prove you can. No wonder this bloody war is dragging on and on."

"I say." He looked hurt. "War is one thing, sportsmanship quite another."

Had I said it out loud? *Fiddlesticks.* I rubbed my eyes.

Clifford slapped his knee. "I still can't straighten the blasted thing."

I'd forgotten he'd taken a bullet. When I first met him, he'd used a cane due to a war injury. He knew as well as anyone the horrors of war. "Sorry, Clifford, dear." I had an idea how to make amends. "How would you like to help me put together the clues I've gathered so far on the Ellen Davis murder case?"

"Murder?" His head jerked and he stared over at me. "I heard it was her heart."

"Where did you hear that?" Of course, I'd heard it too, but I was curious for corroboration.

"It's in all the papers. You really should keep up, old bean." He shrugged. "Plus, I'm friends with the police commissioner." He chuckled. "In fact, one time, Nevil and I were hunting quail out at Birdie Quiddington's country house—"

"Of course you are, and were." I stopped him before he got into one of his stories. "Even if Ellen died of natural causes, there is still the matter of Kitty's attacker, not to mention my hatpin."

"I told you that blessed thing looked bloody dangerous." He snorted.

"Yes, well, it became more so when someone aimed it at the poor woman's neck." I picked invisible lint off my sleeve. "Do you want to know what I've discovered or not?"

"I say." He pouted. "No need to get tetchy. Pray tell."

"You know about the shamrock I found in the dressing room." I was speaking quickly so he couldn't interrupt. "It came off a walking stick belonging to Mr. Jules Silver, who received the Shillelagh, as it is called, from a woman. A woman he is having extra-marital relations with, who also happens to be Molly, the Batterseas' red-headed maid."

"Good Lord." His pipe fell out of his mouth, and he scrambled to catch it, causing the car to swerve.

I grabbed onto the seat and dug my nails into the upholstery.

"Molly the maid gave my hat to Mrs. Kipper by accident. And although Carrie Kipper doesn't remember whether the hatpin was there, I suspect Molly knows." I took a deep breath and picked up my pace. "I visited Carrie Kipper, who was wearing a veil in her own home to cover a bruise on her face. Her husband, your pal Randy, had a similar bruise when I met him at the Dojo." I snickered. "In fact, truth be told, his looked far worse than hers."

"I say." Clifford gave me an outraged look. "You aren't suggesting the man beats his wife!"

"Or perhaps the other way around." I rummaged through my bag, looking for a ginger sweet to settle my stomach. Clifford's driving was quite unnerving. "Anyway, I don't think she had anything to do with either attack. But there was that odd letter from Mr. Kipper to Captain Claude Soughton aka Fredrick Fredricks. Warning of the German Plot in Ireland." I opened my palms. "And here we are. On our way to Dublin." I popped a sweet into my mouth. "What do you know about gardening?"

"As kids, we trapped rabbits in our garden." He chuckled. "This one time..." He was off again, not giving a second thought to the murder investigation.

I tuned him out. Hopefully my cover wouldn't involve rabbits. Apart from my grandmother saying, "You must prune to bloom," my knowledge of plants came from what I learned about poisons on my mission to Ravenswick Abbey. So many beautiful plants were deadly: oleander, nightshade, angel's trumpets, foxglove, lily-of-the-valley, azalea, daffodil, crocus. The list went on. If

Countess Markievicz happened to have a poison garden, I'd be in good shape.

By the time the ferry docked in Dublin, I was completely knackered. Clifford had talked my ear off, and I couldn't wait to get some time to myself. A hot bath, a nice cup of tea, and bed would be perfect. Clifford had booked us two rooms at the Stag's Head Inn, a quaint old pub with warm mahogany walls and ceilings, stained glass windows, and of course a large stag's head mounted above the fireplace.

"Look at that trophy!" Clifford pointed to the stag's antlers.

Leave it to Clifford to find a place decorated with dead animals.

17

THE LIST

The next morning, I got up early to make my transformation from Fiona Figg, counterespionage agent, to salt-of-the-earth Horace Peabody, everyman, and gardener extraordinaire. I took special care with the moustaches and the wig. Hair, especially facial hair, was so important when putting together a disguise. If only I could change my eye color as easily. Shaded spectacles were my answer.

Creating a believable character was as much about gestures and body movements as clothing or hair color. If I didn't alter my behavior, of course I'd be recognized immediately. Alright, perhaps not *immediately* but eventually, once the uncanny sensation of déjà vu wore off. On the other hand, even a slight change in appearance could allow a good actor to pass themselves off as someone else. Having studied acting at North London Collegiate School for Girls, I knew a few tricks for going incognito. My alto voice was just deep enough that I could extend its range into tenor territory to make for a passable man.

Pleased, I smiled at my reflection. Yes, Horace Peabody would do nicely. I rehearsed Horace by taking tea and toast in the Stagg Head Inn's dining room.

When Clifford entered, he didn't recognize me. I smiled to myself. He walked right past, even greeted me, with no sign of recognition. Even the plain-clothed copper who'd followed us all the way from London didn't look up from his breakfast. Success!

"Captain Douglas," I called out.

He turned around. Decked out in his dress uniform, he looked almost handsome.

"Would you care to join me?" I had to bite my lip to keep from laughing.

"I say." He beamed. "Very kind of you. But how do you know my name, sir?"

With all the restraint I could muster, I managed to get out the words, "You, sir, are my best friend," I said, fighting off giggles.

"Good Lord, Fiona." He plunked down across from me.

"Shhh." I put my finger to my lips. "It's Mr. Horace Peabody, gardener extraordinaire."

He shook his head. "What are you up to now?"

"Classified," I said with relish. He knew from his orders that he was to drive me and deliver me to Countess Markievicz's estate. Otherwise, luckily, he was on a need-to-know basis.

"You can tell me." He leaned closer and whispered, "I'm the soul of discretion."

At that, I burst out laughing. "An inveterate gossip, more like."

He got that hangdog look of his and sat pouting until the waitress arrived. It wasn't until his full Irish breakfast landed in front of him and he tucked in that he went back to his old cheerful self again. When he took to smacking his lips over the black pudding, I had to look away. Disgusting stuff.

After breakfast, I instructed him to change into plain clothes, the dirtier the better, and meet me out front. A proper gardener would not be delivered to work by a captain in the British army, for heaven's sake, especially if said gardener was a British spy. If he played his cards right, Clifford could become an older brother to Horace Peabody. Reluctantly and with much grumbling, he did as instructed.

* * *

The entrance to the Markievicz estate was a winding road along the sea. Atop a knoll sat a magnificent old castle overlooking Dublin Bay. Clifford dropped me off at the huge wooden entrance doors. I half expected a moat. Instead, the castle was surrounded by lovely gardens. I stepped out of the car and glanced around.

I recognized that hedgerow from the gossip column in the paper. The camellia was glorious with crimson and pink blooms bursting from the greenery. Along either side of the front door stood giant pots filled with charming lily-of-the-valley sporting bright red berries along with dainty white bells. Jutting out of the center of the delicate flowers were tall cone-shaped stems filled with pink and purple trumpets: foxgloves. Perhaps the countess had a poison garden after all. Both lily-of-the-valley and foxglove plants were highly toxic. Although camellia was not poisonous. In fact, the leaves were used to make tea.

After my investigation of the front garden, I lifted the heavy brass knocker and rapped on the door. A few seconds later, a maid answered. Her brogue was so thick I found it difficult to understand her. She made it clear that I should not be at the front door. Of course, I knew that. But how else would I get a good look at the house? The gardener and other staff always entered through the rear. She pointed. But, seeing how the countess had guests in the back garden at the moment, she would make an exception just this once and bring me in through the front. Good. Just as I'd planned.

As I followed her through the foyer to the kitchen, I took the opportunity to memorize the layout of the castle. The interior of the house was run down and smelled of mildew. Faded carpets and drapes and torn upholstery had seen better days—the days of Saint Patrick, perhaps. I walked very slowly so I could peek into the rooms as we passed.

"You're a right slow-coach," the maid grumbled. "Come on, then."

"What's in there?" I pointed to an ornate wooden door.

"The library, if you must know." She sighed. "We ain't got all day, man."

The library or study would be the place to look for documents. Unless the countess hid the list of Irish Citizen Army members in some other sneaky place in her bedroom. How would I—a mere gardener—gain access to any of those rooms? This assignment was going to be tricker than I thought.

"Wait here," the maid said, leaving me alone in the kitchen.

As soon as she was out of sight, I walked the circumference of the room, taking in the state of the stove, sink, and ice box. Everything looked ancient. Was the countess strapped for funds? I opened a cupboard and looked inside. Chipped ceramic cups and saucers but no hidden lists. I peeked in a drawer. Worn linens and placemats. No secret documents. I tried the ice box.

"Helping ourselves, are we now?" The shrill voice came from behind me.

I whipped around. "No... my apologies... I'm parched from the trip is all."

"Sit yourself down and I'll make you a cup of tea, then." This maid—or was she the cook—was older and wider than the first. She had a hint of a moustache on her upper lip and her hands were the size of a man's. The way she banged around the kitchen, no wonder the china was chipped.

"Thank you." I sat at the small table. "Don't mind if I do."

The tea was strong, and milk was not on offer. The bitter beverage made my tongue shrivel. I liked my tea strong, but this was more like boot polish.

"Drink up." The maid stood over me. "Then I'll take you out back to meet her ladyship."

I drank it down, grateful for the extra fortification for my encounter with the countess. She'd seen me before and I couldn't risk her recognizing me now.

After I drained my cup, the maid led me out the back door into the garden. The back garden was wild and overgrown, nothing like the front. Full of brambles and prickly vines. When was the last time anyone had tended it? Still, it was obvious this spacious green had once been glorious. It lacked a bit of discipline was all. The English touch. No doubt that was why the countess wanted an English gardener. We were known for taming the wildest of nature. A good pair of loppers wouldn't go wanting around here.

In the distance, under a white canopy, sat the countess and her party made up of two other ladies and a gentleman. The countess was again dressed from head to toe in a black uniform. Her sister, Eva Gore-Booth, was laughing and reaching out for the hand of the gentleman sitting across from her. I could see her face but not his. Her bright laughter seemed to float on the breeze. In her pink chiffon day dress, she was attractive, there was no denying it. Next to her sat a young woman who looked every bit the librarian with her severe middle parting and pince-nez and wearing a high lace collar and fitted jacket. She scowled every time Eva touched the gentleman's hand.

As the distance closed between us, an uneasy feeling filled

the air, like a spring mist settling on the dells. Was it déjà vu? Something wasn't right. But I couldn't put my finger on it. Although it did seem a bit odd that the maid would interrupt her ladyship's party to introduce a new gardener, even if the garden was in a state of emergency.

Leading me across the lawn, the maid nattered on about the last gardener's indiscretions. I tried to tune her out and hear what the party was talking about. Peals of laughter pierced the birdsong. They were a gay little ensemble.

Dancing in the mist of my unease, the heady scent of cedar and citrus joined the chorus of wildflower perfume. My chest tightened. The scent of Archie. We were almost upon the countess and her guests. The sounds of his familiar tenor stopped me in my tracks. I felt the blood drain from my cheeks. *What is he doing here? He's supposed to be visiting his sick mother in Wales.*

I wanted to hightail it and run away. But I was trapped. I wiped my sweaty palms on my trousers.

"Are you quite alright?" the maid asked. "You look like you've taken a turn."

"Fine." I took a deep breath. I was far from fine. My betrothed had lied to me. He was laughing and holding hands with the lovely gazelle while I was wearing dirty overalls and a scratchy beard pretending to be a gardener. A male gardener. *Oh, bother. What if Archie recognizes me?* I'd never been able to hide from him. Others might fall for my disguises, but not Archie. *Come on, Fiona. Get a grip.* I couldn't give myself away. "Just fine," I repeated, tugging at my overalls. I must regain my composure and face the party. I took another deep breath. There was no other way. I was on assignment and my mission was my top priority. I'd deal with Archie later.

As we stepped into view of the group, I averted my eyes. I

didn't dare look at Archie. Alright. I stole a glance. I couldn't help it. Big mistake. My stomach roiled and I thought I might be sick.

"Excuse me, your ladyship," the maid said. "The new gardener."

"Thank you, Mary," the countess said, sizing me up. "Mr. Peabody, you've arrived just in time." She waved her arms around as if shooing away bees. "The garden is a disaster."

"*Romaine* calm." I resorted to terrible puns to cover my embarrassment. "Nothing *beets* gardening."

Archie tilted his head and stared at me with a queer look on his face. "Do I know you?"

I shook my head and stared down at my feet. My cheeks warmed beneath my beard. *Please, don't blow my cover.* I said a silent prayer. *Please, please. Don't let him recognize me.*

Eva Gore-Booth stood and took Archie's hand. "Let's leave them to talk about the garden."

Part of me was relieved. If he left, I didn't have to worry about him recognizing me. The other part was appalled. I bit my lip to repress a gasp. Was E. D. Aria right about Archie? Was he two-timing me with the gazelle? If I wasn't seeing it with my own eyes, I wouldn't believe it. I couldn't believe it. "Your garden is full of pricks, er, pricklies," I said, glaring at Archie. "A good pair of loppers and I'll nip them off in no time."

Archie stood and turned to face me. What in the world had happened to him? His left ear was completely covered in sticking plaster.

"Looks like someone beat me to it." I pointed to his ear. Although that wasn't the part of his anatomy I'd had in mind.

He bent to kiss the gazelle's hand and then turned to the countess. "Might I have a word with your gardener?" His lips twitched. "I have a plot that needs tender loving care and I suspect he's just the man for the job." He picked up the black walking stick that was leaning against the back of his chair.

"He's all yours," the countess said, finishing her coffee. "Eva, Esther, and I will be in the morning room."

Archie nodded. "I'll just be a minute." As he waved his walking stick, bronze shamrocks adorning the stick glimmered in the sunlight. *Oh, my word.* My heart sank. Another bejeweled Shillelagh. Suddenly, my world was full of them. I tried to get a better look at the stick. I hoped to heaven it wasn't missing one of its clovers.

After the sisters were out of earshot, Archie glared at me. "Fiona, what are you doing here?" He pounded the ground with his stick.

"What are *you* doing here?" My lip trembled. "Sowing your wild oats before our wedding?" I tried to get a look at the jewels on the head of his stick, but his hand was covering it. "You're supposed to be in Wales with your sick mum."

"I'm on an undercover assignment," he said through his teeth. "You're jeopardizing months of work."

"Me!" I huffed. "I'm jeopardizing *your* cover?" Again, part of me was relieved. His attentions toward Miss Gore-Booth were a charade. The other part was irritated. I too was on a mission. "You're jeopardizing *my* cover." I too was sent by the War Office. And I too had an important undercover assignment. He wasn't the only spy in the field. "I was sent here by Captain Hall himself." I lowered my voice to a whisper. "To find a list of the members of the Citizen Army."

"Then your job is done." He glanced around and then pulled a folded paper from his inside pocket. "Here is your list." He shoved it at me. "Now go home. It's too dangerous for you here. This place is a tinderbox."

"Too dangerous for me but not for you." I squinted at him. "Typical double standard."

"Fiona, please," he pleaded. "Be reasonable. You're a woman—"

"Actually." I cleared my throat and gave him my deepest tenor. "I'm Horace Peabody, *male* gardener extraordinaire." I unfolded the paper and studied the list.

"Stop playing around and go home." He leaned his Shillelagh against the chair, tapped out a Kenilworth, and lit it.

"I'm not playing." I used the list to wave away a cloud of smoke. "Far from it—" I eyed his walking stick. What was I thinking? Had I lost my mind? Of course Archie wouldn't attack Kitty. The idea was ridiculous.

"Calm down." He put his hand on my sleeve. "Just calm down."

Telling someone to calm down rarely achieves that objective. I clenched my jaw to avoid telling him off. I refolded the list and handed it back to him. "Keep your stupid list."

"Please, Fiona." He ran a hand through his hair. "You're my fiancée, soon to be my wife. I love you and don't want anything to happen to you." He sighed. "Please." He took me by both arms. "Fiona, you know I adore you." He picked a stray camellia petal off my jacket. "And if you weren't wearing that ridiculous beard..." He smiled. "I'd show you just how much."

"Like you showed Eva Gore-Booth?" I brushed at my eyes with the backs of my hands.

"That's work." He dropped his cigarette and ground it out. "Please don't make a mountain out of a molehill." He thrust the list at me again.

"Molehill." I stomped my foot. "More like rat's nest" I crossed my arms over my chest.

"Look, Fiona." He closed his eyes. "You know I can't tell you about my mission. It's top secret. Not even Captain Hall knows about it."

"What?" My breath caught. If Captain Hall didn't know about his mission, then he wasn't sent by the War Office. And if he didn't work for the War Office, who exactly did he work for? *Heavens.* Was it true, then? Did Archie really work for MI5? My mind was racing. Then it dawned on me. "You're my contact from MI5."

He nodded. "I suppose I am."

My heart sank. I thought back to all those times Archie had told me his mission was classified. And all those times he'd been following orders to kill. In Manhattan, Archie killed a German agent, and then again in Cairo. In Italy, he'd shot at Fredricks. He'd poisoned Iron Victor in Moscow. He was a killer. A cold-blooded killer. I was engaged to an assassin. "You're an assassin for MI5!"

"Now, Fiona." He sucked his teeth. "Be careful what you say." He took up his Shillelagh and picked at a spot where it was missing a shamrock.

I felt the blood drain from my face. His stick was missing a jewel. The clover I found in the locker room could have been from Archie's walking stick. And yet he wasn't there that day. Was he? He wasn't in the advanced jujitsu class. And why in the world would he attack Kitty? No. It didn't make sense. It wasn't Archie. It couldn't be. I shuddered to think. The jewel I'd found must be from Jules Silver's Shillelagh. I'd never seen an Irish walking stick before in my life. And now suddenly there were two! Missing bronze clovers, no less. And one belonged to my fiancé. I forced myself to put my own feelings aside. Objectivity. I had to maintain my objectivity. A lesson I'd learned from reading Sherlock Holmes. What would Sherlock Holmes do in this situation?

I thought of one of my favorite stories, *A Scandal in Bohemia*.

The king of Bohemia is set to marry a Scandinavian princess but he fears a secret liaison with an American opera singer, Irene Adler, might scuttle his marriage. The king employs Sherlock Holmes to retrieve an incriminating photograph of himself with Irene Adler. I thought of the photograph in the newspaper of Archie with Eva Gore-Booth. Archie wasn't the type to exact revenge. Even if he was, he wouldn't have killed Ellen Davis *after* she'd already printed the article. And he wouldn't attack Kitty. It must have been Jules.

Objectivity dictated that I include Archie on my list of suspects. Luckily, Archie was *not* at the Dojo on the day of the attack, *nor* was he at Lady Battersea's place when Ellen died. A wave of relief washed over me. And yet...

"What happened to your ear?" I touched the bandage. No doubt an injury in the line of duty. Bitten by a gazelle, perhaps.

He flinched. "Nothing."

"I suppose it's classified." I tightened my lips. His secrecy was getting on my nerves.

"Something like that." He shook his head. "Let's just say I was attacked by a stray cat and leave it at that."

"A cat bit your ear!" I couldn't imagine how that could happen. "Where did you get that walking stick? And why is it missing a jewel?"

"Look, Fiona. Take this list." His eyes were hard as he thrust the list at me again. "Now, go home and wait for me." He softened his gaze. "Everything will be different once we're married."

That's what I'm afraid of. Everything would be different. I'd be sent home, and he'd be out in the field doing who-knew-what-with-whom. "Where did you get the Shillelagh?" My voice was stern. "And why is it missing a jewel?" I refused to take the list. I didn't need it. I'd already memorized it.

"It was a gift from the countess and Eva. It belonged to their father. He was a friend of my father's." He admired the stick. "I suppose the jewel came off on one of his many adventures." His countenance hardened again. "Forget about them... that's work. Nothing more." He ran his hand through his hair again. He always did that when he was nervous.

"So, the jewel was already missing from the stick?"

"Yes. It was." He gave me a queer look. "Why does it matter?" He held out the list yet again.

"Keep your list," I huffed. "I don't need it."

He tucked the list back into his pocket and then pulled out a small velvet box. "Look, I was saving this for our honeymoon." He handed it to me. "But I want you to have it now as a token of my love." He shoved it at me. "Take it. And please, please, please, go home."

I stood there blinking at him. He got me a wedding present. I looked into his loving eyes. How could I have let myself get so carried away? He was on a mission. He was a patriot. Like me, he was loyal to king and country. And we were at war. Archie was merely doing his duty. I respected him for that. His gaze was so earnest, so full of love. Tears welled in my eyes. And a pang of guilt stabbed at my heart. How could I have suspected him?

"Well, open it." He smiled.

My pulsed quickened as I opened the box. "Oh, Archie." A gorgeous little charm bracelet with a silver heart and a silver flower dangling from it. "It's beautiful."

He plucked the bracelet from the box. "I'll help you put in on."

I held out my wrist.

"Now will you go home like a good girl?" He fastened the clasp.

I sighed. "Oh, alright." I admired the bracelet and its charms as they tinkled and danced in the sunlight. Even on the wrist of Horace Peabody, it looked lovely.

"Wonderful!" He smiled. "That's my good girl."

Good girl, my fake beard.

18

WOODY THE WOLFHOUND

Two hours later, my alter ego, Mr. Horace Peabody, returned to give his apologies and his notice, telling Countess Markievicz that he had a family emergency back in England. If the countess was suspicious of his sudden departure, she didn't let on.

For my part, I was sorry to let Horace go. I'd just put him on and now I had to take him off. As much as I enjoyed fake beards and moustaches, removing the darn things stung like the Dickens. Archie may have shown me the list and sent Horace away. But he wasn't going to keep me from continuing my investigation into the untimely death of Ellen Davis at the Suffrajitsu tea party.

Back at the Stag's Head Inn, I immediately rang the countess and arranged a meeting. This time as Miss Fiona Figg. Although surprised by my sudden appearance in Dublin, the countess was only too happy to invite me to tea.

I scrubbed my face until the only remnants of the gardener was the bright red rash on my chin and upper lip and then did the best I could to cover the rash with face powder. Thinking of Archie and his undercover—or was it under covers—assignment vexed me no end. I tore off my waistcoat with so much force I popped off a button. Would things change after we were married? Would they change for the better? Would Archie stop cavorting with gazelles and confide in me?

Trying to forget about Archie, I tracked down Clifford in the pub and asked him to take me back to the Markievicz estate.

"Should I go rub more dirt on my clothes?" he asked earnestly.

"No. Put on your nicest morning suit. Not your uniform, though." The uniform might scare off the countess and her sister, seeing how they were founding members of the Irish Citizen Army and wanted the British out of Ireland. "Would you mind posing as my brother, Clifford dear?" He'd done so on other occasions when we were on assignment.

"I say." Clifford beamed. "I'd be honored and delighted, old bean. You know I would." Good old reliable Clifford. Why couldn't I fall for someone like him for a change? He may be boring and a blabbermouth, but at least he wasn't an assassin.

When Clifford and I arrived back at the estate, Archie was gone. Thank goodness. I don't know if I could have faced him again, especially without Horace Peabody for protection. And, in his absence, perhaps I could expand my interrogation of Miss Eva Gore-Booth beyond murder to romance.

The sisters, along with their friend, received us in the morning room. They were still wearing their sharp contrasting outfits from earlier. The older in a black army uniform, complete with collar pins and insignias. The younger in a flowing dress and silk slippers. They couldn't have been more different. And yet they got on so well. From what I could tell, they were practically inseparable. And with their friend, Miss Esther Roper, they made a pretty little trio.

The manly maid served tea while Clifford regaled us with

hunting stories. After he'd sufficiently warmed up the audience, I interrupted and did a bit of warm up of my own.

"May I ask about your uniform, your ladyship?" I smiled. "It's very interesting."

"No need for the ladyship nonsense." She waved her hand as if shooing a fly. "Ten years ago, I was a founding member of the Daughters of Ireland." She gave a nostalgic sort of laugh. "I came to our first meeting straight from a ball at Dublin castle. Imagine what the Irish revolutionaries made of me in my gown and tiara."

"Constance designed the Irish Citizen Army uniform and composed our song, too," Eva said proudly. "She only just got out of prison last month."

"Prison! Good Lord." Clifford nearly choked on a biscuit.

"After the Easter uprising, they commuted my death sentence to life because I'm a woman." She scoffed. "Didn't even have the decency to shoot me."

"Steady on," Clifford sputtered.

"Now, she's running for parliament." Eva beamed. "And she's going to win!"

"Hear, hear!" Miss Roper chimed in.

"I say." Clifford brushed crumbs off his trousers. "Women in parliament. That'll be the day."

"She'll be the first." Eva reached over and took her sister's hands. "Our Constance, making history."

"Congratulations." I smiled. Why shouldn't women run the government? They couldn't do any worse than the men.

"Many a slip between cup and lip," the countess said.

"She's going to win," Eva said, confidently. "Hands down."

"She'd better," Miss Roper said. "I've got a fiver riding on it." She laughed.

"Good for you!" I clapped my hands together. When I did, my charm bracelet tinkled, reminding me of Archie and my mission.

Whether this jubilant moment was the right time to begin my interrogation, I decided there was no time like the present. "The day Kitty was attacked at the Dojo?" I paused to give them a moment to adjust to the change of subject. "Did you see anything or anyone unusual?" I pulled a notebook out of my bag. I figured either they would welcome any topic of conversation to stop the gory details of blood sports, or they were sufficiently amused and disarmed to gain their confidence. Either way, Clifford had served a useful purpose.

The sisters shook their heads. "We were in London for the Suffrajitsu training," the countess said. "I'd like to start something like that here in Dublin."

"Wouldn't that be grand," Eva said. "Ladies can learn to overpower men twice their size."

"Grand," I repeated. She did have a point. Jujitsu training could come in handy.

"Men. Women," Miss Roper declared. "Let's abolish the manly and the womanly and sweep them into the museum of antiques."

"Good Lord," Clifford sputtered. "You're not suggesting men and women are the same?"

"In every way that matters," Miss Roper replied.

I liked her. But I didn't have time to debate the relative merits of the rougher sex. I had an investigation to conclude. "Back to the Dojo, if I may. Nothing out of the ordinary the day Kitty was attacked?" I asked, holding my pencil at the ready.

"No," Eva said. "Archibald dropped us off at the Dojo. We did the course with the suffragettes. And later he picked us up." She turned to her sister. "Right, Constance?"

The countess nodded. "Until Ellen Davis screamed, and you found poor Kitty unconscious, all was as it should be."

"Archibald?" I stared down at my notebook. "You mean

Archibald Somersby from London?" Suddenly, I felt sick. That would mean Archie *was* at the Dojo when Kitty was attacked. He had the means *and* the opportunity. A lump formed in my throat. That hard black walking stick these lovely ladies had given him would make an excellent cudgel.

"Why, yes," Eva chuckled. "Our *friend* from Wales."

The way she said "friend" turned my stomach. "Archie, er, Archibald dropped you off and picked you up at the Dojo?" I asked, just to confirm.

"Do you know him?" the countess asked.

"Of course she does," Eva said. "She's his intended. Or so I've heard." She batted her lashes.

"Quite." I held my tongue. So, Eva did know Archie was engaged to be married. And to me.

"You're not travelling together, then?" the countess asked.

Hot-faced, I sputtered, "Well, we aren't married yet. It wouldn't be proper."

"I suppose you know he's off to London again this afternoon." Eva smiled.

No, I didn't know. "Of course," I said with a forced smile.

"But he promised to be back soon, right, Constance?" Eva turned to her sister.

"Not too soon, I hope," Miss Roper said, taking Eva's hand.

Archie had gone back to London? Why didn't he tell me he was going home? What was he up to? Perhaps he had a surprise in store for me. A surprise wedding present. That had better be it. Unless he was going back to town to finish what he'd started with Kitty. I shuddered. Whatever he was doing, I intended to find out. Just as soon as I got back to town.

"Right, dear." The countess nodded. "He'll be back."

It was clear Eva Gore-Booth was fond of Archie. Thinking of them together produced a sharp pain in my chest. And why did Miss Roper dislike him? That was almost as vexing to me. *Calm down, Fiona.* Concentrate on your investigation. I took a deep breath to tamp down my emotions. Stiff upper lip and all that. I forced myself to return to my line of questioning. "Apart from the suffragette ladies, did you see anyone else at the Dojo?"

"No," Eva said. "Only the suffragettes, Mrs. Garrud, oh, and that Captain Soughton fellow. Right, Constance?"

The countess nodded again. "Yes, he was hanging about the tea house, I think."

"Fredricks," I said under my breath. Of course he was. "And then there was Ellen Davis and the dreadful business at Lady Battersea's tea party." I glanced from one sister to the other, gauging their reactions. "I couldn't help but notice at Lady Battersea's you were very friendly with the maid." I peeked over my teacup, waiting for their response.

"She's from County Wicklow," the countess said. "One of our countrywomen, as it were."

"Did you know her from before?" I asked, tugging off my gloves.

"Ireland isn't some backwater hamlet." Eva laughed.

"Apologies." The last thing I wanted to do was insult the ladies. I needed to gain their trust.

"Don't mind my sister," the countess said. "The girl is the daughter of one of our neighbor's parlor maids. Unfortunately, like great estates and fortunes are passed on in the upper classes, service is passed on in the lower."

"So, you do know Lady Battersea's maid?" I scribbled a note. "Molly."

"No. Not really." The countess sipped her tea. "Only by sight."

"Like my sister said, her mother is in service next door." Eva waved in the general direction of the neighbor's house. "And her father is a craftsman who makes lovely Shillelaghs and canes. He sells them at the local markets."

"We often give them as gifts," the countess added.

Gifts that make excellent weapons. Apparently, both Archie and Jules Silver had been the lucky recipients of such deadly gifts. "Has the girl visited recently?" I asked.

"I couldn't say," the countess replied. "Why do you ask?"

"I'm investigating poor Ellen's demise." I nibbled on a biscuit. "Did either of you notice anything or anybody out of the ordinary that afternoon at the tea party?"

Eva pursed her lips. "It was odd that Lord Balfour was among Battersea's party of gentlemen."

"And why is that?" I took a sip of tea.

"Balfour and Battersea are on opposite sides of the issue of home rule for Ireland," Eva said, putting up her hands. "Everyone knows that."

"I say," Clifford interjected. "Those two chaps are opposite sides of everything except pheasant hunting." He chuckled. "Why, one time—"

"Yes, thank you, dear." I reached over and patted his arm, hoping he would take the hint. "And yet, according to Ellen's gossip column, Lord Balfour covered for Lord Battersea."

"Men always cover for each other when it comes to sex," Miss Roper said.

I coughed.

"Gossip column?" the countess scoffed. "Don't believe everything you read, especially in the gossip columns."

"I don't believe any of it." Clifford clamped his pipe between his teeth. "The things that E. D. Aria said about poor old Battersea would make your hair curl."

"Did you know Ellen Davis was E. D. Aria?" I asked, watching for signs they were lying.

"No idea!" the countess said with a shrug. "Never read that kind of tripe."

"How about you?" I turned to Eva.

She blushed. "I didn't know."

What did it mean that she was blushing? Was she so prudish that mere talk of gossip made her blush? Or was she embarrassed to admit that she read the gossip columns? Perhaps it was because she did indeed know the true identity of E. D. Aria, in which case, she knew it was Ellen Davis who printed the column about her and Archie... although, to be fair, that was after Ellen's death. So, unless Eva killed Ellen to stop her printing the piece (for all the good it did), she was not the killer. Or, if she was, the gossip column was not her motive.

"Did either of you leave the drawing room apart from going upstairs to the demonstrations?" I continued my interrogation. "To use the powder room, perhaps?"

The sisters looked at each other.

"You don't think one of us did it!" Eva's mouth fell open.

"Impossible!" Miss Roper said.

"Good Lord, Fiona." Clifford pointed the stem of his pipe at me. "These lovely ladies couldn't have had anything to do with that ghastly business."

"No, of course not." I demurred—despite the fact I knew full well women were just as capable as men of ghastly business. "I'm just trying to piece together what happened—how it happened—and one of the ladies might have seen something. Something out of the ordinary."

The sisters considered but shook their heads.

"Did the maid give you the correct hats?" I still wondered whether their only connection to Molly the maid was their country of birth.

The countess looked confused. "Whatever do you mean?"

"It was the butler," Eva said indignantly. "And of course he did."

"Hatpins attached?" I drained my teacup.

"Our hatpins were all laid out on a tray," Eva said. "We simply picked them up on the way out when we retrieved our hats."

Odd. Lady Battersea assured us that the butler Toogood would replace the hatpins on the hats. Something was amiss with Toogood and the hatpins.

"That's right. I forgot," the countess said. "Your hatpin was found at the scene of the crime." She flashed a sly smile. "You're trying to clear your name... unless of course you did it."

"Quite."

"Rum do about your hatpin, old bean," Clifford said. "Poor old girl didn't stand a chance."

I squinted at him. "Ellen Davis died of a heart attack." Although the police had ruled it a heart attack, they still insisted I not leave town. Of course, I had left anyway. But only on Captain Hall's orders. I knew it wasn't a heart attack. I knew it was murder. And not just because of my hatpin sticking out of her neck.

"Righto." Clifford nodded. "Imagine if the perpetrator had stabbed her through the eye. That hatpin would make a sneaky weapon."

"Yes, well. He/she didn't and it wasn't." If I could have reached him with my foot, I would have kicked him under the table.

"She did look unwell," Eva said. "Poor dear." She turned to her sister. "Remember? I remarked on how pale she was when she left the table."

"Yes," the countess said. "From my seat, I saw her stumbling down the hallway. She looked half drunk. Wobbling here and there... reminded me of our poor Woody when he got into the foxgloves, poor thing."

"Woody?" I asked.

"Our Wolfhound," Eva said. "Luckily, he spat it out and didn't swallow it. But he was sick for a couple of days, wobbling about, banging into things."

Foxglove could be deadly. If ingested, it could cause shock and slow heartrate, even a heart attack.

I remembered the bright red berries on Ellen's salad. And those odd-shaped leaves. Did the killer use foxglove leaves and lily-of-the-valley to make a toxic salad? Those sweet little red berries could also cause cardiac distress. Foxglove and lily-of-the-valley. A deadly combination. Especially if Ellen Davis had a heart condition. The toxins were found in the leaves of the foxglove plant and lily-of-the-valley. Either one could be deadly in itself. But, combined, they were lethal.

Oh, my sainted aunt! Of course, that explained everything. Well, everything except my hatpin sticking out of her neck. Ellen Davis had been poisoned, which was why she didn't eat her pudding course... and why she had to excuse herself to go to the powder room. The poison was in her salad, which was why she felt unwell. And that was why the coroner's report ruled it a heart attack.

Ellen Davis did indeed have a heart attack. But one caused by a deadly mixture of poisons. Poisons easily found on the grounds of Countess Markievicz's estate.

19

KITTY'S INTERLUDE

Three nights in Reading were more than enough. She had to get answers. She had to regain her memory *and fast*, and that wasn't going to happen tucked away in Reading.

It was nice of Clifford and his mother to take her in. But she didn't need their protection. She could take care of herself. After all, she was a trained operative. That much she remembered. And she was a jujitsu champion. Right. She had a tournament coming up. Unlike Aunt Fiona, she'd been proficient in martial arts, the art of espionage, and more languages than anyone had a right to speak. The boarding school in Lyon was much more than a girls' finishing school. *L'Espion* was the best spy school in the world.

It was coming back to her. She'd been fortunate. On a dreary December day five years ago, Captain "Blinker" Hall had caught her picking his pocket to steal his wallet. She was thirteen at the time. An orphan. Alone with her younger sister, living on the streets of London. Hungry all the time. Always on the make. Funny. She'd never felt desperate, only desire. An overwhelming desire for more. And then on that fateful morning Captain Hall grabbed her wrist and pulled her across town to Whitehall where he handed her over to his wife, who gave her a good scrubbing.

Yes. She was starting to remember. The good and the bad... her secrets. If only she knew her own name. *Jane Archer.* Was that her name? She couldn't get the name out of her head. Why? She had to find this Jane Archer. There was a reason she couldn't shake the name Jane Archer and she intended to find out what it was. Someone close to her? A friend... or associate at MI5?

She made a plan. Tomorrow night, she would wait until Mrs. Douglas was asleep and then creep out of the house. But not before giving Poppy an extra biscuit and a lecture about the importance of being a good girl. She needed to get back to London and find Jane Archer as soon as possible. Jane was the key to everything. She felt it in her gut. If she could find Jane Archer, she could find out who she was... and, more importantly, the name of the mole.

Strange how she was so sure of some things, complicated, secret things. And so unsure of others. Namely, who she was and where she lived.

Even Captain Hall couldn't answer her questions. He merely repeated what Fiona and Clifford had said. He didn't know where she lived either. Captain Hall had ordered her to stand down and rest until she'd recovered. But her work for him was merely her cover. No wonder he didn't know her true identity. Her true mission had been to infiltrate the Irish Citizen Army and get intelligence on their involvement with the Germans, the so-called German Plot. Yes. Her memory was returning. Thank goodness.

But wait. The plot was bogus. There was no plot. But the double agent was very real.

Why couldn't she remember his name? Jane would know.

Whatever his name, there was a mole in MI5. And he was armed and dangerous. An accomplished assassin who was gunning for her. Worse yet, there was a substantial risk that Aunt Fiona could be collateral damage.

20

THE CROSSING

The next morning, after a fitful sleep, there was nothing left to do but head back to London. Clifford and I took breakfast at the inn and then headed to the ferry.

"Penny for your thoughts," Clifford said as he drove us to the dock.

I must have looked more pensive than usual. I took a deep breath. "What is the difference between cold-blooded murder and killing an enemy during war? Or assassinating an enemy for that matter?"

It was this question that had disturbed my sleep last night. If Archie was an assassin for MI5, how was he any different to a cold-blooded murderer? Did it matter if a cold-blooded gun-for-hire was paid by a government or by a criminal? When a man killed dozens of other men in war, he was a hero. But if he killed even one person at home, he was a murderer. No matter how hard I'd tried, I couldn't shake these troublesome thoughts.

"I say." Clifford looked over at me, his eyes full of concern. "It's a little early for deep philosophical questions, isn't it, old bean?" He smiled. "We weren't the aggressors in this bloody war. The Huns started it, not us."

"So, we're killing in self-defense?" I pulled my coat tight against the chill in the air.

"Exactly." He swerved to miss a stray sheep wandering along the road.

"And what about the assassin?" My voice cracked. "Why is he not just a cold-blooded killer?" I held up my wrist and admired the charm bracelet. Shaking my wrist, I listened to the charms tinkle.

"Maybe your assassin was ordered to kill someone so heinous and dangerous that by doing so he actually saves dozens of lives." He raised his eyebrows. "Did you think of that?"

"This bloody war was started by an assassin who probably thought he was doing his duty, too." Every time I'd contented myself with a reasonable answer, another objection crept into my mind.

"Archduke Ferdinand and his wife were hardly dangerous," he scoffed. "They were sitting ducks." He tutted. "Downright cowardly to shoot them in their carriage, if you ask me."

"And what if a British officer was ordered to kill a German spy in his opera booth, would that be cowardly?" I thought of Archie killing a man at the opera last spring.

"All is fair in love and war, old bean." Clifford pulled in behind a line of cars waiting to embark. "We're at war. We do what's necessary to win."

"The ends justify the means?"

"I suppose they do." He shrugged. "Rum do all round."

"Indeed."

* * *

The ferry crossing gave me time away from Clifford to think. He'd gone to the bar for a drink. Wrapped in a shawl, I sat out on the deck soaking in the sunshine, which hardly took the edge off the brisk sea breeze. Professionally, my trip to Ireland had been a success. I'd managed to get the list of members of the Irish Citizen Army, which I had stored in my memory. Personally, on the other hand, it had been a disaster.

The revelation that Archie worked for MI5 had shaken my faith in him. All this time, he'd never once told me. Of course, his assignments were classified. Still, we were getting married. And husbands should not have secrets from their wives. At least not monumental secrets like being an MI5 agent. And, worse yet, an agent assigned to seduce a young lady to gain her trust and learn her secrets. The whole thing was unseemly to say the least. Remembering Archie kissing Eva's hand, frankly, it turned my stomach. The rough seas weren't helping much either.

To distract myself, I went inside and found a cozy spot to take a hot cuppa. Rubbing my hands together, I resolved to turn my attention to Kitty and Ellen's attacker. I removed my notebook from my chatelaine bag and opened my list of suspects. Sipping a rather bitter and tepid cup of tea, I reviewed what I knew so far.

Kitty had been hit on the head with a blunt object by a man. I'd found the shamrock charm at the scene. Jules Silver owned a walking stick missing just such a charm, a stick that could have been used to attack Kitty. Jules had the means and opportunity, but what was his motive? In his post as censor for the War Office, he had passed on a suspicious letter, which meant either he was not good at his job, or he was a spy. Kitty's distrust of the man may be justified. When I'd shown the letter to Captain Hall, he'd vowed to keep an eye on Mr. Silver.

Archie also had a walking stick missing a jewel. A stick given to him by the countess and her sister, I might add. I'd learned from the sisters that Archie dropped them off at the Dojo on the morning of Kitty's attack. So, Archie also had the means and the opportunity. I bit my lip. *Objectivity, Fiona. You must be objective.* How could I? I was marrying Archie soon! I forced all thoughts of Archie as a killer to the back of my mind and moved on to Ellen's death.

As for Ellen Davis... she had died of a heart attack, which I now suspected was induced by foxglove and lily-of-the-valley poisoning. Given my hatpin was sticking out of her neck, it wasn't accidental ingestion but foul play. Her symptoms before she died, combined with the bright berries and odd leaves in her salad, led me to believe she'd been poisoned at luncheon. But why would someone poison her *and then* stab her with a hatpin? Especially since, according to the police, the half-hearted use of my hatpin had only done minor damage in itself. She had to have been poisoned before she left the table, which was why she wobbled as she went. Obviously, she was attacked in addition to being poisoned since she didn't have my hatpin sticking out of her neck when she'd left the table.

My hatpin didn't kill her. The police knew that. And yet why was it at the scene? Did the same person poison and stab her? Or were there two assailants?

As for suspects... I could think of several people who had a motive to kill the gossip columnist. Who had the means? The means would include access to foxglove and lily-of-the-valley to use as poisons and access to Ellen's plate at luncheon. The countess and her sister came to mind. The staff had access to Ellen's plate. But any one of the ladies present—or Ellen's enemies—could have bribed a staff member to poison Ellen's food. I reviewed my notes.

If the poison was in the meal, the killer had access to the kitchen. You couldn't just sneak into a kitchen, no matter how large, and add a few poisonous plants to a plate. I had to get back to Lady Battersea's house and question the staff again. Only someone who worked in the house could have got away with putting poisoned berries and leaves into Ellen's salad. And the killer had to know where Ellen was sitting and deliver the salad to her and not someone else. This narrowed things down considerably. The killer must have been one of the luncheon party or the staff. Someone who'd seen the place cards or Ellen in her seat.

Of course, with the place cards set in advance, everyone in the household would have known where Ellen would be sitting. Only she didn't sit there. But the killer might not have known that. And only someone regularly seen about the kitchen could have added poisoned berries and leaves to a salad without raising suspicions. Randy Kipper or Lord Balfour, for example, couldn't have waltzed into the kitchen unnoticed and done so. The staff would have sounded an alarm, or at least mentioned it to the police. Could one of the suffragettes have done it? How would they make sure the salad was delivered to Ellen and not someone else? My thoughts tumbled in circles. Still, I felt that I was closing in on the murderer.

I kept coming back to the place card. Even with the place card, none of the suffragettes could know which salad would be delivered to Ellen. Therefore, the killer must have been one of the kitchen staff.

I sipped my tepid tea and stared down at my notebook. Something wasn't right. Everyone had a motive to kill E. D. Aria, but no one admitted to knowing she was Ellen Davis. So, who had a motive for killing Ellen Davis?

Only the kitchen staff had the opportunity to poison the salad. But why would any of the staff want Ellen dead? I supposed Lady Battersea could have enlisted her staff to poison the gossip columnist. That was possible. But what about my hatpin? And the fact that the maid—not the butler—delivered my hat to Mrs. Kipper?

"There you are, old bean." Clifford plunked down in the seat across from me. "I've been looking for you from stem to stern, as they say. You're not where you're supposed to be. This is third class and our tickets are for second. You're in the wrong seat." He leaned over the table and peered at my notebook. "What's this? Have you cracked the case?"

"What did you say about sitting in the wrong seat?" I blinked at him.

"Our tickets are for second class and you're sitting in the third-class section." He pointed at a sign. "See?"

"Clifford, you're a genius!" I snapped the notebook shut.

"I am?" he beamed.

"Yes!" I may not have cracked the case. But I was getting close. So close, I could feel it. "Ellen Davis was sitting in the wrong seat!" My pulse quickened. "Of course. The place card was Kitty's." *Oh, my word.* "Kitty was the real target." So, Kitty was the target of both attacks. They were related.

"What?" Clifford swallowed hard. "Then someone really is trying to kill her?" The color drained from his cheeks. "We've got to warn her. And Mother."

I'd never seen him so agitated.

"Quite." I glanced at my watch. Goodness. We had hours left to go on the ferry alone. We wouldn't be back in London until very late. "Don't worry." I reached out and touched his sleeve. "No one knows she's at your mother's house in Reading. She's safe there."

I hoped to heaven it was true.

21

KITTY'S INTERLUDE

She kept to her plan and snuck out after Mrs. Douglas went to bed. She was on her way back to London to find Jane.

Her conscious mind couldn't remember. But she was confident it was all there in her unconscious mind. She'd heard of the inventive Austrian neurologist working on theories of the mind. Wasn't Fredrick Fredricks always going on about Sigmund Freud and unconscious desires and phobias? Didn't that suggest everything was stored deep in her mind? She just had to figure out how to access it.

She'd had several bus rides from Reading back to London to think about it. When Charles Street popped into her head, she ended up in Westminster near the Houses of Parliament. In the hour before dawn, she'd walked up and down Charles Street, hoping her unconscious mind would take her someplace. By the time she sat down on a bench near St. James's Square, her feet were tired, and her hands were freezing. Somewhere out there, someone knew who she was. If only she could find them.

Watching the sun rise over the statue of Florence Nightingale, she remembered the address on Charles Street. Number sixteen.

Yes. That was it. She was certain she would find Jane Archer at number sixteen Charles Street. She only had to wait until the offices opened. Pulling her coat tight around her torso, she walked back to Charles Street. Glancing over her shoulders, she paced back and forth in front of number sixteen. Eventually, Jane would arrive at work. Would she recognize Jane? Her memory was coming back in bits and pieces. But she still didn't have a clear sense of how they fit together or the whole puzzle.

She continued walking to keep warm. Hopefully, she wouldn't be arrested for loitering before Jane showed up. Or worse, be hunted down by the MI5 assassin.

22

THE GERMAN PLOT

After yet another restless night—at least this time in my own bed
—I got up early and was at the War Office first thing. Clifford had
gone off to Reading to warn Kitty. I would have gone with him
except that Captain Hall needed the list of names of the Citizen
Army from Dublin. I paced the floor, hoping Clifford found Kitty
safe at his mother's house. No one knew she was there. I took a
deep breath and reassured myself that she was safe. She had
to be.

Room 40 was deserted. The men wouldn't arrive for another
hour. I went to the kitchenette and put the kettle on. I tried to
ignore the sink full of dishes. But I could no more ignore them
here than I could at my own home—not that I'd ever let dirty
dishes pile up at home. I may not be much of a homemaker, but I
liked things neat and tidy. After cleaning the kitchenette and
making a cup of tea, I went back to my desk to wait for Captain
Hall's secretary to arrive.

From memory, I wrote out all the names I'd seen on the list. I
glanced at my watch. Sitting at my desk with a strong cup of tea, I
was looking forward to the look on Captain Hall's face when he

saw me back already and with the list of Irish Citizen Army members in hand.

While waiting, I rang Lady Battersea and asked if I might stop by for tea... and another interview with her maid. Reluctantly, she agreed. But not until the end of the month and then only if I put in a good word about her and her husband with Captain Soughton, "seeing how you're such *close friends*." I didn't see the point in contradicting her, especially if agreeing could get me what I wanted. Trouble was, I couldn't wait until the end of the month. Neither could the police. I needed answers now.

"Perhaps I could just pop in later today," I persevered. "For just a few minutes."

"Under usual circumstances, I would be delighted, but we have workmen around giving the old place a much-needed touch up." She paused. "I'm leaving for our country house today to get out from under foot and the dust and mess. I won't be back until the end of the month, or I'd be happy to host you."

"I see." Workmen. That gave me another idea. A better idea. Especially considering Lady Battersea and his lordship would be away. "Thank you. Until the end of the month, then."

"From what I hear," she chuckled, "you'll be Mrs. Archibald Somersby by then. I'll send around an invitation to you both."

"Very kind of you." *Mrs. Archibald Somersby.* How different my life was going to be soon.

Once I was off the telephone, I tidied up my desk for the third time this morning, made yet another cup of tea, and waited. The limbo of waiting always put my mind in an awkward state of relaxed agitation.

An hour later, finally I was sitting across from Captain Hall.

"Why aren't you in Ireland?" His lashes fluttered a mile a minute.

"I got the list, sir."

"My God." He slapped his desk. "That was quick. Good job!" He stabbed the air with a finger. "And brilliant work discovering Jules Silver was a spy." He beamed. "He's being arrested as we speak." He tugged at the hem of his jacket. "I wonder, how did you come across that suspicious letter?"

"Ah, er, I purloined it from Fredrick Fredricks." My cheeks warmed.

"You're still on his tail." He waved his hands as if directing an orchestra. "As it should be. We can't let the scoundrel out of our sight."

"No, sir." More like the scoundrel didn't let me out of his sight.

"Thanks to your dogged intelligence work, we learned of the German Plot." He nodded his approval. "You've become an asset to the department."

"Thank you, sir." I smiled and fished the list out of my chatelaine bag. "Here's the list you wanted." I handed it to him. When I did, my charm bracelet tinkled.

"Wearing a warning bell now, like a cat?" He looked stern. "You won't catch many birds that way."

I couldn't tell if he was joking. I laid my hand in my lap and looked down at the bracelet. It was true. I wouldn't be sneaking up on anyone wearing this.

Behind his large desk, the small man pursued the list. "Good work, Miss Figg." He turned to the second page. "We'll start rounding them up immediately."

Rounding them up? "You're arresting them, sir?" Would the countess and her sister be arrested, too? Having spent time in prison myself, I wouldn't wish that on them. Although it would get the gazelle out of the way. Archie would have to kiss her hand through prison bars.

"I'm not." Lashes fluttering, he chuckled. "I'll send Basil Thomson and the boys from Scotland Yard. We won't leave a single one of them there to agitate and collaborate with the Germans. We'll haul them all off to jail."

Goodness. "Yes, sir."

"Nice work." He gestured toward the door, a signal our meeting had come to an end. "You might get a promotion out of this."

"Er, actually, sir." I cleared my throat. I felt bad taking credit for Archie's list. "I got the list—"

"Yes, fine," he interrupted. "You're dismissed." Ignoring me, he shuffled some file folders on his desk.

"But—"

"You're dismissed!"

"Yes, sir."

Back at my desk, I buried my guilt in another cup of tea. I found a tin of biscuits in the kitchenette and helped myself to one... and then another. I considered it payment for cleaning up after the tin's owner. I was heading back to the kitchenette for a third biscuit when Clifford flew in. His hair—what little he had—was sticking up and his coat was askew, the result of being misbuttoned.

"What's wrong, Clifford dear?" I asked as he followed me into the kitchenette. "Biscuit?" I held out the tin.

"It's Kitty." He waved away the tin. "She's disappeared."

"What do you mean, disappeared?" A lump formed in my throat. What had the girl done now? She was supposed to be safely tucked away in Reading.

"Mother called me this morning and told me Kitty has flown the coop." His lip trembled. "Thank God, Poppy is alright."

"Kitty didn't take Poppy with her?" *Oh dear!* This was serious. The girl never went anywhere without her dog. "Did she say where she was going?"

He shook his head. "Slipped out in the night."

"Good heavens!" I held up my biscuit. "She could be in danger."

"We have to find her." Clifford paced the length of the kitchenette. "Poor girl, out there alone."

Poor girl, my half-eaten biscuit. Kitty was a force of nature. "Where shall we start?" I fetched my coat and hat from the coat rack. If anyone could look after themselves, it was Kitty. Still...

I'd just got my arm in a sleeve when a grimy boy wearing a newsboy's cap appeared out of nowhere. "Telegram for a Miss Fiona Figg." He held out the telegram.

What now? I grabbed it. Was it from Kitty? I unfolded it and read it. I stood paralyzed on the spot.

"What is it?" Clifford asked.

"It's from Fredricks." I reread the telegram:

THE LIST IS A FRAUD AND SO IS YOUR FIANCÉ. UNDER NO CIRCUMSTANCES GIVE THAT LIST TO YOUR SUPERIORS.

Too late.

"What does he say?" Clifford moved closer and tried to read over my shoulder.

I ignored him and refolded the telegram. The boy was still standing there blinking at me. "Oh, sorry." I went back to my desk, fetched my purse, and handed the boy a coin. Clutching it in his grubby hand, he grinned and took off.

"Wait for me here," I said to Clifford, putting my coat back on the rack. "I'll be right back and then we'll go after Kitty." How we were going to find her, I didn't know. A terrible thought crossed my mind. Maybe she was kidnapped.

I ran back up the stairs to Captain Hall's office. I didn't know if Fredricks was telling the truth. But I knew I'd better alert the captain. What was I thinking? I stopped on the landing. Of course, Fredricks wasn't telling the truth. Of course, Archie wasn't a fraud.

"Miss Figg?" Captain Hall's receptionist stepped out of the office. "Did you forget something?" she called down the stairs.

The telegram was practically burning a hole in my hand. "No. Never mind."

I stood paralyzed. Who should I trust? Archie, my fiancé? Or Fredricks, a known spy? Hard to believe at this point, it was fifty-fifty, Archie or Fredricks was telling the truth. I resolved to put my faith in the man I was going to marry. Anyway, my priority had to be finding Kitty. I headed back downstairs. If she *was* an MI5 operative, her life was in danger. And if either Archie or Fredricks could help me find her, all the better.

MI5 operative. I had an idea. If Archie really was back in London, he could help. He worked for MI5. He'd know what to do. Maybe he knew where to find Kitty.

Tinkle. Tinkle. I grabbed the bracelet to silence it as I dashed back downstairs to collect Clifford. I persuaded him to stop at my flat before we went anywhere else.

Clifford waited with the car while I ran upstairs to ring Archie. I had to trust him. I was marrying him for heaven's sake. It was ridiculous not to. And this was an emergency. If anyone could, Archie could help us find Kitty.

As the telephone rang, I held my breath. What if he wasn't home? Then again, what if he *was*? The last time I'd seen him, he'd kissed another woman's hand, revealed he was secretly working for MI5, and told me he'd ring when he was back in London. According to the gazelle, he was back in London. But I hadn't heard a peep.

"Come on, Archie," I said under my breath. "Answer."

Ring. Ring. Ring. I let my thoughts drift. All those times I'd longed to see him again. Lieutenant Archie Somersby, handsome pilot. That irresistible lock of chestnut hair that fell across his forehead. Those soft green eyes.

"Hello, Somersby here." His smooth tenor startled me.

"Thank goodness." I inhaled. "It's me, Fiona."

"Fiona, darling, is everything alright?" His voice was full of concern.

"Kitty's gone missing." I fought back tears and explained everything. Her amnesia. Her delusions of working for MI5. Her insistence that someone was trying to kill her, perhaps even someone from MI5. "With your MI5 connections, maybe you can help—"

"Slow down, Fiona," he said, interrupting my flow. "I'm sure she's fine. Kitty can take care of herself."

"That's true," I sighed. "Still, she's not fully herself. She needs medical care. Can you help me find her?"

"Of course, sweetheart." He gave a little chuckle. "I'll find her. Don't you worry your pretty head."

"She left Poppy at Clifford's mother's place in Reading." I bit my lip. "She never leaves that dog. I'm worried about the girl."

"Don't fret. Leave it to me." He sounded confident.

Just hearing his voice was reassuring. I didn't want to hang up. "Thank you, dearest Archie." I had so many questions for him. But they would have to wait. Right now, we had to find Kitty. "Ring me if you locate her and I'll do the same." If anything happened to that girl... I shuddered to think.

Given the task at hand, I went to my closet and changed out of my heels and into my practical Oxfords. I grabbed a sensible hat while I was at it. Dashing around my flat, I made sure I had everything I needed, including my belted chatelaine bag.

In my hurry, I nearly missed it. If I hadn't stepped on it, I probably wouldn't have seen it. An envelope. *What in the world?*

Apparently, while I was on the telephone, someone had slipped a note under my door. I picked it up and ripped it open. *Oh, my word!* It was from Kitty.

Aunt Fiona, meet me this afternoon at the Piccadilly Dojo for the final competition at 3 p.m. I have important news. Kitty

She must have been here within the last ten minutes. I opened the door and looked up and down the hallway. No Kitty.

Alright. At least I knew where and when to find her. That was a relief. I exhaled and leaned against the wall to catch my breath. Piccadilly Dojo. After the competition. The silly girl didn't plan on competing, did she? She was still recovering from a serious blow to the head. Good grief. That girl was vexing.

Maybe Clifford had seen her enter the building. Perhaps they were together now, waiting for me out front. I grabbed my bag, stuffed the note inside, fastened the belt around my waist, and dashed downstairs again.

Clifford was nowhere to be seen. How irritating. I glanced up and down the street, hoping to get a glimpse of Kitty. I saw shop-girls sweeping pavements, and shoppers looking in windows, but I didn't see Kitty. Blast it all. Where was Clifford?

I'd best let Archie know I'd found Kitty... sort of. At least I knew where to find her. Later today. The Piccadilly Dojo at the final competition. I ran back upstairs and rang Archie back again. He was delighted with the news.

"I told you not to worry," he said. "And she'll win that competition, hands down."

"More like feet up!"

He laughed. "You're quite a girl, Fiona, you know that?"

"When will I see you again?" We had so many things to discuss before the wedding, not the least of which was why

Fredrick Fredricks would send a telegram saying the list was a fraud and so was Archie. Of course, I didn't believe it for a minute. And I wasn't about to tell Archie. Not now anyway. Not until I confirmed the list for myself and told Captain Hall about the telegram… at least the first part of the telegram.

He laughed. "I'll see you tomorrow at the wedding."

How could it be here already? I stood gaping into the telephone like a fish out of water. I wasn't ready. My gown. I had to at least pick up my gown. Everything else had better take care of itself.

"Fiona, are you there?"

"Yes."

"I'll see you at the chapel, my darling girl." He made a kissing sound. "Now, I should ring off. Captain Hall is expecting me at the Old Admiralty."

"Captain Hall?" *But wait*. Archie had said he didn't work for the War Office.

"My cover, remember," he whispered. "Shhhh…"

"Be careful, dearest." I closed my eyes. With this bloody war, you never knew whether you'd see your beloved again.

"You, too, darling." More kissing sounds. "I can't wait until we're married."

"Me too." I tightened my grip on the receiver.

"By this time tomorrow, you'll be Mrs. Archie Somersby." He sighed.

Tomorrow. The word stung like a hornet. How could our wedding be tomorrow already? I wasn't ready. Blast it all. Nothing I could do now except float downstream with the current and hope I landed safely ashore.

"Until tomorrow," I said, closing my eyes. After we hung up, I held the phone to my chest for a few extra seconds. It was all happening too fast.

I didn't have time to worry or fret. My cold feet had better get moving. Clifford had to be back by now. I would run down and tell him to wait while I changed my clothes and then he could drive me to Lady Battersea's.

When I got downstairs, Clifford was waiting for me. He claimed he'd been driving around the block rather than obstruct traffic.

"Good Lord," he said. "Kitty was here, and I missed her? Dammit."

"Indeed." At least we knew she was safe. "Could you wait for me here while I run back up and change and then drop me off at Lord Battersea's place?"

Time to implement my new plan. Horace Peabody would not be wasted. This time, he would not be a gardener but an expert draper. I rubbed my hands together. I couldn't wait to return to the scene of the crime to get to the bottom of the mystery of those bright red berries and strange leaves in the dead woman's salad.

23

KITTY'S INTERLUDE

At nine o'clock sharp, a petite young woman wearing a trench coat and cloche hat entered the building at sixteen Charles Street. Although Kitty couldn't be sure the woman was Jane Archer, her gut told her to follow. She raced across the street and entered the building.

The woman she hoped was Jane Archer pushed the button to call the lift. When the door opened, she followed Jane inside.

"Good morning," she said to Jane.

"Where have you been? Are you alright?" Jane was speaking so fast, she couldn't get a word in. "I've been worried sick..."

"So, you do know me?"

"Of course, silly. You're my sister." Jane tilted her head. "Are you alright?"

Sister. Jane Archer was her sister. "I have amnesia." Kitty sighed. "Losing one's memory is the most vexing and uncanny sensation. My body knows things, but my mind is a blank."

"Oh, dear." Jane took her by the elbow. "Come with me."

"Is my name Kitty Archer?" she asked.

Jane furrowed her brows. "Archer is my cover name. Your

name is Baker. Eliza Baker." She put her arm around Kitty. "Are you alright, sweetie?"

Eliza Baker. Her name was Eliza Baker. The lift doors opened, and Jane led her down a hallway to an office. The office had a row of desks outfitted with typewriters. Jane took off her coat and hat and hung them on a coat rack just inside the door and then went to the first desk. Kitty followed. Had she been in this room before? Seeing Jane Archer had jogged something in her memory.

"You're a secretary?" Kitty asked. She'd been sure Jane Archer —her sister—was an MI5 agent. "You're not an agent?"

"I wish." Jane laughed. "Maybe someday. If I play my cards right, I'll be as good an agent as you." She lowered her voice. "But, as you know, I *do* have access to the files, and I *do* keep up with the latest intel." She smiled. "Speaking of which, what have you got for me? And what can I do for you? Tit-for-tat, sis."

Kitty told her about the attack at the Dojo, her amnesia, the mysterious hospital visitor, the address in Finsbury, the man she'd shot, the mole, the agent who'd been assigned to kill her.

"Slow down, sis." Jane's eyes went wide. "Who is trying to kill you?"

"I have a partial print off the walking stick used to attack me." Kitty laid her case on the desk and removed the imprint she'd made of the fingerprint found on the clover. "I suspect it will match the print on this." She pulled his gun out of her coat pocket. The one she'd used to shoot the mole. "The question is, whose fingerprint is it? Do you have access to MI5 agents' prints on file?" If only she knew his name...

"I do." Jane narrowed her eyes. "But why would an MI5 agent be trying to kill you?"

"Because I discovered he's a mole." She blew at her fringe. "A double agent. That's the case I was working when I was attacked."

"Blimey." Jane leaned back in her chair. "You did it. You found the mole. Impressive, sis."

"Trouble is, I don't remember his name." Kitty shook her head. "But if we can identify his prints..." She glanced around and then laid the gun on the desk. She took out her brush and dusting powder and dusted the weapon for prints. Of course, she'd fired it, so her prints would be there. But so would the man's from Finsbury. "Tell me everything you know about me." She continued dusting, hoping Jane Archer—her sister—could fill in the blanks in her memory. More to the point, was the man from Finsbury also the man whose prints were on the shamrock? Then again, he'd had her dead-to-rights back at his flat. If he'd wanted her dead, he could have killed her then. All the more reason she needed to learn his identity. She had a connection to the Finsbury man. The man she'd shot. If only she knew what it was!

"Your name is Eliza Baker. Your best friend is a Pekingese named Poppy, or Poppy-poo as you call her." Jane sounded like she was reciting from a book. "You use the alias Kitty Lane, among others. You're a highly trained MI5 agent and the only woman agent in the field. Your dog is highly trained, too."

"That adorable dog is a trained agent?" And her best friend. She shouldn't have left the poor thing out in Reading. After the jujitsu competition, she'd scoot right back out there and pick up the little darling.

Jane nodded.

"How did I become an agent?" Using tape, she lifted prints off the gun.

"You tried to pick Captain Hall's pocket." Jane laughed. "After Mum died, we were homeless and living at St. Martin's church. You did your best to scrouge up enough to feed us." She shook her head and chuckled. "You were a darn good pickpocket."

Kitty had a vague memory of begging for pennies, but stealing, that she didn't remember.

"Captain Hall hauled you in, but instead of arresting you, he sent both of us to school in France. After our stint at the espionage school in Lyon, I came to MI5 and you went to work undercover at the War Office trailing Fiona Figg." Jane tilted her head. "You call her Aunt Fiona. And, yes, your latest assignment was to find a mole in MI5." She took a breath. "A mole compromising our operations in Ireland."

"Ireland?" No wonder she woke up speaking Irish "Was I undercover in Ireland?"

"Dublin, to be precise." Jane studied her. "Sis, you look terrible. Shouldn't you be resting or something?"

"I'm fine." She held up one of the prints she'd lifted off the gun.

"In Dublin you learned one of our agents is protecting the Irish Citizen Army, essentially operating as a double agent." Jane shrugged. "That's the last I heard about you and your mission, until now."

"So, that's how I knew the list was bogus." Kitty exhaled. "Right. Now I remember. I was in Dublin undercover. I met another operative there. He was procuring a list of ICA members. But I discovered it was fake. How? I can't remember." She tightened her fist. "But it makes sense. He made a phony list to distract us from the real ICA." No wonder he'd tried to kill her. She had discovered his list was phony. She was on to him. She'd discovered he was the mole. And when he'd learned she knew, he'd tried to kill her. First at the Dojo by hitting her on the head with that club. And then in his flat with the gun. This gun. If she was right, then the print on the gun should match the print on the bronze clover Aunt Fiona found at the Dojo. Kitty laid the print from the gun atop the print from the clover. "Let's see if I'm right." She compared the two.

Wait. What? Not a match. They weren't the same. She was wrong. They were definitely different. She tried another print from the gun. Not a match. There was no doubt about it. The man from Finsbury was not the person belonging to the clover print from the bejeweled walking stick. He was not the man who attacked her at the Dojo. If the mole wasn't her attacker, who was?

24

THREADS

Dressed as Horace Peabody, complete with wig, moustache, beard, overalls and cap, I had Clifford drop me off at Lady Battersea's house. At least I would get another use out of my disguise. This Horace was a draper specializing in the restoration of old houses. Of course, I knew nothing about drapery or old houses, except for basic carpentry I'd picked up on my grandfather's farm. I hoped the staff knew even less than I did.

Clifford offered to wait for me in the car, but I sent him on his way. I had no idea how long I'd be. I planned to examine the powder room and hallway, retrace the maid's steps to the coat closet, and snoop around the kitchen. I glanced at my watch. Not yet eight o'clock. I had seven hours before I had to meet Kitty at the Dojo. Plenty of time to investigate. I winced. And plenty of time to prepare for my wedding? There was the little matter of collecting my wedding gown. The shop didn't close until evening. Anyway, right now, I had a murder mystery to solve, which was more exciting than a dubious wedding.

Although I now suspected Ellen Davis was poisoned during luncheon by lily-of-the-valley berries and foxglove leaves in her salad, I still didn't know how my hatpin fit in. Except, if it weren't for my hatpin, her death would be deemed the result of a heart attack, natural causes, rather than murder. In a way, it was lucky someone had stabbed her in the neck with my hatpin. The question was, how? How was it possible for anyone to stab her in the neck given where her body was found—by me—blocking the door? It wasn't. The locked-room aspect of this murder mystery wasn't lost on me. The powder room door opened inwards, and the body was flush up against the door. The killer could not have attacked Ellen Davis and left the room because Ellen's body was holding the door shut. I cringed, remembering the yellow chiffon strewn across the lavatory floor.

Clearing my throat, I pressed the doorbell.

Mr. Toogood, the butler, answered the door.

"Horace Peabody, at your service," I said in my best cockney accent. "Here about the drapes."

"Drapes?" He stood blinking at me.

"Lady Battersea hired me special to see to the new drapery." When I straightened to my full height, I had a good inch on him. "I'm here to do measurements." I patted my new leather bag. Fredrick's clever gift doubled as a toolbelt of sorts.

Toogood squinted at me for a few more moments. "I see," he finally said. "Come this way."

The house was buzzing with workers coming and going. It was the perfect opportunity for me to do some detective work while undercover as one of them. Lord and Lady Battersea were having the entire place redone with new carpet, wallpaper, and fresh paint. Nothing like a murder in the powder room to inspire redecoration.

Once the butler left me to my own devices, I made a beeline to the powder room. To my chagrin, the old wallpaper had already been removed—and no doubt with it the remnants of any clues. On hands and knees, I crawled around searching the tiles and floorboards for... for what, I didn't know. Something, anything, to tell me what happened to Ellen Davis in this room on her last day on earth. Someone was in here with her. The person who stabbed her in the neck with my hatpin. How did that person leave this room without moving Ellen? And why stab someone who'd just been poisoned. Unless... there were two people involved. One poisoned her and another stabbed her.

A stray thread stuck to the bottom of the door caught my eye. It matched the ones I'd found attached to the bottom of the door on the day of the murder. I removed the magnifying glass from my bag and took a closer look. Next, I took a pair of tweezers and plucked the fibers from the door and tapped them into one of Kitty's small glass vials. Maybe she could test the fibers for me. Unfortunately, her tests couldn't answer the most pressing question, which wasn't *what* they were or *where* they came from but *why* they were stuck to the bottom of the door.

Sitting on the bathroom floor, I compared the threads. The one I'd just found stuck to the bottom of the door and the one I'd pulled off the door on the day of the murder. Yes. They looked exactly the same. Both white. Both linen. Indeed, they both looked like threads from a linen bath towel, not unlike the hand towels hanging from the hook next to the sink. I fetched one of the hand towels and compared its threads. They looked the same, even under the magnifying glass.

It always surprised me that posh towels weren't all that different from the coarse flour sacks used by my grandmother. My grandmother was very clever and reused everything. Nothing went to waste on the farm. She always said, "Waste not, want not." She reused flour and sugar sacks for everything from bath towels to fabric for aprons or nightgowns. She even used them as pads to move furniture. She was a stout strong woman and could move a large hutch by herself so long as she put its feet on a flour sack and pulled it across the floor.

Golly! That gave me an idea. What if the murderer had used a towel to pull Ellen Davis across the floor? I crawled back to the door and looked under. There was a bit of white fuzz stuck to the floorboards... as if someone dragged a towel under the door, a towel carrying the dead weight of Ellen Davis. *Bingo!* That had to be how the killer stabbed Ellen and then left the room. Of course. The killer loaded Ellen onto a bath towel, dragged the edge of the towel out the door, shut the door, and then pulled the towel out from under Ellen and out from under the door. Voila! Impossible murder revealed to be all too possible. Very clever. Pleased with myself, I stood up and brushed off my overalls. Very clever indeed.

Having discovered the how—an ordinary towel—I needed to find the who. I'd already deduced the murderer had used poison, likely from Countess Markievicz's gardens. The person had access to the food and knew where it would be served. Had the countess and/or her sister hired one of the kitchen staff to poison Ellen's salad? They could have brought poisonous foxglove and lily-of-the-valley from their garden, given it to their country-woman, the maid, and told her to poison Ellen's salad.

The place cards. Ellen was sitting in Kitty's spot. Whoever poisoned the salad thought they were poisoning Kitty.

Next stop, the kitchen to question the cook and serving maids. Of course, there was still the unsettling missing link between the poisoning and my purloined hatpin. Why spoil a perfectly good poisoning by stabbing your victim in the neck with another guest's hatpin?

In the kitchen, I found one of the maids scrubbing dishes. It was the freckle-faced, red-headed Molly. The very maid who had admitted to having a liaison with Jules Silver. The maid who had given Mrs. Kipper my hat. I stopped on the threshold and closed my eyes. In my mind's eye, I recalled my notes. What did I know about Molly the maid?

She had given Jules the walking stick. Possibly the one used to attack Kitty. She was from Ireland and was known to the countess and her sister. She could have visited the Markieviczes recently and returned with poisonous plants. On the day of Ellen's murder, instead of serving luncheon and then clearing up, she had been near the coat closet handing out hats. In my mind, I turned the page of my notebook, and concentrated on my notes from my interview with Carrie Kipper. What else had Mrs. Kipper told me about Molly the maid? I focused my mind's eye on the page. The page came into view. *Yes. That's it!* Mrs. Kipper had seen the maid in the hallway outside the lavatory. Carrying... carrying a towel! Mrs. Kipper said it was a dirty towel. *Crikey!* A towel dirty from being dragged across the floor carrying the body of Ellen Davis?

Like my grandmother, Molly the maid could have moved the heavy body of Ellen Davis by rolling her onto a towel and then pulling it across the floor. She could have slid the towel under the door and pulled it out, leaving the door shut and Ellen's body up against it. Blimey! Locked-room mystery solved. *Good job, Fiona!*

"Excuse me, Molly," I said, brushing dust off my overalls. "May I have a word?"

Her hand to her heart, she whirled around. "You scared the living daylights out of me." She stood blinking at me. "Do I know you?"

Right. She didn't know me dressed as Horace Peabody. I touched my beard. *Quick, Fiona. Think.* I glanced around the kitchen. Who would she talk to? Confide in? "I'm a friend of Jules." *In the way Judas is a friend.*

"Oh." Her mouth hanging open, she stared at me.

"He sent me to tell you he's sorry." I went out on a limb. I didn't know where I was going, truth be told. But I suspected Molly and Jules were working together, or at least having an affair. Jules was a married man. And judging by the little bulge in her apron, Molly was in the family way. I recalled the notation *Maid's affair* from Ellen's notebook. I wouldn't be surprised if next week's gossip column featured an elegant man-about-town and Lady Battersea's parlor maid given that obviously Ellen had her columns submitted for publication weeks in advance.

Hypothesis number one: Jules used his Shillelagh to hit Kitty on the head at the Dojo. He mistook her for Ellen Davis and not the other way around. Then Molly poisoned Ellen's salad. The couple wanted to silence Ellen and her gossip column before she broadcast their liaison. Jules Silver had the most to lose from such a revelation. But he could have made promises of marriage to poor Molly to cajole her into helping him.

Hypothesis number two: Kitty was Jules's target at the Dojo and Molly poisoned Ellen thinking she was Kitty. But why would they want Kitty dead? Because Kitty had discovered Jules was a double agent and he wanted to stop her before she reported him. That could explain why Kitty thought someone was after her. Jules attacked her at the Dojo and, when she survived, he continued his attempts on her life. Thank goodness Captain Hall had him arrested and Kitty was safe. I liked this theory since it also had the advantage of exonerating Archie. Not to mention, confirming Kitty's ravings about an assassin as sane.

Molly's upper lip started to tremble. "He should be sorry." She put both hands on her stomach.

Oh dear. I was right. She was with child.

"He promised to marry me." She sniffled.

"But now he's been arrested." I shook my head. "I'm so sorry."

"Arrested!" she scoffed. "That's not possible."

"He was arrested his morning, I'm afraid." I thought she knew.

"He lied to me." Her eyes were wild. "He made me do a terrible thing and he lied."

Now *my* eyes went wide. "What terrible thing?"

"That soldier." She slumped into a chair next to a pile of newspapers. "He came here that morning and threatened Jules."

Soldier. The word hit me like a lorry. I dropped into a chair next to her.

"He threatened to have Jules arrested for treason unless I helped him." Her shoulders were shaking. "I did help him. I did it. What he asked. I put those berries and leaves in Miss Kitty Lane's salad," she sobbed. "I didn't know it was poison." She looked up at me through her tears. "I swear I didn't know."

"Which soldier?" I asked softly. "Who asked you to put the berries in Ellen's salad?"

"I thought she was Kitty Lane." She wiped her nose on her sleeve. "At the hospital, she was in the bed and the place card said Kitty Lane. How did I know it was another lady?"

Oh, my word. The hospital. The redhead who peeked in Kitty's room asking for Kitty. The Irish woman. It was Molly. And Ellen had been sitting on Kitty's bed and had answered her. Of course. She thought Ellen was Kitty. And then the place card. That confirmed it. So, Kitty was the target. But why? I steeled my nerves and continued. "Of course, dear," I said reassuringly. "It wasn't your fault. How could you know?" I patted her arm. "Who asked you to do it? What is the soldier's name?"

She shook her head. "I don't know."

"Who sent you to the hospital?" I surmised she'd gone to stalk Kitty. Was she doing Jules Silver's bidding?

"Ummm." She squirmed in her chair. "The soldier?"

She was hedging. Probably to protect her lover.

"It's alright." I took a deep breath. "Tell me what happened. Everything. Who sent you to the hospital and who asked you to do a terrible thing?" I gave her an encouraging look. "What did you do, Molly?"

"Is Jules going to hang?" Her lip was trembling again.

What could I say? If he was spying for the Germans and found guilty of treason, then yes, he would. "I don't know—"

"I can't live without Jules!" she wailed. "Our baby won't have a father." She broke down again.

"It will be alright, child." I pulled my handkerchief out of my chatelaine bag and handed it to her. "Here. Wipe your face and then tell me what happened. Maybe I can help."

She took the hanky but didn't use it. Instead, she sat staring down into her lap, troubling the edge of the fabric. Tears streamed down her cheeks.

"Jules sent me to help you," I lied, reaching out and touching her sleeve again.

Her face was red and blotchy. When she looked at me with those sad, swollen eyes, I felt sorry for her. I knew Jules Silver never had any intention of marrying her. He was already married. Poor girl. She was pregnant and then used to commit murder. The question was, by whom? "Tell me everything and I'll do whatever I can to help you," I said, and I meant it.

"The soldier told me if I didn't do what he asked then he'd have Jules arrested and hanged for treason," she repeated, then blew her nose. "On the day of the luncheon, he brought the berries and leaves and told me to put them in Miss Lane's salad." She sniffed. "I did what he asked."

Every time she said "soldier," I cringed. There was one particular soldier who kept coming to mind. I pushed thoughts of Archie away and continued my questioning.

"And then you followed her to the powder room to make

sure the poison was working." I took a gamble. "She was ill but still alive. So, you stabbed her with a hatpin. When she collapsed, you used a towel to drag her body and make it look like she'd been in the room alone... and must have stabbed herself."

"I didn't stab her." She looked at me with terror in her eyes.

"I know this is difficult." I gave her a sympathetic look. "But you don't want to be arrested for murder." I patted her hand. "Tell me the truth, the whole truth, and I'm sure I can put in a good word for you with the police." Not that my word would matter.

"The police!" Her teeth were chattering.

"At this point, telling the truth is the best bet, my dear." I gave her hand another pat.

"I was afraid for Jules and our baby," she whimpered. "So, I did what he asked."

"Did he ask you to stab her?" I said gently.

"I didn't stab her." She shook her head. "Jules did." Her voice broke off and she started crying again. "He took the longest, sharpest hatpin." Her voice was shaky. "Then he pulled her body on the towel and had me take the towel to the laundry."

"Why did Jules stab her if she'd already been poisoned?" I asked softly.

"He didn't know." Her eyes flashed. "The soldier made me swear not to tell anyone, not even Jules."

"I see." Actually, I didn't see. Had Molly and Jules tried independently to kill Ellen? Molly thinking Ellen was really Kitty. And Jules knowing it was Ellen. "Why did Jules Silver stab Ellen Davis?"

"I don't know. I think it was because of us." She grimaced. "I heard them whispering." She sniffed. "I recognized Jules's voice, so I stopped and listened." Finally, she used my handkerchief and blew her nose. "The lady said if he didn't pay her one thousand

pounds, she would publish her article in the newspaper for all
the world to see."

"Blackmail," I said under my breath. Good heavens. Ellen
Davis was blackmailing Jules Silver. Surely, she didn't blackmail
all the targets of her column. Blackmail was an excellent motive
for murder. But why start blackmailing now? *Wait a second*. I
remembered her telling Clifford, "Even journalists need money
to live on." Maybe she needed the money. Her clothes were worn.
Perhaps she couldn't afford new ones. And what about the
soldier? Who, if she was telling the truth, blackmailed Molly into
poisoning Ellen Davis (thinking she was Kitty)?

"Can you describe this soldier?" I kept my voice calm and
level despite the tempest in my chest. "This soldier who threatened to tell on Jules."

"Umm... Tall. Green eyes. Brown hair." She sniffled. "Nice
looking."

Green eyes. Brown hair. Nice looking. I got a sick feeling. She
could be describing Archie. "Are you sure you don't know his
name?"

She shook her head. "I'm just the parlor maid."

"Do you remember anything else about him?" I had to identify this mysterious soldier.

"Are you married?" She sniffed. "Do you have a girlfriend?"

My cheeks warmed. I'd almost forgotten I was dressed as
Horace Peabody. "We're talking about you, not me."

"I can cook for you." She gave me a weak smile. "I'm a good
cook."

Oh dear. Poor girl.

"I can do other things for you, too." She batted her lashes.

Blimey.

"Ah... I'm getting married," I stuttered. "Tomorrow, actually."

She scowled. Looking contemplative, she sat there a minute.

Suddenly, her face brightened. "If I remember his name, will you promise to help me and the baby?"

"I promise." I swallowed hard. I wished I could do something to help her. But if she'd helped Jules or this mysterious soldier commit murder, then she was an accomplice and just as guilty as they were.

"His name is Lieutenant Archibald Reginald Somersby." She smiled at me. "Now will you help me?"

I tightened my lips. Archie! I squinted at her. How could she suddenly remember his name? And not just his Christian name or his surname, but his entire name. Complete with a middle name I'd only just learned from E. D. Aria's gossip column.

"How do you know his full name?" I asked, incredulously.

"I heard another soldier call for him." She blushed. "First he called out Lieutenant Somersby, but when the soldier didn't answer, he used the full name."

I closed my eyes and sucked in air. I felt lightheaded. Was it possible? Archie blackmailed this poor maid into poisoning Kitty. And Ellen Davis got the poisoned salad by mistake. Then Jules Silver tried to kill Ellen by stabbing her with my hatpin. It was all too much.

My head was spinning. I cringed. A lump of regret sank in my stomach like an anvil.

The telephone call. Kitty's note.

Oh dear. If Archie was trying to kill Kitty, I'd just told him where to find her.

25

THE FINAL MATCH

The bus back to my flat seemed to take forever. I sprinted the three blocks from the bus stop and then ran up the stairs. By the time I turned the key in my lock, I was out of breath. Without stopping to take off my cap or beard, I went straight to the telephone and rang Archie. I had to confront him. To find out what was really going on. There must be a reason. Some explanation. Molly must have been mistaken. It could have been any lieutenant. There was a whole regiment practicing in the park that day. Yet, she knew his name. I winced.

Oh, Archie. What kind of bride was I, jumping to conclusions about my fiancé? Suspecting him of murder. I wasn't fit to marry him.

Panting, I waited. "Come on, answer!" Archie had killed people before. I knew that. He'd been ordered to kill them. The German agent in New York, another in Cairo, and Iron Victor in Moscow. How many others had he killed? Was it true? Was he a cold-blooded assassin? But Kitty? Why Kitty? She wasn't a German agent. Surely he wasn't ordered to kill her! My head was starting to hurt.

"Answer the darn telephone!" It was no use. He wasn't home. Now what?

Should I tell Captain Hall? Tell him what? That his favorite lieutenant is a fraud who is trying to kill his favorite niece?

The telegram. From Fredricks. I pulled it out of my bag and reread it.

THE LIST IS A FRAUD AND SO IS YOUR FIANCÉ. UNDER NO CIRCUMSTANCES GIVE THAT LIST TO YOUR SUPERIORS.

Good grief. No wonder Archie wasn't answering the telephone. A shiver ran up my spine. He was lying in wait for Kitty.

Fredricks. He would know what to do. Where was he when I needed him? I didn't have the foggiest idea how to get hold of the bounder. I paced the length of my kitchen. Blast! My thoughts were so jumbled I couldn't think straight. Should I ring the police? And report Molly. That poor girl. Pregnant and alone. Wasn't that enough? Then again, she poisoned an innocent woman, even if she didn't want to. She didn't know what she was doing. She did it to save her beloved. Then there was Jules. He'd stabbed the woman with my hatpin. My new hatpin. Thankfully, Captain Hall had taken care of him.

Confound it, Archie! How could you do this to me? And to Kitty? And Ellen Davis? And who knows who else!

Our wedding was tomorrow. What wedding? Tremors coursed down my limbs. Oh dear. The wedding. Of course I couldn't marry Archie if he was trying to kill Kitty. What kind of aunt would that make me? Even a fake aunt couldn't abide a murderer. But the invitations had gone out. It was literally the eleventh hour and too late to notify everyone the wedding was off. I dropped into a chair. I'd have to show up at the wedding and make an announcement in person. Mortified, I put my head in my hands.

How in the world had I got tangled up with MI5 and assassins? Why couldn't I have been happy being plain old Fiona Figg, file clerk? What happened to the halcyon days when my greatest pleasures were alphabetizing and perfecting my filing system? The bloody war. That was what happened. And then there was the earthquake that shattered my self-esteem, discovering my husband canoodling with his secretary. Until today, I thought my life couldn't get any worse than that day. The day I'd discovered his infidelity. But I was wrong. This was worse. Much worse. My fiancé was trying to kill my protégé—or was I her protégé? And the wedding was tomorrow.

I went to the cupboard and fished out some headache powders and added them to a glass of water. Drinking them down, I noticed my watch. Heavens. It was after one o'clock already. Confound it. I'd better get to the Dojo and warn Kitty.

* * *

When the driver pulled up in front of the Dojo, I tossed him some money, jumped out of the car, and dashed inside. A matronly receptionist at the front desk stopped me. Blast. I didn't bring my membership card. When I told her my name, she looked at me funny. Right. I was still dressed as Horace Peabody.

"Long story." I patted my beard. "I need to get to the gymnasium right away. My friend is in danger."

"Who is your friend?" she asked, peeking over thick spectacles. "What's his name?"

"*Her* name..." Good question. "Kitty Lane but she might have signed in as Eliza Baker... or even Jane Archer."

The receptionist scowled. "You don't know your friend's name?"

"Young women these days." I shrugged. "They're complicated."

She thumbed through a list attached to a clipboard. "Aha!" She looked up at me. "Kitty Lane is scheduled to compete in the women's final match." She smiled. "Don't worry. The sport takes strength and stamina but rarely is anyone seriously injured."

I wished she was right. But I knew better. My worries weren't for the competition—Kitty would win—but for a far more dangerous game. The game of cat and mouse with MI5.

"The men's final match is finishing now. And the women's is next." The receptionist waved me in. "Please enter quietly so as not to disturb the contestants or spectators."

"Of course," I assured her.

I opened the gymnasium door as quietly as possible. A couple of dozen people filled stands on both side of a mat in the center. I tiptoed along the stands to get a better view of the spectators. Hopefully, Kitty was in the crowd. When I reached the edge of the stands, I had an unobstructed view of the competitors. *Oh, my heavens!*

Kimono flying, Fredrick Fredricks did a cartwheel maneuver into Mr. Garrud's torso. The jujitsu instructor bent backwards as if he were made of rubber. When he sprang forward again, his jaw met a snap punch from Fredrick's fist. With his black hair tied up at the back and his muscular form on display even through the canvas robes, Fredricks was as graceful and elegant as a panther. Watching him in action was so distracting I almost forgot why I was there.

When he saw me, he broke into a huge grin. Unfortunately, his opponent took the opportunity to kick him in the head. I cringed. How did he know it was me? On the bright side, his fall reminded me why I was here. To find Kitty... and Archie. I surveyed the stands, looking for Kitty's telltale blonde ringlets. Everyone was intent on watching the match, which gave me the chance to stare shamelessly into their rapt faces.

No Kitty. No Archie.

Wherever they were, I hoped it wasn't together.

26

KITTY'S INTERLUDE

Kitty sat in the Ladies' locker room at the Dojo. Her heart was racing. In a few minutes, she would be competing for the Piccadilly Dojo jujitsu championship. She prayed her body remembered what to do and her mind would follow suit.

Her visit with Jane Archer had been helpful, as always. *Of course*. Jane was her sister. But, more than that, Jane supplied her with top-secret information from the MI5 files and in return she supplied Jane with intel from the field, intel to prepare Jane to become an agent herself. They were more than sisters. They were friends. Good friends.

Head in hands, she took several deep breaths. She would win this and regain her confidence and her life. Maybe another blow to the head would straighten her out. All she needed was a name. *His name. The name of the mole*. The double agent working for the Irish Citizen Army. The one who had given the bogus list and concocted the ludicrous story of the ICA collaborating with the Germans. The so-called German Plot. It was nonsense. Why would this agent concoct such a rumor? What purpose did it serve? If he was protecting the ICA then why malign them with rumors of them working with the enemy? She shook her head, hoping to clear her thoughts.

Only a few more minutes now. She'd better stretch and get ready. She stood up ready to bend to touch her toes. The hairs on the back of her neck stood up too. She had the uncanny sensation of being watched. The faint scent of cedar and citrus was a warning. She dropped to the floor and rolled. Jumping to her feet, she held up her hand ready for a knife hand strike.

"You!" She lunged at him. "You'll not hit me again, you bastard." She took him down with one pass. Pressing her knee into his chest, she raised her fist above his face. "Who are you? What is your name?"

"Kitty, calm yourself!" He lifted his palms in surrender. "It's me, Archie." His brows narrowed. "Archie Somersby? We work together. MI5."

Somersby. That name was familiar. She glared down at him. "You're the mole." Holy moly. Archie Somersby was Aunt Fiona's fiancé. He was marrying her tomorrow. She had to stop him. Fiona couldn't marry this man. He was a mole and a traitor.

"No. Not a mole." Puffing, he shook his head. "Just let me up and I'll explain everything."

She pressed down harder. He grunted.

"You're an assassin sent to kill me." She tightened her fist, ready to bring it down into his face. "To keep me from reporting you as a double agent." Now she knew his name, after the match, she would report him. She put all her weight on the knee on his throat.

"I'm not trying to kill you." His face was red and his voice was hoarse. "I'm trying to protect you." He was having trouble getting the words out.

"I don't believe you." When she stared into his green eyes it was almost as if she were looking in the mirror. An uneasy feeling crept into her chest. "You're lying."

"Let me up." He pushed both of his hands against her knee. "I can explain."

She pressed harder.

"I'm on your side," he said, gasping for breath.

"Why should I believe you?" She eased off a tiny bit.

"Because I'm your partner," he said through clenched teeth. "We work together at MI5. Now, please let me up."

Stunned, she stood up and stared down at him. "I don't have a partner." She raised her hand, ready for a knife strike.

Panting, he crawled to his hands and knees. "You do. And I'm him." He looked up at her and held up his hand palm open. "I wish you'd get your blasted memory back." He pulled himself to his feet. "Your amnesia is deuced inconvenient and bloody dangerous!" He ran his hand through his hair. "Look, how about I narrate your life for you. Your mother—"

She cut him off. "Is dead." She lowered her hand.

"Is dead," he repeated. "She left you and your sister Jane orphaned to live by your wits on the street."

Kitty's lip trembled. She didn't know whether to believe him or smack him. "Was it you who came to the hospital?"

"I came to check on you, but you weren't in your bed." He sighed. "Then you showed up at my flat and shot me." He touched his ear. "With my own gun, I might add."

Memories came flooding back to her. "We were working together in Dublin." She sat down on a bench. "You falsified the list of ICA members. You spread false rumors about the ICA working with the Germans, the so-called German Plot. Why?" Her muscles tense, she looked up at him, ready to attack if necessary.

"I never spread any rumors." He tapped out a cigarette. "That was all Kipper and Balfour. They wanted to discredit the Irish and home rule." He lit the cigarette and took a long drag. "As for the list, it's complicated." He blew out a cloud of smoke. "Oh, sorry." He tapped out another cigarette and held out the pack. "Want one?"

She couldn't remember whether she smoked, but, since he was offering, she must do. She took the cigarette, and he lit it for her. She inhaled and then started coughing. If she did smoke, maybe it was time to quit. She pinched the end of the cigarette. "The list. Why did you give the War Office a phony list?"

"Eva." He sighed. "And her sister Constance, Countess Markievicz."

"Aren't you engaged to Aunt Fiona?" There was something about this Archie Somersby she didn't like. She couldn't quite put her finger on it. But she didn't trust him. "Is the gossip true, then? You're two-timing Fiona with Eva Gore-Booth?"

Bong! Bong! Bong!

The gong sounded, signaling it was time for the women's championship to begin.

"I've got to go." She took a deep breath. "But I'm warning you. Stay away from Aunt Fiona." She levelled her gaze at him. "I'm not letting Fiona marry an assassin and a traitor."

"At least let me explain." He pressed his palms together. "Please."

She glared at him. "If you go through with the wedding," she hissed, "I'll turn you in for treason. You'll hang."

"You wouldn't..." He put both hands on his head.

"You leave Aunt Fiona alone, you hear me!" She shook herself all over like a dog after a swim, and then sprinted out of the locker room.

She had a match to win.

27

THE CONFRONTATION

Since I didn't see Kitty in the stands, I went to the locker room. From the hallway, I heard raised voices. I recognized them. Kitty's and... Archie's. I quickened my pace. She was yelling. I heard my name. At least if he was trying to kill her, he hadn't yet succeeded.

Just as I reached the locker room, Kitty burst out of the door, did a double-take, and then blustered past me.

So much for my disguise. "Be careful, Aunt Fiona," she said as she passed. "He's not what he seems."

"I was coming to tell you the same." I stopped and watched her march down the hallway. "Are you alright, dear?" I called after her.

"Fine." She waved but didn't turn around. "I'll meet you back here after the match."

"Good luck," I called to her as she rounded the corner and disappeared.

"Fiona! Or should I say Horace?" The scent of cedar and citrus lingered in the air. "I was hoping to see you."

When I swirled around, I was face to face with Archie.

He chuckled. "Nice moustache."

"What are you doing in the Ladies' locker room?" I narrowed my eyes.

"Having a chat with Kitty." He ran a hand through his hair.

"Why are you following her?" I didn't know how to ask if he was trying to kill her. What if I was wrong? What if the maid meant someone else and not Lieutenant Somersby?

"I came to watch Kitty win the championship." He flashed a weak smile.

"Look, Archie, it's time you levelled with me." I stood facing him, arms akimbo. "I know the ICA list you gave me was a fraud." Provided Fredricks was telling the truth. At this point, I judged the bounder more reliable than my own fiancé! "Lady Battersea's maid, Molly, says you asked her to slip poisonous berries and leaves into Kitty's salad." I held up my hand to stop him interrupting. "And, last but not least, I can't get over that business with you and Miss Eva Gore-Booth."

"Why don't we go someplace where we can sit and talk?" He reached for my hand, but I pulled away. "Please, Fiona, don't be like that."

"I'm not going anywhere with you until you tell me what's going on." My chest tightened. I wasn't sure I really wanted to know. But I needed to know. And I needed to know right now. "Spill it or I'll never speak to you again."

"You're right." He tapped out a Kenilworth. "You deserve to know everything."

I nodded.

"About the business with Eva." He lit his cigarette. "She's the daughter of a close friend of my father's." He blew out a cloud of smoke. "On an expedition to the Arctic, her father saved my father. They were like brothers." He reached for my hand.

I flinched and took a step backwards.

"Eva and Constance are like sisters to me." The weak smile

appeared again. "Anyway, Eva's preferences don't lie with my sort." He raised his eyebrows. "You met Esther Roper. That is Eva's, ah, *friend*, close friend."

"Oh." My cheeks warmed. Deep down, I knew Archie wouldn't cheat on me. I shouldn't have let my jealousy cloud my judgement. "I'm sorry I suspected—" Suspected him of what? Infidelity? I still suspected him of murder, for heaven's sake!

"No." He waved me away. "I'm sorry. I should have told you."

"So, you provided a false list of ICA members to protect your friends Eva and the countess." Fredricks was telling the truth! Blast it all. I had to tell Captain Hall as soon as possible. He was out of the office until tomorrow. Fiddlesticks. I was going to have to pay him a visit on my wedding day. I almost laughed out loud. What was I thinking? What wedding?

"The countess and Eva are like family to me." He took a deep drag of his smoke.

"So, you made up a list of low-level operatives to misdirect Scotland Yard away from the countess and her sister and other leaders of the Irish resistance."

"That's right." He shrugged. "You're a clever girl."

"By protecting the countess and Eva, you made me look bad." I tightened my lips. "Captain Hall will blame me."

"I'm sorry." He took my hands. "I didn't mean for you to get involved. I just wanted to keep you safe. To get you out of Ireland before everything exploded."

"I appreciate that, but—"

"Thank you." He reached out and took my hands. "You're a real brick."

"What about the German Plot?" Was it a fraud, too? Fredricks had said so. "Is it a fraud, too?"

"I tried to warn Captain Hall." He dropped his cigarette and ground it out. "The German Plot was nothing more than a rumor started by hardline home rule opponents in order to undermine the ICA by painting them as enemies in cahoots with the Kaiser."

"If you warned him, then why is the captain having Scotland Yard round up dozens of people from that list?"

"Let's just say," he shook his head, "sometimes the captain is overzealous."

"So, you *do* work for Captain Hall and the War Office?"

"My work is classified." He closed his eyes and sighed. "But it's not worth losing you over. Yes, to the public, I work for Captain Hall. But, secretly, I also work for MI5."

"And Kitty?" I cleared my throat. "Did you have the maid put lily-of-the-valley and foxglove from the Markievicz estate in her salad?" He'd picked flowers for me from the estate and brought them to London. Why not poisonous plants, too? He could have brought them to Lady Battersea's in advance of the tea party. Or had his good friends the countess and her sister deliver them. I thought back. Had the sisters arrived with a bunch of flowers? Good heavens. They had. I remembered. The centerpiece. The one Jules Silver admired.

"What?" He looked confused.

"Molly, Lady Battersea's maid, told me you blackmailed her into poisoning Kitty, who turned out to be Ellen." I regretted it as soon as I'd said it.

He stood gaping at me, a puzzled look on his face. "I have no idea what you're talking about."

"Is your full name Archibald Reginald Somersby?" I peered into his eyes, searching for the truth.

"What?" He shook his head. "You know my name. And my middle name is not Reginald. It's Fitzwilliam." He let out a little laugh. "Oh my God. This is that gossip columnist again, isn't it?"

"What do you mean?" Now I was the one who was puzzled.

"She got my name wrong." He sighed. "She printed my

middle name as Reginald. Is that what this is about?" He took a step closer. "I've explained. I was on assignment. Eva and the countess are dear friends. Nothing more." He tapped out another cigarette.

So, it wasn't Archie. Of course it wasn't. "Molly was lying to protect Jules Silver." I let out a sigh of relief. The soldier to whom the butler had given a glass of water was just that—a thirsty soldier. He wasn't Archie, and he didn't blackmail Molly. She must have seen Archie's name in the newspaper. In Ellen's gossip column. That was why she got his middle name wrong. She'd invented his involvement to divert attention from her lover, who was the real villain.

"Jules Silver." He held his cigarette out in midair. "You know about Silver?"

"I'm pretty sure he attacked Kitty." I sucked my teeth. "And then cajoled his mistress into poisoning Ellen, thinking she was Kitty."

"Yes. That makes sense." He ran his hand through his hair again. "Kitty knew there was a mole in British Intelligence. She has been after him for months."

"At least Jules Silver is behind bars." I tried to look on the bright side.

"That's just it." He paced a few steps and turned back to me. "He escaped custody. He's flown the coop, I'm afraid." He sucked his teeth. "But I'll find him. And when I do—"

"Are you an MI5 assassin?" I shuddered just saying the word. "Tell me the truth."

"I have on occasion..."—he blew out a cloud of smoke—"had to dispose of high target enemy spies."

"Are you going to kill Jules Silver?" I held his gaze. "Don't you dare lie to me. Not now."

"Yes," he said matter-of-factly.

I stood blinking at him. I didn't want to believe it. But I knew it was true. My mind was racing. I thought back to my assignments over the past year. He'd always turned up when I least expected. Had he been following me, too? "All those times you showed up on my missions, were we working together or not?"

"Please believe me, Fiona." He gazed into my eyes. "I will never work against you. I adore you. And I can't wait until you're my wife."

About that...

Before I could say anything, his lips were on mine. Soft and warm.

"After we're married, we can have everything we've always dreamed of..." He smiled down at me. "A house, a family, whatever you want."

"What about the bloody war?" *And my physical defects.* I cringed.

"After the war." He pulled me closer.

"As long as we're confiding secrets," I whispered. I closed my eyes and took a deep breath. The moment of truth. I had to tell him I couldn't have children.

"Let's forget about the past." He held me out at arm's length. His eyes were bright. "Our future together is what matters now." Dimples budded on his cheeks when he smiled. "I love you and tomorrow we'll be married and live happily ever after, just like in the fairytales."

As much as I wished he were right, I couldn't help but wonder if everything he'd told me was a fairytale. I didn't know what to say. Paralyzed by uncertainty, I just stood there, blinking up at him like an idiot.

"We'd better get out to the gym." He took my hand. "Or we'll miss Kitty's match."

Overwhelmed, I nodded and let him lead me down the hall.

Sitting in the stands, I couldn't concentrate on the match. Instead, I tried to sort through my thoughts—and more importantly what to do about them. Immediately after the match, I would go to the police. I would tell them everything. Namely, that Molly had poisoned Ellen Davis. And Jules Silver had attacked Kitty. The pieces were falling into place. Jules attacked Kitty to stop her reporting his espionage activities. She suspected he was a mole and he tried to dispose of her. Then he killed Ellen to stop her publishing the article about him and Molly in her gossip column. It was complicated, but it made sense.

If Archie had wanted to harm Kitty, he could have when they were alone in the locker room. Maybe he was telling the truth. Even so, he'd falsified an important list solicited by Captain Hall and the War Office—I was sympathetic to his reasons but still it was wrong.

A loud thud from the center mat got my attention. Kitty had delivered a cartwheel kick that sent her opponent to her backside on the floor. Her opponent shook her head and jumped up again. Across the gymnasium, a pair of dark eyes pierced the crowd. Fredrick Fredricks. He'd won his match, of course—despite my distracting him. He wasn't watching the match. Instead, his gaze was trained on me. When our eyes met, I averted mine and pretended to focus on the match.

Her opponent crouched into position and Kitty did the same. They looked like two cats circling each other. Kitty lunged and the pair were tangled together in a jujitsu hug. When Kitty let go and stepped back, her opponent fell to the floor like a sack of potatoes. Gasps rippled through the crowd. What just happened?

Kitty knelt next to the fallen woman. She put two fingers to the woman's neck. Her mouth fell open and she glanced wildly around the room. She dove to the edge of the mat and rolled into the aisle next to the stands. What in heaven's name had got into the girl?

Tap. A pellet—no, a dart—hit the mat. Where did it come from? Several more followed. *Tap. Tap. Tap.*

"Get down!" Archie shouted to the crowd. He turned to me. "See you at St. Olave's tomorrow morning." He kissed my cheek and then took off like a bullet. Kitty was right behind him. They flew through the exit and disappeared.

I went to the fallen woman. Kneeling, I felt for a pulse. That was when I saw them. Several small darts were sticking out of her neck. Poisoned darts, I surmised. Fredricks joined me at the poor woman's side. She groaned and reached for her neck. Her pulse was slow and her breathing was shallow, from the exercise or the darts, I didn't know. "Someone call for an ambulance," I shouted.

Mrs. Garrud waved at me. "On it!" She sprinted out of the gym.

"Why would someone want to kill a jujitsu finalist?" I said more to myself than anyone else. I held the poor woman's hand.

"Are you sure the dart wasn't meant for her opponent?" Fredricks asked.

"Kitty!" Alarm bells went off in my head. I looked at Fredricks. "The MI5 assassin." The assassin was Jules Silver. I'd been so stupid! Thinking Archie had attacked Kitty. I gasped. Of course. Kitty's opponent was not the target. Kitty was. And the silly girl had gone chasing after the man who was trying to kill her.

Blast it. As long as Jules Silver was on the loose, Kitty was in danger. I had to stop him before Mr. Silver finally finished the job.

"We have to go after him!" I stood and tugged at Fredricks's sleeve.

"He's long gone by now." He gestured at the door.

"I'm going anyway." I dashed toward the exit. Fredricks was right behind me.

Outside the Dojo, I glanced up and down the street. In the distance, I made out a white kimono flapping in the breeze. Kitty pursuing her attacker. I took off. Weaving in and out of shop-keepers sweeping pavements, women pushing prams, and soldiers taking a stroll, I kept my gaze trained on Kitty's kimono.

Where was Jules Silver heading? If a killer wanted to escape, what was the best way? I shielded my eyes with my hand and surveyed the direction he was heading. The Thames. He was heading for the river. For the docks. Did he plan to escape by boat? I had to stop him. But how? If he was going get away by boat, he'd have to go to St. Katharine docks. It was too far to go on foot. He would have to hail a taxi. The taxi rank on Lower Regent Street. Following my hunch, I veered off Piccadilly and cut through an alley. If I was right, I could head him off before he reached the taxi rank.

Sucking in cool evening air, I sprinted up the alley to the corner. Just as I rounded the corner, I saw him. Jules Silver. "Stop!" I raced toward him. "Jules Silver, stop!"

He turned to face me. Desperate to stop him, I charged ahead.

"Fiona, no!" Fredricks's voice played in the back of my mind as I hurled myself at Mr. Silver.

I slammed into his torso with such force that he stumbled backwards. Clutching at his jacket, I fell forward. He pushed me away. I staggered into the street and tried to regain my balance. He lifted his walking stick over his head. I shielded my face with my hands. *Holy Mother of God.* I said a silent prayer. The stick landed on my shoulder. Ouch! The force and the pain were crushing. I collapsed in a heap in the street.

Whoosh. A rush of air raged past me. Fredrick Fredricks flew past like a winged beast. With him went Jules Silver. Fredricks tackled him and put him in a jujitsu grip.

A horn sounded. I looked in the direction of the sound. Good heavens. A lorry was barreling down Regent Street, coming right at me. I tried to stand, but the pain forced me back down. The lorry's tires squealed. *This is it.* Time slowed down. As if in slow motion, strong arms lifted me up. It was Fredricks. He cradled me in his arms and carried me to the pavement. The lorry's horn wailed as it roared past. Fredricks had saved me. Just in the nick of time. Shaking, I put my arms around his neck and buried my face in his shoulder.

Although I was in no condition to give chase, I insisted we go after Jules Silver. The killer had jumped into a taxi and was gone. Fredricks persuaded me it was no use. I was injured and Jules was out of our reach.

"Are you alright, *ma chérie*?" Fredricks set me on my feet.

Rubbing my shoulder, I nodded.

"Nothing broken?"

I hoped not. I shook my head. "I'll be fine."

He insisted I go with him for a brandy at Fortnum's. Shaken to the bone by this afternoon's events—not to mention revelations—I could use a brandy to calm my nerves.

"Are you sure you don't need to go to hospital?" His arm around my waist, Fredricks led me into Fortnum's.

"I'm sure." My shoulder hurt like the Dickens. "I'm going to have a dandy bruise though." I clamped my hand on my shoulder to stifle the ache. "I'm more worried about Kitty."

"Your *good lieutenant* went after her," Fredricks said. "Plus, with her jujitsu skills, her feet should be classified as weapons."

Yes. My good lieutenant and fiancé had disappeared... again.

Fredricks gave me a reassuring smile. "She'll be fine." He asked the hostess to be seated in a quiet corner near a window. I was glad for the privacy. With so many thoughts racing around in my mind, I needed someone to confide in. Why not Fredricks?

My wedding to Archie was tomorrow. And I had a monumental decision to make. Not that Fredricks was a disinterested party. But he was the only person interested enough in me and my affairs to care.

"Don't worry, *ma chérie*." Fredricks reached across the table and took my hand. "Your brave lieutenant will catch Mr. Silver and Miss Lane will return unscathed."

"Kill Mr. Silver, more like." I closed my eyes. "Archie is an ass—"

"I know what he is." He held up his free hand. "I've been telling you for months, but you didn't believe me."

"So, you sent me that telegram, telling me the list was a fraud and so was my fiancé." I sipped my brandy.

"I hoped you would heed my warning and keep the list to yourself." When he shook his head, black curls fell around his shoulders. "I knew you were planning to give it to your superiors, and I didn't want the bad intel to reflect poorly on you."

"Thank you." I wished Archie had thought of me before he'd shown me the blasted fraudulent list.

"Perhaps..." Fredricks let out a long sigh. "The *good lieutenant* does want to marry you out of love. But I suspect he has another motive. Taking you out of the field. Out of the action." He tightened his lips. "To protect you, yes. But, also, to keep you contained."

Contained? Was he joking? "What am I going to do?" I felt tears welling in my eyes. "My wedding is tomorrow, and I've just confirmed my fiancé is an ass—"

He cut me off again. "Best to keep that bit of intel to yourself, too."

Overwhelmed by emotion, I felt like I might burst. "That's not all." My lip trembled. "He wants a family and... and... I can't." I lowered my head.

"If he loves you, then you'll be enough." Fredricks took my hand in both of his. "You're enough. You will be his family." He caressed my hand. "Lucky sod," he said under his breath.

"I heard that," I sniffed. "He wants me to quit my job and stay home." I sighed. "While he's running across the globe on secret missions." I had the sudden sensation we were being watched. I looked around and everyone was staring at us. I withdrew my hands from Fredricks. Good grief. No wonder. I was still Horace Peabody.

"Maybe he'll change his mind once he realizes how important your work is to you." Fredricks reached out and wiped a tear from my cheek. "Don't worry, *ma chérie*. Everything will turn out as it's supposed to." He smiled. "You'll make the right decision."

"And what if I don't?" I said with a sniff.

"You are the most beautiful and brilliant woman of my acquaintance... even with that bushy beard and moustache." His eyes sparkled with moisture. "I have confidence in you. I know you'll do the right thing. You always do."

"Hardly." I picked at the edge of the tablecloth. "Marriage should be for life... until death do us part and all that rubbish."

"Love is not rubbish, *ma chérie*." His voice was earnest. "Love is a sunrise over a clearing fresh with the dawn of hope." He lifted my hand to his lips. "Love is a rock cliff, stalwart and steady for all eternity." He gazed across the table into my eyes. "Love is a cloudburst that drenches us with life itself." He kissed my hand.

Tears streamed down my cheeks, but I didn't care. "Should I call off the wedding?" I kept my gaze trained on his. "Tomorrow. Should I go to the church and tell the guests to go home?"

"Setting my own desires aside, *for once*." Fredricks sighed. "If you love your lieutenant, you should marry him." He gave me a resigned smile.

"I don't know..." Unsure of how to finish the sentence, I let my voice trail off.

"Don't make a rash decision. Sleep on it." He reached for my hand again. "Go home, take off that beard, and climb into bed with a nice hot water bottle." He winked. "And if you prefer naughty and hot, I volunteer my services." He flashed a cheeky grin.

The cad.

I couldn't sleep yet. I still had to pick up my gown and go to the police station. I stood up. "I've got to run." Unfortunately, it wasn't a metaphor. I literally was going to have to run.

First stop, the bridal boutique. I couldn't put off picking up my gown any longer. Whether it would fit properly was another matter.

Second stop, the police station. Obviously, I couldn't get married until I told the police about Molly the maid and cleared my name.

Whew. Then, first thing tomorrow—*before the wedding!*—I'd report back to Captain Hall and tell him the list I gave him was a sham.

A conversation I dreaded more than my upcoming nuptials.

28

KITTY'S INTERLUDE

Zigzagging through the crowded pavement of Piccadilly Circus for what seemed like miles, Kitty finally caught up to the rotter who'd fired the dart during the championship match. She recognized him from the War Office. Jules Silver. The German mole working in the censorship office. Carrying a walking stick in one hand and a valise in the other, he climbed into a taxi. She ran full tilt, hoping to catch it before it pulled away from the curb. Dammit. She was too late. The taxi pulled out into traffic. She jumped in the next taxi in line.

"Follow that taxi!" She pointed at the car containing the villain. What had happened to Lieutenant Archie Somersby? He'd taken off after the killer before she had. And yet he was nowhere to be seen. She looked out the window, watching for him. *What the heck?* Aunt Fiona was being carried up the pavement by Fredrick Fredricks. Kitty craned her neck for a better look. They must have gone after Silver, too. Now, it was up to her to catch him.

She wished the taxi driver would go faster. Her heart was racing. If only the driver would keep up. "Faster!" The tail of

Silver's cab was receding into the horizon. "We're losing him." She stomped her foot into the floorboard. "Double fare if you catch him."

That got the driver's attention. He jammed his foot on the accelerator. They caught up to Silver at St. Katharine docks on the Thames. Whatever the blackguard was planning, he wouldn't get away with it. Not on her life.

He jumped out of his taxi and ran toward the docks, swinging his stick as he went. She paid the driver double and hopped out. Shielding her eyes with her hand, she watched where he went. He boarded a large dazzle-painted ship sporting huge geometric shapes. She'd heard of these Flower-class sloops painted to confuse the enemy. She took off toward the ship. HMS *Saxifrage* was painted on its side.

Stevedores trudged up and down the gangplank loading the ship. She followed one of them up, keeping her head down and avoiding any eye contact. She was still dressed in her jujitsu kimono, so she didn't exactly blend in.

The sun was setting and long shadows fell across the Thames. It would be dark soon. Judging by the activity on the ship, it was about to sail. She had to catch up to Jules Silver before then.

She was almost to the end of the plank. The ship's deck was only a few steps away. Arms firmly at her side, teeth clenched, she stared down at her feet and stayed as close as possible to the stevedore in front of her. When she was about to step onto the deck, a uniformed officer stopped her.

"You there!" He grabbed her by the arm. "Where do you think you're going?" He scoffed. "What have we here?" He pulled her aside. "A girl in a dressing gown?"

She yanked herself free.

"Stowaway!" the officer shouted as she took off.

She sprinted back down the plank, almost smacking into another soldier on the way.

"After her!" the officer's voice echoed off the water. "Stowaway. Catch her."

A stevedore grabbed at her as she passed by. She whirled around and knocked him off the plank into the water. The distraction served her well. While his mates were busy trying to fish him out, she made her way back to the dock and quickly glanced around, looking for a hiding place. She tucked herself inside an empty barrel and watched and waited.

With no moon to illuminate the night, darkness fell fast. The activity on the gangplank had slowed and the ship's engines were running. The HMS *Saxifrage* could set sail any minute.

Jules Silver was somewhere on that ship. If she didn't stop him, he would get away. And if he got away, she'd be looking over her shoulder for the rest of her life, wondering when he'd make his move.

This was her last chance to catch the mole and her attacker. She crawled out of the barrel and made her way to the water's edge. She stripped down to her smalls and then dove in. The frigid water took her breath away. She swam to the ship's anchor. Latching onto the heavy chain, she heaved herself out of the water. Shivering, she clamped her feet tight around the huge chain link and started to climb. One link at a time. The chain was wet and slippery. She clung to it with all her might, hoping they didn't pull anchor with her on it. Moving as quickly as she could up the slippery chain, winded, she finally reached the top. She flung herself into the anchor hold and rolled out of the way of the chain. And just in the nick of time, too. Creaking and groaning, the chain started to move. She pulled herself to her knees to catch her breath. Now to find her way to the deck.

Dripping, her underwear clinging to her, she crept along the hull until she came to a ladder. She climbed the ladder and gingerly opened the hatch at the top. Peeking out, she saw the silhouette of a man crouched behind a bench near the bow. Jules Silver? Was he hiding out until the ship set sail? The boat lurched. With a noisy growl it chugged away from the shore.

Dammit. She had to nab Silver and get off this blasted ship. Otherwise, who knew where she'd end up? She'd miss Aunt Fiona's wedding and, for some reason she still didn't comprehend, she was Aunt Fiona's bridesmaid.

It was now or never. Kitty took a deep breath. She exploded through the hatch and lunged at the shadow. She tackled him from behind and pinned him to the deck. Panting, she stared down into his face.

"What the..." she huffed. Pinned underneath her was Lieutenant Archie Somersby, her so-called partner.

"Where's Silver?" She let him up. "How'd you get on board?"

"I'm an officer." He tugged on his jacket to straighten it. "Let me guess." He shook his head. "You swam."

She wrapped her arms around her torso. "Where is he?" She wanted to find him and get off this bloody ship as soon as possible. "We'd better find him or you'll miss your wedding." Not that she cared whether he made it or not. Aunt Fiona might be an odd duck, but she didn't deserve to be saddled with an assassin and a traitor who falsified top-secret documents.

He ran a hand through his hair. "I'm not going to let that happen."

A sharp pain exploded across the back of her skull. She whipped around and then ducked.

Jules Silver wielded his walking stick like a club.

Kitty staggered to the railing and held on. Stars circled before her eyes. She clung to the rail, for how long, she had no idea.

Time stood still. When she regained her balance, she took several deep breaths to combat the pain in her head.

Archie grabbed the end of the walking stick and tore it out of Silver's hands. He lunged at Silver and took him down. Wrestling on the deck, the two men grunted and snorted like animals.

She held her head in both hands. Behind the pain was something else. A clearing. Everything came flooding back. She remembered. Everything. She stood stock still, letting the memories return: It was Jules Silver who attacked her at the Dojo. After months of field work, she'd determined *he* was the mole in British Intelligence. Not Archie. When Silver found out she was onto him, he attacked her to shut her up.

Aunt Fiona. Uncle Clifford. Poppy-poo. Everything came back to her. Poppy. Dear, sweet, little Poppy. How could she have done it? She'd left her best friend in Reading. As soon as she got off this ship, she was going back to get her beloved doggie. "Poppy, I'm sorry," she whispered.

"I could use some help here," Archie croaked as he rolled around the deck with Jules Silver.

Watching for an opportune moment, Kitty tensed her leg muscles. When Silver had Archie pinned and was about to strike a blow, she whirled around and landed a kick to the side of his head. He hit the deck with a thud.

"We've got to stop the ship." Archie sounded desperate. "I'm not going to miss my wedding."

"Good luck with that." She glanced around. "We're well on our way. They'll never turn around too. We've gone too far."

"I'm going back." He pointed to the rail. "You take care of Silver."

"Are you mad?" She laughed. "You can't swim all the way back!"

Stripping off his shoes and then his jacket, he ignored her. He unbuckled his belt.

"Sorry about this, old boy," she said under her breath. "But it's for your own good." She wheeled around and delivered a kick to the side of his head. He fell to the deck like a brick. "And for Aunt Fiona's, too." She looked down at him. With his eyes closed and pink cheeks, he looked like he was sleeping—sweet, even. You'd never know he was one of MI5's most deadly assassins.

Jules Silver groaned.

Kitty turned around and picked up the walking stick. She put her foot on Silver's chest. "Don't move or I'll give you a taste of your own medicine." She lifted the stick over her head. "I know you're the mole."

"You think you're pretty smart, girlie." He spat out the words. "If it weren't for you, I'd still be the Kaiser's golden boy in London."

"Try golden boy in prison." At least until her partner, the assassin, came to. "You tried to kill me to keep me quiet about your treason. But why did you kill Ellen Davis?"

"Molly was supposed to poison you but got the old gossip lady instead," he scoffed. For someone with his neck under her boot, he was darn cheeky.

"Who is Molly?" She pressed harder on his chest.

"The maid." He squirmed under her boot. "Molly was supposed to give you a couple of berries, but I heaped a whole bunch of leaves and berries onto the old bird's plate. Still, I had to finish her off with a hatpin, the old cow."

"You're in no position to get cheeky with me." Kitty ground the heel of her boot into his chest. "Why? Why kill Ellen Davis? When you stabbed her, surely you knew she wasn't me." She waved the walking stick at him.

He put his hands in front of his face. "Alright. Alright."

She waved the stick a little closer to his head. "Why Ellen?"

"Look, I'm a married man." He tried to wriggle out from under her boot. "I had a good job. A family. Between you and that horrible gossip woman, my life was ruined."

"Explain." She tapped the stick on the deck next to his ear.

"Alright." He winced. "The old bat was threatening to publish about me and Molly in her daft newspaper." He grimaced. "I couldn't let her do that. Then she made me pay her off to keep it out of the paper."

"You mean she was blackmailing you?" That was a pretty good motive for murder. "Because you were having an affair with the maid? This Molly person."

"Yes," he sputtered.

"What's going on?" Archie sat up and rubbed his head. "What happened? Why are you all wet? And where are your clothes?"

"Tie him up." Shivering, Kitty pointed the stick at Silver. "We're in for a long trip." She glared down at the mole and murderer. He'd be a lot less trouble if he were unconscious.

29

THE WEDDING

After a fitful night, I woke early and padded into the kitchen to make a cup of tea. Sitting at the table half asleep waiting for the water to boil, I let my mind relax into the grey fog of blankness. The kettle screamed and jolted me out of my stupor. Crikey! Today was my wedding day. I pushed thoughts of marital bliss—and despair—to the back of my mind. I had yet to show Captain Hall the telegram—the one from Fredricks claiming the list, and its author, were frauds. I gulped down my tea and prepared to confess to the captain. Whether or not I went through with the wedding, I planned to keep my job. I only hoped Captain Hall obliged. The bogus list was a major cockup. I sighed. *Please, don't fire me on my wedding day.*

In a hurry to get to the War Office, I grabbed the same clothes I was wearing yesterday, which happened to be my Horace Peabody outfit, sans facial hair. I threw on the clothes, tugged on my favorite wig, dashed downstairs, and went to the corner to wave down a taxi. I didn't have time for the bus. Luckily, my street was always busy and it was easy to find a taxi. I asked the driver to wait for me.

My plan was to run in, tell the captain, and then hurry back to my flat and get dressed for the wedding. The moment of truth. Will the gown fit? When we got to the Old Admiralty Building, I asked the driver to wait for me. He agreed, but only after I promised to pay triple fare. So be it. Desperate times.

I dashed up the stairs to the captain's office. I told his secretary it was imperative I see Captain Hall immediately. After looking me up and down and tutting a few times, she asked me to wait in the reception area. She came back with the news that he'd see me. Thank goodness.

When he saw me, his eyes went wide, and his lashes came to a standstill. "What kind of get-up is that!" He laughed. He could make fun of my "get-ups" all he wanted, but they'd come in handy on many occasions.

"My cover in Dublin, sir." I looked down at my overalls. "Horace Peabody, gardener extraordinaire." I laid my palms on my cheeks. They were hot. Too bad I didn't wear the facial hair to hide my embarrassment.

"About that." He picked up a folder and tossed it across his desk. "The intelligence you brought back is completely bogus. The list is nothing but schoolboys and shopgirls." He shook his head. "I'm deeply disappointed, Miss Figg." He let out a big sigh. "Scotland Yard have rounded up dozens of them already but none are older than eighteen. And none are the leaders of the protests or the ICA."

I felt like I'd swallowed broken glass. The captain had confirmed it. Fredricks was telling the truth. And Archie sent me up the river. Did it mean Fredricks was right about the other part, too? Archie was a fraud. "Sir, about the list." I bit my lip. "I got it from Lieutenant Somersby, my MI5 contact in Dublin." If I felt guilty ratting out Archie, I felt worse that he'd hung me out to dry.

"Somersby!" he scoffed. "He works for me. My right-hand man if you must know."

"That's just it, sir." I swallowed hard. "You're his cover. He actually works for MI5."

"Lieutenant Somersby no more works for MI5 than you do, Miss Figg." He tapped a pencil on his desk. "Are you trying to shirk your responsibility? Blame him for your shoddy work?"

"No, sir." I stared down at my lap. "I need to show you a telegram I received yesterday, just after I delivered the list to you. I came back, but—"

"Alright," he interrupted, wigging his fingers at me. "But make it quick."

I dug the telegram out of my bag and held it out to him. I winced as I watched him read it. What would he think of his right-hand man being called a fraud?

"What is the meaning of this?" He stood up. "Fredrick Fredricks again." He came around his desk and paced back and forth. "How did he know the list was no good?" He slapped the telegram into the palm of his hand. "How is that bastard always one step ahead of us?" He stopped and stared at me. "Miss Figg, for some unknown reason Fredricks trusts you. You've got to stay on him. Stick to him. Don't let him out of your sight. From now on, your top priority is getting close to him. As close as you can. Learn everything about him. I want to know what kind of after-shave he uses. His favorite fruit. Whether he drinks tea or coffee."

"Rosewood. Peaches. Both." I regretted opening my mouth as soon as I'd spoken.

Glaring at me, he dropped back into his desk chair. "Most of all, I want to know where he gets his intel," he bellowed. "And why he's always ahead of us!" He pounded his fist on the desk. "Stay on top of him. That's an order!"

Startled, I jumped a little. "Yes, sir. Stay on top of him, sir."

"Can you do that, Miss Figg?" He lowered his voice. "Learn what makes him tick and how he always knows more than we do. Report back on all intercourse with him."

"Yes, sir. Get close. Very close. On top of him." My cheeks weren't the only part of my anatomy on fire. "All intercourse with him. Yes, sir."

"And no more silly disguises." He waved his hand at me. "Enough of dressing up like a man. You're a woman, for God's sake. Dress like one."

I tightened my lips. Promising to stick to Fredricks was one thing, giving up my fake facial hair was quite another.

"Is there anything else, Miss Figg?" The way he asked made it clear he'd had enough of me.

"About Kitty, sir." I cleared my throat. "Your niece. A man tried to kill her. Jules Silver. She's in danger. MI5 may have sent an operative to—"

"Yes, yes." He waved me away again. "I know all about Kitty and MI5."

"You do?" What a relief. Did that mean everything was alright? Kitty wasn't in danger. I hoped to heaven he was right. Especially since she was meeting me in an hour to help me dress for my wedding. Not to mention, she was my maid of honor. "And Jules Silver. Has he been arrested?" Or killed by an MI5 assassin?

"Of course. Do you think me a fool?" His lashes fluttered faster than ever. "MI5 keeps me in the loop."

"Yes, sir," I gulped. "I mean, no, sir." Of course, he wasn't a fool. Still, I was beginning to wonder how much he really knew.

"Look, Miss Figg, overall, you've been an asset, a fine agent, most of the time. But I won't stand for any more bad intel." He stabbed the air with his pencil. "Now track down Fredricks and find out how he knew the list was bad." He went back to the papers on his desk. "Don't let him out of your sight."

"Yes, sir." I stood up. "If that's all, sir."

He waved me away. I hightailed it back downstairs to my desk. Now to get home and prepare for my wedding. Good grief. I was far too busy to be getting married.

At least Captain Hall had reassured me that Kitty was safe. Or did he? Come to think of it, what did he mean, "I know all about Kitty and MI5"? Did he know she worked for MI5? That she was being chased by MI5? And why had Archie told me he worked for MI5 when Captain Hall was adamant that he didn't? Maybe Archie was having me on, making a joke. Then again, maybe Archie did work for MI5.

I glanced at my watch. Oh, fiddlesticks. The taxi! It was still waiting for me... and costing me a week's wages.

Back at my flat, I put the kettle on. I couldn't face wedding preparations without a strong cuppa to fortify me. Clifford would be here in just over an hour to pick me up. Kitty was supposed to be here to help me get dressed, but I hadn't heard from her since she took off after Mr. Silver yesterday.

Of course, I still hadn't decided whether to go through with it. On the one hand, it seemed a shame to waste the flowers, cake, and champagne. On the other hand, my groom was a mysterious assassin who wanted a family that I couldn't give him. At the very least, I had to show up and explain to the guests. I let out a long forlorn sigh. Where was my grandmother with her words of wisdom when I needed her?

I ran a bath and added a few drops of rose water. While waiting for the bathtub to fill, I laid out my dress, a simple pongee ivory silk with panels of French lace, full lace sleeves, a nipped waist with a lovely satin sash tied into a bow. Yesterday, after the tragedy at the Dojo and just before I went to the police station to report Molly the maid, when I'd gone to pick up the dress, the seamstress at the bridal shop had refused to hand it over. I'd missed my last fitting and she "wouldn't be responsible." I assured her it was good enough and I'd take full responsibility. Hopefully I could say the same for my marriage.

After soaking in the warm rose-scented water for longer than I should have, I stepped out, toweled off, and wrapped myself in my robe.

I set to work packing my bags for the honeymoon, just in case. Archie still hadn't told me where we were going. Like everything else with him, it was a big secret. I didn't know whether to pack for a south sea island or the North Pole. Not that it mattered much. It was our honeymoon, after all. Most of our sightseeing would be in the bedroom. Wherever we were going, I'd have my lovely lavender silk pajamas and the ravishing georgette crêpe chemise I'd bought when Clifford wasn't looking. I smiled to myself as I gently folded them into my suitcase.

I might as well get ready. Hopefully, I'd know what to do once I was at the church.

I had to get into the dress and somehow fasten it on my own. And, of course, the problem of my hair. With so many missions disguised as a man, I'd kept my naturally auburn locks closely shorn. Seeing myself in the mirror, hair sticking up in all directions, I looked like a hedgehog. Archie had never seen my real hair. What would he think when he realized he was married to a shorn sheep? I could never take off my wig. I'd have to wear it without fail until my own hair grew back.

Now, which of my wigs was Archie's favorite? He only ever remarked on my moustaches. I decided to wear *my* favorite, a strawberry-blonde bob. Assembling my various undergarments —lingerie, corset, and petticoat—was no small feat. Cinching a corset on one's own was like rowing a boat wearing a straitjacket. I slipped on the dress and slid my arms into its gorgeous lace sleeves. Twisting myself into a pretzel, I managed to fasten the hook at the back of the gown. I tied the sash at the waist and admired my reflection in the mirror. Some face powder and lip rouge wouldn't go amiss. Using all the ammunition in my arsenal, I powdered and painted, trying to achieve the smooth pale look of a lady, if not a gazelle.

With another contortionist's maneuver, I fastened the charm bracelet around my wrist. Waving, I listened to the charms tinkling. Captain Hall was right. I'd never sneak up on my enemies wearing this. But Archie wasn't my enemy.

I went back to my wardrobe to fetch a pair of shoes. Unfortunately, my practical Oxfords were not an option. Hopefully, my wedding wouldn't require a quick getaway. I'd purchased a lovely pair of cream satin court shoes that would do nicely (unless, of course, I had to run to catch a villain). Sliding my foot into the shoe, it hit me. I was about to make a lifelong commitment to a man I hardly knew. If I loved him, would that be enough? *Did I? Did I love him?*

Here I was, an hour before the wedding, wearing my bridal gown, and I still didn't know if I could go through with it. If I didn't, I would embarrass myself for life by showing up at the church and announcing it was off. And poor Archie. That wouldn't be fair to him.

Come on, Fiona. You can't marry a man just to avoid embarrassment.

The butterflies in my stomach had become bats fleeing the light at dawn. My hand trembled as I applied the lip rouge. What should I do?

A knock on my door sent my heart into my throat. *Oh, dear.* For once Clifford was early. Today of all days. When I needed more time. I took one last look in the mirror, adjusted my wig, and went to the door.

Clifford looked sharp in his morning suit and slicked-back hair. "I say, old bean." He beamed. "You look marvelous."

"Thank you, Clifford dear." I wished I felt marvelous. It was my wedding day, and I was miserable. I retrieved my suitcase and left it by the door to pick up later. Enveloped in a suffocating cloud of paralysis and regret, I fetched my coat and hat. Stepping over the threshold, I took Clifford's arm to steady myself. The moment of truth was upon me.

* * *

From the outside, St. Olave church looked more like a railway station than a church. Long and narrow and made of red bricks, if it weren't for the belltower, you'd never know it was a church. Inside, though, the church was magnificent with Italian marble floors and ornate columns leading to a gilded altar below a baby-blue paneled domed ceiling.

I was practically hyperventilating as Clifford led me inside. I peeked into the church on our way to a private office where I was to wait for the wedding march as the signal for Clifford to walk me down the aisle. Who were all these people? They must be friends of Archie's—although there were an inordinate number of countesses and society ladies. Archie had insisted on a big wedding in the church. I had to admit, filled with well-wishers and flowers, the chapel was lovely. It almost put me in the mood to get married. *Almost.* Clifford left me alone with my thoughts and went to greet the guests. He promised to return as soon as the groom and his party arrived.

Sitting alone in the small office, surrounded by old tomes and icons, I closed my eyes and fingered the lace on the hem of my sleeve. A year ago, I would have never guessed I'd be dressed in silk and lace waiting for my betrothed to arrive for my wedding. My second wedding. Would it go any better than the first? I winced. So much had happened over the last year. I'd gone from a happily married housewife to a divorced and widowed file clerk turned espionage agent. I'd gone on missions to Paris, New York, Cairo, Italy, and behind enemy lines in Austria.

What had been the lowest point in my life—my ex-husband's infidelity and then horrible death from mustard gas—had opened the door for the greatest adventures of my life. *You never know what is waiting around the corner*. As my grandmother used to say, "When the door locks behind you, find the nearest window and crawl out." The War Office and my disguises had been my window out of that dark room of despair. And what amazing adventures I'd had once I'd dried those tears. What a difference a year makes.

Now, I had Archie. The handsome pilot who loved me. Who desperately wanted to marry me. Why, I didn't know. Was I doing the right thing? He was a good man despite being a cold-blooded killer. And he only killed for the cause of justice.

Pipe in hand, Clifford poked his head in the door. "Lieutenant Somersby is not here yet."

Where was Archie? What if something had happened to him? I hoped he was alright. Last time I'd seen him, he was chasing after a suspected murderer and German spy. Archie had got out of tighter spots. And so had Kitty. It was typical of Archie to disappear and then reappear without warning. He would show up. I knew he would. He wouldn't miss his own wedding, for heaven's sake.

Clifford glanced at his watch. "The ceremony was supposed to start ten minutes ago." He stood in the doorway looking at me. "Are you alright, old bean?"

"Give him time." I nodded. "He'll be here." I said it with more certainty than I felt. He'd promised he'd be here. But, if I knew anything about Archie, it was that he vanished and reemerged like a magician's rabbit. I never knew when or where I'd see him again. Surely he'd show up for his own wedding! For *our* wedding!

My nerves were frayed wires. To calm myself, I got up and paced back and forth in the small office. Silently, I read the titles of the old books to further distract myself. My heart was racing and it was hard to breathe. *The Catechism of the Counsel of Trent. Confessions of Saint Augustine. City of God Saint Thomas.* The religious tomes weren't helping.

"Of course he'll be here, old thing," Clifford said, puffing on his pipe. "Did I ever tell you about my brother's wedding?" He chuckled. "I was his best man, you see. And it was raining cats and dogs. On the way to the chapel, the carriage got stuck in the mud." He laughed. "We had to get out and push the bloody thing. By the time we reached the church, we were both covered in mud up to our knees." He snorted. "Poor old William slipped and had mud from stem to stern." He took a puff. "Can't get much worse than that, I'm afraid."

For once, I was glad for his stories. Good old Clifford. He was a dear friend indeed. I smiled at him. "Thank you, Clifford dear. You are a good friend."

"I say." He blushed.

For the next twenty minutes, he told stories about his brother and their hunting adventures growing up. I tuned in and out, happy for the calming sound of his voice.

"Excuse me." The priest knocked at the doorframe. "The natives are getting restless." He entered the room. "When do we expect the groom?"

"Any minute." I fiddled with the lace on my sleeve. "Hopefully."

"I'm afraid we can't wait much longer." The priest gave me a knowing smile full of sympathy. "The church is needed later this afternoon for another wedding."

"Just give him another ten minutes." I glanced at my watch. The priest was right. Archie was already forty minutes late. My heart sank. Was I being jilted at the altar? Maybe he'd been shot or kidnapped or killed. He'd better be incapacitated or I'd kill him myself when I got my hands on him.

"Five is all we can spare." The way the priest looked at me, you'd think I'd been condemned to the firing squad.

I nodded. My stomach churned. My head was pounding. Now what? I took a deep breath. I'd have to bury my pride and make an announcement. "The wedding is off." I steeled myself for the inevitable.

"I'm sorry, old bean," Clifford said. "Rum do about your missing groom."

"Indeed," I huffed. "Well, here goes nothing." I lifted the hem of my wedding dress, skated out of the office, and marched into the church.

The din of chatter echoed through the narrow chapel. Standing at the entrance, I surveyed the crowd. No sign of Archie or Kitty. But, there in the back row, Fredrick Fredricks caught my eye. He smiled and came to me.

"Fiona, *ma chérie*." He lifted my hand to his lips. "You look stunning."

Our eyes met. "He didn't show." My lip trembled as I tried to speak. "I have to call it off." I felt tears welling in my eyes. "What should I do?"

"Leave it to me." He took my hand. "I'll take care of everything."

I nodded.

He led me up the aisle.

When we reached the front of the church, he held up a hand. "Ladies and gentlemen." He raised his voice. "Ladies and gentlemen. May I have your attention, please?" He clapped his hands together a few times. "Your attention please. Our lovely bride has an announcement."

My cheeks were on fire as I looked out at the audience. Fanning themselves, the society ladies gazed at me expectantly. My chest was tight and I felt lightheaded. "Thank you all for coming." I cleared my throat. "Apologies..." *What can I say? That I've been jilted at the altar?* It was all too mortifying. "I'm sorry..." I sputtered, trying to get the words out. Overcome with dizziness, I reached out for Fredricks's arm to steady myself.

"Apologies for the delay," Fredricks whispered in my ear.

His voice was reassuring. "Apologies for the delay," I repeated.

"You came here for a wedding party," he whispered.

I took a deep breath. "You came here for a wedding party." I waited for his next cue.

"Despite not getting the wedding, why waste a good party!" he said into my ear.

I repeated what he'd said.

"And while we're at it, why not make it an engagement party," he whispered.

Confused, I met his gaze.

"And why waste a lovely bride?" He smiled. "*Ma chérie*, will you do me the honor of becoming my wife?" He took my hand, raised it to his lips, and kissed it. "Will you marry me?" he whispered.

"Really?" I squeezed his hand. "You want to marry *me*?"

His dark eyes were moist. "More than anything in the world." He lifted my hand to his lips again.

"As much as world peace?" I grinned.

Again, he kissed my hand. "Having you by my side, as we work together for peace, would make sense out of this nonsensical world." He interlaced his fingers in mine. "Shall we?" As he led me back down the aisle, I was smiling so hard it hurt.

He put his arm around my waist and pulled me closer. "*Je t'aime, ma chérie.*"

"I love you, too." Tears welled in my eyes, but this time they were tears of joy. Even my step felt lighter. "Thank you, dear Fredricks." I was practically floating.

"Don't you think it's time for you to call me by my Christian name?" he grinned. "Fredrick."

"A rose by any other name..." Like a silly schoolgirl, I grinned back at him. "You're not asking me out of pity, are you?"

"Marrying you would be the greatest honor of my life." His dark eyes gleamed. "We will make a formidable team, *ma chérie.* Pity the fools who get in our way."

At the back of the church, we met Clifford, who had been watching the scene play out.

"Steady on, old bean," Clifford sputtered. "You can't be serious."

"Deadly serious." I leaned closer and whispered in his ear. "I'm just following orders."

"You were ordered to marry Fredricks!" Clifford chuckled. "I say, the great hunter has finally been caught." He patted my hand. "Well done, old bean."

I didn't know if I'd caught Fredricks or he'd caught me, but it was going to be fun finding out.

Fredricks instructed the guests to move next door to King's Square, where the reception was waiting.

Standing under the stone arches, dressed in his morning suit, his ebony hair flowing over his broad shoulders, Fredricks's smile was contagious. He took both my hands. "Until death do us part," he said.

"With you, death could be around any corner," I grinned. "Which makes life all the more exciting."

Fredricks slipped the panther ring off his pinky and slipped it onto my ring finger. "You haven't answered." He gazed at me expectantly. "Will you marry me?"

"Why not?" Actually, I could think of a million reasons why not. But, at this moment, I didn't want to countenance them. I'd just been jilted at the altar. And the most gorgeous man of my acquaintance was standing before me, asking me to marry him. "Let me count the ways..." I dramatically lifted the back of my hand to my forehead.

Fredricks encircled me in a gentle embrace. "I do love you, *ma chérie*. With all my heart and soul." He smiled down at me. "You are the most beautiful person I've ever met. Especially when"— he bent closer until his breath tickled my ear—"you're practicing jujitsu as my cousin Monsieur Marcel Désiré from France."

"In the words of cousin Marcel..." I put my hands around his neck and pulled him closer. "*Tais toi et embrasse moi*," I whispered. "Shut up and kiss me."

EPILOGUE

After the reception and much champagne and dancing, Fredricks had a carriage waiting to take us back to my flat to fetch my suitcase for the honeymoon. He said we could get married on the way. Full of excitement, he described a honeymoon trip to India to meet a peace activist there. Someone called Mahatma Gandhi.

"Given we're not married yet," I said, straightening myself, "aren't you putting the cart before the horse?" I had to admit, it all sounded thrilling. And I was under orders, after all.

When the carriage hit a bump, the seat squeaked in such a peculiar fashion it sounded like a small animal. I clutched my hat.

Passionate about our "future together," Fredricks talked about "our life's adventure spreading peace"—and no doubt agitating— "all over the globe." He spoke of Mr. Gandhi in India, Margaret Watts and the Australian Peace Alliance, Laura Lunde the peace activist in Canada, Jane Addams and Lillian Wald in America. Fredricks knew everyone. Everyone who was anyone. He had contacts all over the world. One thing was certain, our life together wouldn't be boring. As I listened to his plans, his passion for peace was contagious. The trouble was his beautiful lips were devilishly distracting. And I found it difficult to concentrate on what he was saying.

We hit another bump and I nearly fell into his lap. I leaned against him and took in the spring flowers and the scent of jasmine and horses. The sounds of the street—automobiles, lorries, horses, carriages, street vendors—were amplified riding in the open air. Despite the symphony of the street, I kept hearing a tiny cry coming from under my seat. Perhaps I'd had too much champagne at the wedding reception and was imagining things.

"Don't you want to end the war?" He looked at me earnestly.

Always the idealist, Fredricks claimed together we could end the war. I wanted the war to end as much as he did. But, at this minute, I wanted him more. I leaned into his warmth and put my hand on his knee. He turned and smiled at me. Our eyes met. He kissed me. Breathless, I kissed him back. A passion for peace wasn't the only passion we shared. There it was again. That tiny peeping sound. I tried to ignore it and continue the pressing business at hand. By the time we reached my building, I was dewy with expectation.

When the carriage stopped, Fredricks reached under the seat and pulled out a small parcel covered with a cloth. Was he about to perform a magician's trick? At this point, nothing would have surprised me.

"What's that?" I asked, pointing to the cloth.

"A wedding present." He smiled.

"But I didn't get married." I grinned. Knowing Fredricks, he'd somehow delayed Archie and planned the whole thing.

"An engagement present, then." He helped me down from the carriage. "I didn't think I'd ever be so lucky as to have a real chance with you. Fiona, *ma chérie*, you've made me the happiest man alive." He carried the mystery parcel in one hand and led me up the stairs with the other.

When we reached my door, he waited while I unlocked it.

"I believe it's customary for the groom to carry the bride over the threshold." He raised his eyebrows in a most mischievous way.

"I'm not your bride." I leaned into him. "Not yet."

"Thus, the blushing bride doesn't appear too eager to consummate the marriage."

"So, she has to be carried?" I rolled my eyes. "Against her will." On tiptoes, I reached up and kissed him. "And what if she is eager?" I nuzzled his neck. "Awfully eager. Terribly eager. Urgently eager," I whispered breathlessly.

With one hand, he scooped me up, and still kissing me, carried me into the flat. Once inside, I pushed the door shut... with a bit too much force. The bang scared whatever was in the mysterious cage and it let out a loud meow.

"For you, *ma chérie*." Fredricks held up the cage. "Uncover it." He beamed like a proud father.

So, *I* was to be the magician. I whisked off the cover. "Oh, my word." My heart melted. Inside a gold cage sat the most adorable kitten I'd ever seen. White with a black mask and a pug nose. When I opened the cage, the little darling climbed out into my hand. I snuggled her to my chest. "I love her." I looked up at Fredricks. "She's perfect. And so are you."

Glowing, Fredricks wrapped us both in an embrace. "Our little family."

Either the kitten generated an excessive amount of heat or the proximity to Fredricks and the scent of rosewood was going to my head. Slowly, I untied his bow tie and began to unbutton his shirt. He bent down and kissed me with such passion I had to hold onto his shoulders to keep from falling over. I felt like I might combust.

"Perhaps we should show the kitten the bedroom," I said breathlessly.

"Excellent idea." Fredricks untied the sash at my waist. He nuzzled my neck. "Fiona, you smell delicious." When he inhaled it sent tingles down my spine. "Like sweet peaches."

I led him through the flat to my bedroom. I put the kitten on the floor. With its little tail pointed skyward, it sniffed and explored until it found a feathered slipper. It reared up and pounced. Fredricks and I both broke out laughing. While the kitten played with my slipper, I played with a lock of Fredricks's beautiful black hair.

"I'll be back in a second," I said, tearing myself away. I had plans for the lacy chemise waiting by the door in my suitcase. I dashed out, retrieved the case, and took it into the lavatory. My chest was buzzing as I quickly tore off my wedding dress and most of my smalls and slipped into the delicate chemise. I glanced in the mirror. Oh, what the heck. I pulled off my wig and then washed my face clean with rose-scented soap.

"I miss you, *ma chérie*," Fredricks called from the bedroom. "Hurry back."

I stared at myself in the mirror. Did I really want to be Mrs. Fiona Figg Fredricks? There were worse things I could imagine. Mrs. Fiona Figg Fredricks. It was a bit of a mouthful... but so was Fredrick Fredricks.

I smiled, thinking of Captain Hall's orders. "Stay on top of him. Don't let him out of your sight." I giggled. How far would I go for my country? We were about to find out.

I fastened the belt and chatelaine bag around the waist of my chemise. I might need my notebook and pencil to record "all intercourse." I smiled at my reflection. I was a sight. Shorn hair.

Barely clothed. A belt and bag around my waist. Fredricks would be amused if nothing else. I replaced my notebook. I didn't need it. "Not this time," I said to myself. Thankfully, my photographic memory would allow me to keep my hands free. And I had a feeling that I would need both hands on deck to stay on top of Fredricks. I couldn't stop giggling. I planned to memorize every inch of him. Stick to him, the captain had ordered. And I was a stickler for following orders.

"Pussy and I are both getting cold without you, *ma chérie*," Fredricks called.

"I'm coming!" I called back.

For fun, I pressed my Horace moustache onto my upper lip with a dab of spirit gum. I laughed out loud. What fun!

I headed for the bedroom. Halfway there, I stopped. I dashed back to the coat rack, removed my new hat, and withdrew the emerald hatpin. The one Fredricks had given me. Espionage was a dangerous business. I tested the tip against my index finger. *Ouch*. It was sharp. Fredricks had better behave himself or I'd show him the tricks I'd learned at the Suffrajitsu demonstration.

I tightened my lips to keep from laughing and then tucked the weapon into my holster. "I'm coming." Repressing a fit of giggles, I dashed back into the bedroom.

Oh, the things I do for king and country.

AUTHOR'S NOTE

Many of the characters in this novel are inspired by real-life people, although the story itself is mostly made up. To sort the fact from fiction, here is a bit of information about the real people who inspired this story.

Ellen Davis is inspired by gossip columnist Eliza Davis Aria (1866–1931), who was a London fashion writer and gossip columnist known as Mrs. Aria. She grew up in a literary family and of her seven brothers and sisters, many were writers or actors. Her own literary and artistic friends included Oscar Wilde, H. G. Wells, and Rebecca West, among many other London luminaries of the day. She was known to call everyone of her acquaintance "darling." She died at the Adelphi Theatre just before the curtain went up.

Sylvia Pankhurst is of course based on the famous suffragette, Estelle Sylvia Pankhurst (1882–1960). In addition to her work on behalf of women's rights, she fought for workers' rights in London's East End. Unlike her mother Emmeline Pankhurst and her sister Christabel, Sylvia didn't settle for votes for only land-owning married women over the age of thirty (land-owning, married, English women over thirty got the vote in 1918; full voting equality took ten more years to achieve). She wanted enfranchisement for all women and better working conditions for men and women. Between 1913 and 1914, she was arrested eight times. The so-called Cat and Mouse Act allowed the prison to release suffragettes who went on hunger strike and wait until they were healthy and then arrest them again and put them back in prison. Pankhurst regularly worked with Irish suffragettes and home rule activists against conscription and for workers' rights.

Suffrajitsu was practiced by many suffragettes who were encouraged to learn self-defense. Sylvia Pankhurst did have jujitsu-trained bodyguards, the suffrajitsus. Edith Garrud trained suffragettes in the martial art jujitsu at the Dojo owned by her husband William.

The character of Jules Silver is loosely inspired by the real-life Jules C. Silber (1885–1939), who was a German spy and mole who worked for British Intelligence in the censorship office during the Great War. He was never caught and emigrated to Germany in 1925.

In 1902, Lord Balfour's government did secretly protect Cyril Flower (known as Lord Battersea) from prosecution in a sex scandal involving underaged boys, although Balfour and Battersea were on opposite sides of the political spectrum, with Balfour against suffrage for women and against Irish home rule and Battersea in favor of both. Lord Battersea's wife, Lady Battersea, was Constance Rothschild, who was a socialite and philanthropist, as well as a women's rights activist.

The "German Plot" was real in the sense that British Intelligence received bad intel and Captain "Blinker" Hall ordered over a hundred members of Sinn Féin to be rounded up and arrested on 12 April 1918. It turned out there was no collaboration between the Irish and the Germans. Furthermore, the list was of moderates and the revolutionary leaders were tipped off and got away. The arrests backfired and made people more sympathetic to the cause of home rule.

Randy and Carrie Kipper are *very loosely* inspired by Rudyard and Carrie Kipling. Rudyard Kipling was an important English poet and novelist known for *The Jungle Book* duology. Kipling was born in British India. Although his writings were very popular during his lifetime, his conservative politics and Imperialist ideology have been the subject of contemporary criticism. He married Caroline Starr Balestier, the sister of his good friend and collaborator, Wolcott Balestier, after Wolcott died suddenly of typhoid in 1891. Carrie was from a wealthy, if unconventional, New England family. Reportedly, they had a tumultuous marriage, in which Carrie was unhappy. Some biographers fault Carrie for being overbearing, while others fault Kipling for being overbearing. Kipling was decidedly anti-suffragette and anti-home rule.

At the age of eighteen, in 1916, Jane Archer (born Sissmore, 1898–1982) was appointed to MI5 as a typist and clerk. In 1929, she became the first woman officer in Britain's Security Service, MI5. She married Wing Commander John Oliver Archer in 1939 on the eve of World War II. She did important work during World War II, including serving under and then working to expose double agent Kim Philby, who was secretly working for the Soviets. By all reports, she was a formidable interrogator. In 1940, she was dismissed for insubordination when she criticized the then director of MI5.

ABOUT THE AUTHOR

Kelly Oliver is the award-winning, bestselling author of three mysteries series. She is also the Distinguished Professor of Philosophy at Vanderbilt University and lives in Nashville Tennessee.

Sign up to Kelly Oliver's mailing list here for news, competitions and updates on future books.

Visit Kelly's website: http://www.kellyoliverbooks.com/

Follow Kelly on social media:

 x.com/KellyOliverBook

 facebook.com/kellyoliverauthor

 instagram.com/kellyoliverbooks

 tiktok.com/@kellyoliverbooks

 bookbub.com/authors/kelly-oliver

ALSO BY KELLY OLIVER

A Fiona Figg & Kitty Lane Mystery Series

Mystery in Manhattan

Covert in Cairo

Mayhem in the Mountains

Arsenic at Ascot

Murder in Moscow

Poison in Piccadilly

Poison
& Pens

POISON & PENS IS THE HOME OF
COZY MYSTERIES SO POUR YOURSELF
A CUP OF TEA & GET SLEUTHING!

DISCOVER PAGE–TURNING NOVELS FROM
YOUR FAVOURITE AUTHORS &
MEET NEW FRIENDS

JOIN OUR
FACEBOOK GROUP

BIT.LYPOISONANDPENSFB

SIGN UP TO OUR
NEWSLETTER

BIT.LY/POISONANDPENSNEWS

Boldwood

Find out more at www.boldwoodbooks.com

Follow us
@BoldwoodBooks
@TheBoldBookClub

Sign up to our weekly
deals newsletter

Made in the USA
Las Vegas, NV
15 January 2025

16388455R00144